GROWTH

GROWTH

JEFF JACOBSON

PINNACLE BOOKS
Kensington Publishing Corp.
www.kensingtonbooks.com

PINNACLE BOOKS are published by

Kensington Publishing Corp.
119 West 40th Street
New York, NY 10018

All Kensington titles, imprints, and distributed lines are available at special quantity discounts for bulk purchases for sales promotions, premiums, fund-raising, educational, or institutional use. Special book excerpts or customized printings can also be created to fit specific needs. For details, write or phone the office of the Kensington special sales manager: Kensington Publishing Corp., 119 West 40th Street, New York, NY 10018, attn: Special Sales Department; phone 1-800-221-2647.

ISBN-13: 978-0-7860-3080-4
ISBN-10: 0-7860-3080-1

First printing: July 2014

10 9 8 7 6 5 4 3 2 1

Printed in the United States of America

First electronic edition: July 2014

ISBN-13: 978-0-7860-3081-1
ISBN-10: 0-7860-3081-X

SATURDAY,
JUNE 30th

CHAPTER 1

Bob Jr. thought the whole thing was a big joke right up until Dr. Deemer shot the Vice President of Marketing in the neck.

The day hadn't started out that bad. Hell, Bob Morton Jr. fully expected it to be one of the greatest days of his life. He'd been promised a party, and by God, he was ready for one. Up early, not too hungover, he joined his superiors on the exclusive little café on the roof of their hotel as the sun broke over Port-au-Prince. Then a short ride to the city's international airport where a sleek Gulfstream was gassed and ready to go.

Bob Jr. had never been on a jet that small or luxurious. He tried not to let the awe show on his face as he strapped himself into the leather seat. His employer, the genetically modified–seed giant Allagro, owned an entire island almost fifty miles to the west, and flew their executives back and forth all the time. Their proximity to Haiti and its laws gave the corporation quite a bit of flexibility regarding certain safeguards and scientific protocol. Before they had even taken off, the stewardesses, all perky local girls, brought everybody fresh oranges, giant frosted glasses full of hand-chipped ice, and nearly frozen bottles of Iordanov vodka.

Bob Jr. limited himself to just one screwdriver. He was one of the newest members of the upper echelon at Allagro and he didn't want to get too drunk too fast in front of the rest of the twenty or so other executives, all heavy hitters within the corporation. There was still a tour of the facilities and a whole mess of backslapping and glad-handing to get through before the real party began.

It hadn't been said aloud, but the message had been received loud and clear. Bob Jr. understood that all of the speeches, all of the presentations—everything—was simply a series of formalities meant to be endured before heading back to Port-au-Prince, where the booze, drugs, and women were all waiting.

And oh good Lord, the women. Bob Jr. had had to bite the inside of his cheeks to stifle a shit-eating grin. Somebody high up in the corporation had clearly spared no expense in showing their appreciation for a job well done. Viagra had been passed around like after-dinner mints. There was a damn good reason no wives had been invited on the trip.

The five-mile island was curved into a little comma. Cornfields covered most of the thin sliver of land. The jet landed smoothly on the airstrip that split the island in half and Bob Jr. got his first good look at the acres and acres of corn. As he disembarked, he couldn't help but feel a little unsettled. He'd grown up in cornfields; his dad had used to joke that he should have had corn silk for hair. But something was off. It felt *wrong*, somehow, to see all these endless, perfectly geometric rows of cornstalks with the pale blue Caribbean ocean in the background.

Six air-conditioned Range Rovers whisked the executives down dirt roads to the main campus, a sprawling cluster of massive greenhouses, a four-story office building, and what looked like a large, imposing warehouse. The office building was first, where a waiting contingent of on-site personnel were full of slick smiles and fawning congratulations. A troop of secretaries handed out mimosas spiked with rum-soaked pineapple wedges.

Then it was on to the laboratories.

Bob Jr. couldn't help but feel that shit just got real when they had to take turns going through a no-nonsense airlock. Everybody had to slip into surgical masks, sterile blue scrubs, and disposable booties fitted snugly over their custom alligator- and ostrich-skin shoes. The subdued, expensive paintings and wood walls disappeared, giving way to gray cement and pipes that clung to the ceilings; corrugated rubber mats protecting evenly spaced drains in the cement floor replaced the ornate rugs on hardwood. There was no doubt they were now squarely in the heart of Research and Development's territory.

Inside, the air tasted flat and stale. The rest of the tour was a dizzying blur of exotic scientific instruments and freezers and test tubes and obscure machines. They peered through thick Plexiglas into stark white rooms devoid of anything except heat lamps and a couple of cornstalks planted in ten-gallon buckets. Bob Jr. found he was having a hard time concentrating after the Caribbean heat and all the deceptively powerful drinks. The information their guides gave became nothing but endless, confusing blather.

He understood the basics, though. Of course he did. He'd been drilled, first from his father, then from the rest of the executives at Allagro, and finally from the men upstairs who never appeared at any meeting except on speakerphone. He barely knew these men's first names. He'd never actually met them in person. He didn't even know what they looked like.

It didn't matter, though. They certainly made sure he got the message.

These latest corn seeds were something brand new, going so far beyond the current cutting edge in technology that nobody even had a classification for them yet. They represented nothing less than the future of crop management. These special seeds had been armed with a sleeping genetic defense that only became active if the corn plant was attacked by some sort of pest, such as the European corn worm. This was a particularly troublesome moth whose larvae, voracious caterpillars, ate through the stalks, causing the entire plant to fall over and rot.

It had been patiently explained, over and over, that this genetic response was a kind of cocktail fungus grenade, a stew of fungal species that had been programmed to attack and destroy the corn worms. The whole thing was some kind of super-duper, top-fucking-secret. And though Bob Jr. had no idea what the Latin names actually meant, the eggheads certainly had been proud of their accomplishments. They'd combined a healthy dash of *Ophiocordyceps unilateralis*, a sizable chunk of *Beauveria bassiana,* a little contribution from *Paecilomyces cicadae*, and a sprinkling of God-knew-what.

How they did it exactly, Bob Jr. got a little shaky on the specifics.

All he really knew was that the men upstairs had decided to turn away from their profitable pesticide arm of the company. They sold that for billions and focused their genetic division of the corporation instead solely on organic responses to pests.

The new seeds were the harbinger of the future—a truly "green" solution.

When the tour of the labs had finished, the executives were shown into a plush conference room, and while Bob Jr. was thrilled to accompany the big boys to the island for the grand rollout, he hadn't realized how many stultifying speeches he would have to endure. One speaker after another had stepped up to the podium to explain, in soul-crushing detail, how their own unique vision had contributed to the success of the new seed. Everybody wanted his own moment in the spotlight.

At first, Bob Jr. had tried to pay attention, but the presentations were taking forever. His chair had become impossibly comfortable and the surface of the conference table had become a glazed, hypnotizing brown sea. The massive table had been built as a stylized replica of the actual island, with the sharp edges smoothed out, curves and angles minimized, until it resembled a thirty-foot quarter moon, curved in sync with the floor-to-ceiling windows that looked out across a spotless white beach, revealing a seemingly endless tropical paradise—nothing but sand and waves. The alcohol and the heat were making his head fuzzy, and he was more than a little worried that he was about to fuck up and do something truly stupid, like fall asleep in front of everybody.

He tried to distract himself by watching the gray clouds piling up over the soft blue Caribbean water through the expansive windows behind the podium. The gorgeous view should have been enough, but the gentle rolling waves just made time pass slower. He shifted instead to picturing his fiancée, who was waiting for his return to Chicago, hopefully in something sheer and revealing.

Then he thought of his parents on their farm, and even though he had chosen not to stay and farm the land, they had to be so proud that their only child, a son no less, had at least chosen to pursue an extremely lucrative career in crops—corporate, genetically modified crops, in his case. He was bound and determined to fulfill his father's vision of returning the American farmer to his rightful, exalted position of honor in the greatest country on God's green earth.

The Vice President of Marketing was up at the podium, grinning like an egg-sucking shark. "Imagine, gentlemen, a corn seed booby-trapped with its own built-in pest control. No more pesticides, no more chemicals. This will improve our image among the organic fruitcakes and hippies whining about all these so-called 'genetically modified Frankenseeds.' No. That era is over. We are—"

That's when Dr. Deemer or Beemer or something

lurched through the whisper-quiet double doors to the conference room, waving an old German Luger around. The scientist shouted something unintelligible to someone out of sight beyond the doors.

Bob Jr. recognized the gun because his father had one just like it. Supposedly Great-Granddad had brought it back from someplace in France or Germany just after D-Day, depending how much booze the story-teller had swallowed when the pistol was taken out of the family safe and passed around. Bob Jr. always got an extra swallow of beer after he held the pistol and aimed it; it always reminded him of Han Solo's blaster in *Star Wars*.

And because he was the new guy, Bob Jr. thought at first it was just a gag, some kind of lame hazing prank. He'd almost laughed out loud when the scientist had staggered into the room, waving the handgun in one hand and a bottle of Jameson in the other.

The gun-toting man, one of the leading eggheads who had actually developed all the genetic codes that lay dormant within the seeds, moved as if he were being forced to dance halfheartedly to music only he could hear, almost as if he needed to create momentum to keep going. It didn't look like the old man had gotten the memo that this was a triumphant, joyful occasion. His face, framed by unruly tangles of gray hair, had a haunted, lost quality. The skewed, smudged glasses didn't help the impression.

Given the circumstances, Bob Jr. figured the man was probably drunk. It made the most sense. After all, this whole trip, the tour, the conference, it all was one big celebration.

Either that, or he was having a stroke.

The scientist shuffled to the front of the room like someone in physical therapy learning how to walk after a serious car accident. He leaned into the podium at the head of the gleaming teak table and took a moment to catch his breath. If he was drunk, he wasn't a happy drunk, like everybody else.

The VP of Marketing finally edged back in and said, "Dr. Deemer?"

Dr. Deemer was either having hearing problems or ignoring the questioning tone. He glared at the twenty or so executives and said, "I hope you all are enjoying yourselves, but I am afraid I have some bad news." His voice barely rose above a whisper and the microphone only caught every third word. "Because this," he waved the pistol around, ". . . this, this is all a mistake. It is over. Finished."

"Perhaps it is," the VP said smoothly, gesturing at the table. "Nevertheless, we want to make sure everyone involved understands how vitally essential—"

"Shut your mouth, you simpering mongrel." Dr. Deemer's arm flopped over, and suddenly the barrel of the Luger was aiming in the direction of the VP. Even then, even when Bob Jr. should have known to run for the doors, he still thought it was all fake. Despite all of his instincts, he thought he was invulnerable. He was his father's son, and there wasn't anything he couldn't tackle. He knew the Luger, and even though he hadn't looked at the real thing since he was a child, he still thought it wasn't happening; he had convinced himself the gun in Dr. Deemer's hand was plastic, that it was a stupid cigarette lighter or even one of those gag toys where a little banner that said "BANG" popped out when you pulled the trigger.

Bob Jr. was hoping Dr. Deemer would snap out of it and cough and laugh and admit that it was all just a joke. After all these speeches, Bob Jr. had been promised a thirty-six-hour binge of drinking, women, and food, and maybe even a few illicit drugs. He had been focusing on these particular thirty-six hours for weeks now. Nothing would come between him and total hedonism. Nothing.

That's why the next logical choice was that it had to be a gag, part of some goofy ritual. Everybody would have a good laugh at the nervous looks on the couple of new executives, and then the lead scientist would follow the program and proclaim how these new seeds were officially vastly superior to all of the previous strains.

Goddamn, Bob Jr. was willing to drink to that. These new genetically modified corn seeds were going to make them all millionaires, if not fucking billionaires.

And the thing was, all this pomp and circumstance, all the dull speeches, all of it was unnecessary. The safety and effectiveness of the seeds had been cleared months ago by the internal research and development geeks. Hell, Bob Jr. had quietly shipped off a package to his parents once he'd heard that the seeds had been declared safe after the first round of test results. That was three, four months ago. His father owned one of the largest farms in Manchester County and couldn't wait to get the seeds in the ground. Allagro protocol demanded that the rest of the time was spent in equally useless further tests and buying off their pals in the Department of Agriculture. The whole process was like being wrapped in red tape and falling into bureaucratic quicksand, until finally, finally they were permitted to start test trials off the island.

Hence the celebration.

The punch line to the joke never came. Nobody broke character. Dr. Deemer said, "We are reaping what we have sown, gentlemen." He took a long swig from the bottle, swallowed, and wiped at his face. Bob Jr. was shocked to see tears streaming down the old man's face, spilling along the contours of the wrinkles.

There was a banging on the conference room doors.

"I warned you!" Dr. Deemer shouted at the doors, and then, without any further hesitation, turned and shot the VP of Marketing.

Everybody flinched.

And even then, Bob Jr. thought it was staged. There was no deafening blast, no explosion of blood that splattered across the wall behind the VP like in the movies. No, it was just a little pop, and the marketing guy twisted, giving the surprised, harsh grunt of someone who'd had the wind knocked out of them.

Bob Jr. didn't know whether to grin or react in horror.

The VP clutched at his throat, took two steps toward the wall, and collapsed. He kicked once or twice in mindless spasms, gurgling his last breath as he slid down the wall and sprawled on the floor.

The doors were silent.

Now that he had everybody's attention, Dr. Deemer said, "This, this is one time where I will not be interrupted." He took the time to meet each executive's eyes, like a snake waiting for a mouse to emerge from under a log; and only until he had stared each of them in the eyes for a long two or three seconds did he move on.

When he met Bob Jr.'s eyes, Bob Jr. felt like he might piss his pants.

Dr. Deemer straightened. Put the Luger on the podium. "I hate to rain on your parade, as they say. However, I am afraid I have some bad news. The . . . organisms contained within this new seed have developed in reaction to its environment in remarkable, unpredictable forms."

"So this, this fuckup is your fault, is that what you're telling us?" the CFO, Howard Slade, asked with an air of patient nonchalance. He had an antique pocketknife out and seemed to be paying more attention to cleaning his fingernails than to the gun.

Bob Jr. suddenly found that his own hands were the most interesting thing he'd ever seen. He was sitting next to Slade, and did not want Dr. Deemer looking their way. Bob Jr. had been around enough firearms in his life to know when he was in the line of fire.

"I am saying our experiments have produced an organism far more . . . *voracious* than planned, and the results have been catastrophic." Dr. Deemer coughed, hacked up a wad of dark phlegm, and spit it on the table. Everybody avoided looking at the slimy gob of mucus.

Dr. Deemer gave a soft chuckle or sob, Bob Jr. wasn't sure which. He shook his head, as if dislodging water in his ears.

"You say the results have been catastrophic. Elaborate." Slade said.

Dr. Deemer took another drink from his bottle. "There has been a Level Five Containment Breach."

Bob Jr. heard Slade clack his teeth together. He had no idea what a Level Five Containment Breach was. He figured it must be serious, the way some of the older executives were reacting. Probably bad news for the corporation.

Bob Jr. put on a concerned expression, mostly to be a part of the team. It didn't matter a whole hell of a lot to him one way or another; the only thing that worried him was that the party might be affected.

"For those of you who have no idea what I am talking about," Dr. Deemer's gaze swept across the table, "please believe me when I say to you that there is something altogether unnatural on this island. Something that does not belong anywhere on earth." Dr. Deemer started to cough, the way a cat hacks up a hairball.

He cleared his throat enough to breathe. "The results of our work were not foreseen. Certain safety measures . . . did not work. It appears that the fungal defense has been successful in jumping from species to species. Last night, we discovered that this . . . new species of fungus is not only able to spread between species as vastly different as insects and mammals, but that it can also latch on to the somatic nervous system, thereby controlling individual muscle groups within an organism." He started retching again, until he could barely keep his feet; he doubled over, dry heaving spatters of wet air, until the rasping sounds grew more liquid and he suddenly vomited half-digested blood all over the podium.

"I think this has gone on long enough," Slade said, snapping the pocketknife blade shut with one hand as if that would provide the necessary authority to back up his statement.

A few of the executives stood up and started moving to the front of the table, getting closer to the doors.

Dr. Deemer spit clots of blood onto his shoes and whipped his gaze back up to the long scythe of a table. His skin glowed a ghastly white in the soft tropical light from the windows. "Sit down."

Everybody slowed down until they were almost standing still, but none went back to their chairs.

"I said sit *down*." He pulled the trigger six times, hitting two executives. One caught a bullet in the head, another in the elbow. The rest of the standing men dropped to the floor while everybody still at the table froze. "Listen to me very carefully. This may be difficult for you to comprehend, at least at first. However, you deserve to know the truth. Every single one of you have been infected since the moment you landed on this island and took your first breath."

Something that looked like slick black blood oozed from the corner of his mouth. He wiped at it absent-mindedly, the way a toddler will wipe away drool. "Even now, you may be feeling a little warm, a little dry mouth, clogged nose, a little tickle in the back of your throat, like nothing more than a summer cold." He gave a slow, sad smile. "I am truly sorry. I wish . . ." He shook his head and looked at the bottle in surprise, as if he'd never seen it before. He took another long drink. "You do not understand." He gave a horrible gagging gasp, as a toe-curling dry heave wrenched its way through his torso. "You . . . *We* are all dead." He hacked again, and another torrent of whiskey and thick blood splattered across the sticky podium.

"You all just don't know it yet." He spoke with the conviction of a borderline alcoholic pleading with his maker for mercy as his body expelled the poison. "I'm so sorry," he gasped. "I am, truly."

His breathing increased, until it caught for a second, stuttered, gaining volume as it spiraled around the vocal cords, and the pitch grew higher and higher, till he sounded like a little girl having an asthma attack. His arms whipped at the air in grabbing motions.

None of the executives moved.

Dr. Deemer pulled off his glasses with a shaking hand. He dropped them and shivered. Straightened. His hands twisted inward and his arms folded into his chest as if he were trying to imitate the corpse of the funky chicken. Something marched up his spine, cranking it backward, vertebrae by vertebrae. The whine built to a shriek as the muscles ripped his shoulders and head back, arching his back until his entire body strained against itself in a crude mockery of the curved table.

The howl drained his lungs of oxygen and he did not take another breath. His body swayed for a moment, but he did not fall. He opened his eyes far too wide and a blackened, thick tongue emerged from between his cracked lips. He struggled to breathe through his nose.

Everyone heard a muffled crack that sounded like stepping on a rotten board in a carpeted staircase.

Dr. Deemer trembled. He pivoted slowly, as if he wanted to admire the view, then jerked away from the windows as if repelled by the light. The table recoiled. Blood flowed through the scientist's wispy gray hair at the back of his head. Bob Jr. thought he could see the jagged edges of broken, bare skull.

His face was now nearly unrecognizable, as pressure

built inside, driving the tongue out even farther. His eyes bulged until they all could hear two soft pops in quick succession as his eyes erupted like two small land mines, vaporizing the muscles and nerves and jelly, spraying a fine mist into the air. Whatever life was left in his body vanished, and it collapsed.

A gray cloud floated out of the empty, moist eye sockets.

CHAPTER 2

Fred Lockwood, head of the International Relations division, was the first one to break for the doors. Three more immediately followed. The rest of the executives looked at each other with wide, calculating eyes. The slow trickle to the door became a flood. Even the exec with the shattered elbow managed to run.

Bob Jr.'s first instinct was to follow the rest of the herd, but Slade grabbed his arm. "You help me out of this building, I'll get you off this island. Please. Help me."

Bob Jr. looked down at the sixty-year-old man, a skeleton trembling with a mixture of anger and anxiety. Slade might have been frail, but he was way, way up the corporate totem pole. He could be a hell of an asset to Bob Jr.'s career. And he might know about a back door somewhere. "Okay. Where?"

"Wait. Just wait. Let these fools run," Slade said. "They will undoubtedly attempt to reach the jet. If there truly is a Level Five Containment Breach on this island, then measures have already been taken. Nothing will be permitted to leave. Even if they manage to take off, it will be shot out of the sky."

Slade caught Bob Jr.'s look of astonishment. "You do realize, don't you, that a containment breach of this magnitude demands an armed response? There is a scorched-earth policy in motion."

Slade could tell that Bob Jr. still hadn't gotten with the program. He shook his head. "I can't believe your father talked Henry into hiring you." His clawed hand snatched at Bob Jr.'s tie and yanked him closer. "This company will leave nothing to chance. They have the men and the means to come here and burn everything. This company will protect itself. They will burn everything. This island will cease to exist." Spittle landed on Bob Jr.'s cheek.

Bob Jr.'s thought process moved sluggishly in the best of times, and these latest developments had really thrown a wrench into the gears of his mind, leaving him nearly paralyzed with incomprehension. Finally though, current events snapped into understanding, and panic bloomed in his eyes like a match dropped into a back-yard grill.

He edged around the table to check on Dr. Deemer.

Something was growing out of the old man's skull. Gray and bulbous, it seemed fragile and dense at the same time. It reminded Bob Jr. of the body of an oc-topus somehow, as if the creature had been quietly growing inside Deemer's head and had gotten too big for its cage. Bob Jr. used the tip of his shoe to nudge the scientist's knee.

The gray sac wobbled with the movement, but did not break.

Bob Jr. blinked. Had it gotten bigger since he was standing here?

He looked around. Except for the two men and the three corpses, the conference room was now empty. "We gotta go," Bob Jr. said.

"No. Now is precisely the time to be patient. Let the rest distract whatever measures the company has prepared."

"Look at him. C'mere and look! There's something growing inside his head. We need to get out of this room. We gotta get far away."

Slade peered at Dr. Deemer and thought about it for a moment. "Very well." He pushed away from the table and struggled to his feet. His cane tumbled to the floor. "Help me up, dammit!"

Bob Jr. didn't need any more encouragement and half-lifted, half-dragged the older man out of the room. The hallways were empty and quiet. There were no alarms. No screaming people rushing around. Except for a few white pages scattered on the floor where the hallway intersected a wider corridor, there was nothing to suggest an island-wide evacuation.

No, not an evacuation, Bob Jr. reminded himself. If what Slade said was true, then this was more like a hunt, or flat-out extermination. Even if he didn't quite believe it was happening, the rest of the executives sure as hell did, and that was enough to kick Bob Jr.'s self-preservation instincts into high gear. He slung Slade's left arm around his neck and pulled the old man along. "Where? Where to?"

"Through the labs, out to the greenhouses," Slade said, gasping for breath. His glasses had slid down to the end of his nose in a slick sheen of sweat, despite the frigid air-conditioning.

"Then what? Tell me you've got a plan." Bob Jr. felt a little sick when they came upon an airlock that stood wide open. After all the precautions they had to tolerate just to pass through the membrane, seeing it gaping and exposed now was, in some ways, almost worse than seeing the VP get shot.

God knew what all was in the air.

"We have to hurry," Slade said.

No shit, Bob Jr. thought. *It'd be a lot faster if I didn't have to drag your lame ass.* Out loud, he asked again, "What's your plan?" Bob Jr. was starting to wonder if he even needed the old man once he knew where they were going.

But Slade didn't claw his way up near the top of the Allagro food chain by being an idiot. He knew damn well what Bob Jr. was thinking. He would have done the same thing, except he would have gotten the plan back in the conference room. He said, "Shut up and keep going."

They found the first bodies soon after. Three of them, all wearing the protective scrubs, slumped in their chairs around a low table strewn with a frantic storm of print-outs and graphs. One had fallen to the floor and lay twisted and tangled, one arm propped against the wall.

Bob Jr. noticed all three had empty coffee cups nearby and faltered, trying to put the pieces together.

"I told you this was no joke. Keep moving," Slade said.

The second airlock was closed, not that it mattered. It hissed open upon command and they stumbled through, feeling the temperature rise at least fifteen or twenty degrees. The greenhouses were close.

The next body they found, some local wearing the uniform of one of the fieldworkers, was on his stomach in the middle of the corridor. He had a small hole in the back of his head and a gaping, ragged maw where his face used to be. Bob Jr. had to look away. Before today, he'd only seen one dead person in his entire life. That had been when he was twelve, at the open-casket funeral of his church's former pastor. That man had looked asleep, at peace.

These people looked interrupted, violated.

The corridor started up a gentle incline, and Bob Jr. and Slade struggled on, both drenched in sweat. Bob Jr.'s sides hitched and he could feel the morning's rum threatening to boil back up his throat. Slade's arm kept slipping, so they switched sides. Slade's thin fingers were surprisingly strong, and Slade wasn't shy about using his fingernails to sink his grip into the side of Bob Jr.'s neck.

Sunlight appeared through the glass doors at the end of the corridor. At first, it was so bright it washed out the artificial lights down there, but as they got closer, it grew dim for some reason, as if heavy storm clouds had covered the sun.

The panic swelled within Bob Jr., sending bursts of herky-jerky twitches through his muscles, making him lurch along as if he were stepping on exposed electrical currents. Slade's fingernails left bleeding trails on Bob Jr.'s neck as he struggled to hang on.

They both heard the distant rattle of automatic gunfire.

* * *

The island burned.

They had reached the glass doors and saw that the cornfields were on fire. Boiling black smoke filled the sky. Another stitch of gunfire.

They heard a muffled whump, and a mushroom cloud of fire appeared, roiling above the corn before transforming into a bubbling fountain of smoke. "Fuel truck," Slade said.

Bob Jr. craned his head and saw one of the Range Rovers, stalled at an angle across the main road. Smoke seeped from under the hood, the doors hung open, and the bodies of men in bloody gray suits were clustered around it as if a bunch of drunks had all staggered from the vehicle and passed out.

A man dressed as a lab tech, his blue scrubs startlingly pale against the vivid red and black chaos, moved into sight from behind the SUV. He carried an assault rifle. Another man, a fieldworker, darted at the lab tech with a machete raised over his head.

The lab tech turned and calmly fired a burst of bullets into the fieldworker's chest. The fieldworker hadn't even hit the ground before the lab tech turned back toward the facility's main entrance, moving with a methodical, unhurried precision. The burning fields threw skittering shadows around him, as if he were illuminated by false gods while a black funeral shroud cloaked the noon sun above.

Bob Jr. shifted Slade to get a better look. "He . . . he works here. He must. Who the hell is he?"

Slade panted, struggling for breath. "A mole. Somebody kept here just in case."

"In case of what?"

"In case of something like today."

"But you said they would kill everyone on the island."

"They will."

"But he's . . . that's suicide. Isn't it?"

Slade gave a slight shrug. "Sometimes suicide is the preferred option. Perhaps he's here to repay a debt. Perhaps he is willing to die so his family does not." Bob Jr.'s face made it clear he could not fathom dying intentionally. Slade smiled, a cadaverous, sick expression. "It's a big, bad world out there, farm boy."

They watched as the man strolled through the koi ponds and the sweeping lawns that had been clipped more carefully than most putting greens. The lab tech stopped for a moment, then leaned over a low hedge.

One of the secretaries rose from her hiding place behind the hedge and tried to run on wobbling high heels. The lab tech emptied the rest of his clip into her back and reloaded. He moved out of Bob Jr. and Slade's line of sight, heading for the main entrance.

"Whoever he is, they had him here for a reason," Slade said. "I'd be willing to wager he is not the only one. Let's move, before the rest of the team gets here. Their arrival is imminent, make no mistake."

Bob Jr. eased open the door and they moved cautiously into the murky light. Blackened flecks of corn leaves and gritty ash floated in the gentle breeze. The air smelled of smoke and ash. Bob Jr. shifted his grip once again on Slade, putting the old man between himself and the main entrance, and dragged him along the flagstone walk as it curved around to the massive greenhouses.

This was the only upside to hauling the old man around; he might provide a shield for any bullets.

Slade realized this as well and said again, "Hurry up, dammit!"

The greenhouses had been built along a low cliff and looked down on a boulder-strewn shore. "A boat is waiting down there," Slade said. "It is secret, hidden, and reserved for upper management, regularly maintained in case of emergency. I would say that today certainly qualifies." Slade caught Bob Jr.'s eyes. "Understand this. You will not gain access without me. The stairway is locked with a code. I know the code. Get me to the boat and you will live."

"That's the plan," Bob Jr. lied.

The doors to the greenhouse had been sealed in red biohazard tape. A short chain encircled the handles, secured with a padlock. The distant lights of the sun and fires reflected in the myriad windows, making it impossible to see inside. Bob Jr. didn't want to think about what that meant. He stopped short. "We can't go in there. We'll have to find another way around."

"There is no other way. The stairwell to the dock is inside."

"Then how? It's locked."

Slade shot Bob Jr. a withering stare. "Break the glass, moron."

Bob Jr. didn't want to make any more noise than necessary, so he lugged Slade around the far side of the building, near the cliff, leaned the older man against the wall, and lifted a football-size rock out of the border separating the bushes from the grass. He held his breath.

Slade looked back to the main building. "Do it. Now."

Bob Jr. heaved the rock at the nearest pane. It bounced off.

"Oh, for Christ's sake," Slade said.

Bob Jr. retrieved the rock, lifted it over his head, and threw it so hard both feet left the ground. This time, the rock smashed through the glass with a tinkling explosion. Spinning red lights flickered to life inside, and a deep, insistent buzzing erupted. Bob Jr. felt his insides go watery.

"Go, go!" Slade said, clutching at his arm and pushing him inside. Bob Jr. tried to ignore the broken glass in the soft dirt and crawled into a forest of cornstalks. A cobweb smeared across his face but he couldn't stop to wipe it away. Some of the strands pulled taut across his tongue, then broke free, drying against his teeth. He gagged and spit, hating the feeling of the threads disintegrating in his saliva even more than the glass slivers in his palms.

He turned back and wasn't gentle about dragging Slade through the shards. If the old fuck got cut, then he deserved it.

Slade was tough enough to keep quiet and not complain. They pushed through the glass and dirt, cracking cornstalks as they crawled deeper into the greenhouse. The temperature wasn't much different from outside. If anything, it was cooler.

They slid over a wooden partition, landing in an aisle of some kind. Rows of corn stretched into the gloom, lit only by the spinning red lights high above. The deep, throbbing buzz of the alarm reverberated through Bob Jr., rattling his bones. He caught sight of his bleeding hands and knees and whirled on Slade. "Where's that goddamn staircase, old man?"

Slade wiped soil and cobwebs from his eyes. "Down . . . down there. I think."

"You better be fucking right," Bob Jr. said, hauling Slade to a standing position.

Their leather soles scraped concrete as they struggled down the aisle. The greenhouse was full of corn and nothing else. Most seemed to be healthy, mature stalks, bursting with nearly ripe ears of corn. The only thing that felt out of place was the abundance of cobwebs, glistening in the spinning red lights. Husks of caterpillars hung in the strands. The webs stretched everywhere, even across the walkway, and the two men had to plow through the intricate designs as they shuffled along.

Bob Jr. didn't think much of it. Fucking spiders. Nothing more. He was focused on the boat.

And so he didn't notice the movement along his arms, his back, his hair.

"Where? Where!" Bob Jr. demanded. His tongue felt dry and thick, too big for his mouth. There was a tickle in the back of his throat.

For the first time, Slade looked like he was about to panic. "They told us . . . it's supposed to be around here."

Bob caught a glimpse of some dark insect, a spider of some kind, creeping through Slade's silver hair. He ignored it and spun them in a circle. Webs encircled their bodies. "There's nothing here. They lied to you, old man. They lied."

"There!" Slade shouted, his voice full of triumph. Bob Jr. followed his finger and saw a metal door, crusty with rust, sunk into the wall. There was no traditional door handle; instead, a two-foot iron pipe crossed the door, waist-high. A number pad enclosed in a greasy-looking plastic cover waited next to the door.

Slade said, "It runs off a different system. It's an older grid, not on the books anymore."

Bob Jr. decided that the old man was getting one chance to get the fucking code right. If the door didn't open immediately, he was going to ditch the old fart and get out of this awful greenhouse. No doubt the alarms had drawn the fake lab tech with the automatic weapon. And there was no way in hell he was going to sit around and wait to get shot.

Slade broke the seal on the plastic cover and hit six digits. He waited a moment, then pushed two more.

A solid *chunk* came from behind the door.

Bob Jr. wrenched the handle out of the locked position and slammed it down. They heard a dusty click inside the doorframe and glanced at each other.

Bob Jr. swung the door out, opening it on a fire escape and the sky. He could smell salt water. Below, hungry waves lunged against the rocks. When he saw the black Zodiac tied and secure, bobbing around in a tidal pool at the bottom of the fire escape, he couldn't help himself and blurted, "Sweet fuck." He went back and slung Slade around his shoulders again. They left the greenhouse and started down the steep steel steps.

Bob Jr. shook out his free arm and pulled webs out of his hair. They stuck and broke, leaving a tacky net across the left side of his head. He felt something crawl under his collar near his tie and slapped at it, feeling it pop, almost like a rotten pea. He spit again, just to get the taste of the spiderwebs out of his mouth.

The engine started on the first pull. Bob Jr. crawled over Slade in the bow of the rigid inflatable boat, clearly something left over from Allagro's military contract days. He ignored Slade's protests and fished around in

Slade's pockets, finally pulling out the knife he'd seen at the conference table.

It made a muted, dense click when he snapped the blade open. Bob Jr. liked that. He didn't bother trying to untie the knots, and slashed the mooring ropes, then sat back next to the engine and steered the Zodiac straight into the eastern winds.

The first wave blasted warm salt water around the bow, soaking Slade. The old man bounced and flopped as the boat smashed against the incoming waves. The ride settled out once they turned south into the deeper swells.

The engine, a black outboard Bob Jr. figured must be military grade just like the boat itself, churned through the sea with a hushed whir. He could still hear the alarm back in the greenhouse. And something else, coming from way back beyond the buildings, something higher pitched, like some swarm of pissed-off Weed Eaters and lawnmowers.

He cranked the throttle over as far as it would twist. The Zodiac dutifully soldiered up one swell after another. Bob Jr. coughed. His mouth was curiously dry, as if he'd taken five or six bong hits and was so stoned he wasn't sure if he was sitting or standing. He scraped the top of his tongue against his top teeth and didn't like the feel of the slime that now coated his teeth. He coughed again.

An open knife didn't belong in an inflatable boat, so he snicked it shut and handed it back to Slade. Slade was sitting up now, digging around in his nostril with his thumb. He closed one nostril and tried to blow out whatever was in his nose. A tiny spatter of blackened mucus landed on his knee.

Bob Jr. coughed again and bent over between his knees, really hacking. He tried to swallow. Globs of wet clay seemed to be clogging his throat. "Hey. All that shit back there that Deemer told us, you don't think he meant us or anything, right? I mean, we didn't breathe in anything. We didn't, right?"

Slade didn't answer. He closed his fist around the knife and pointed.

Bob Jr. twisted and saw distant helicopters, looking like a dozen dark dragonflies rising over the island, incinerating everything below. Streaks of light leapt from the buzzing insects. When they struck the island, fire bloomed so bright it darkened the sky itself. He heard the immense crackling thunder a half-second faster than he felt the impact, a hot blast of wind that lifted his hair and dried his eyes.

He thought he heard a dense, muted click behind him.

If he hadn't turned back to shield his face from the explosions, Slade would have been able to slit his throat. As it was, Bob Jr. had turned just enough to catch the old man's movement and shot his hand out. The blade sliced through the outside of his palm, but then Bob Jr.'s hand had slipped past the knife and grabbed Slade's bony wrist. He wrenched his fist over and Slade cried out, releasing the pocketknife.

It bounced on the wooden floor of the boat.

Bob Jr. let go of the throttle and snatched at the knife. The engine's pitch dropped to a low murmur and the boat spun as he knocked the tiller sideways. Anger sparked and roared in his clogged head, and for a moment, rage obliterated everything. Still clutching Slade's wrist, he wrenched the older man even farther off balance and drove the knife into his chest. The three-inch blade punctured the thin sternum with a sound like the snapping of a plastic fork.

Slade tried to catch his breath. It hitched and snagged.

Bob Jr. yanked the knife out, plunged it in again.

Again.

And again.

When Bob Jr. finally stopped, the wooden floor was slick with blood. Slade's chest was a shredded patchwork of blood, ripped fabric, and meat. The old man's head was thrown back, dead eyes staring at the sky.

Bob Jr. rose to his knees, gathering his bearings. The island was off to the right now, and the relentless waves were pushing them closer. He hit the throttle again, knowing that he had to keep moving, put some distance between him and the island.

He coughed again. This time it felt like something ripped in the back of his throat, and he swallowed before he could stop himself. A thick lump the size of a peach pit, wet and smooth, slid down his esophagus. He couldn't breathe through his nose.

Soon as he hit land, he was gonna have to find some antibiotics or something.

That brought him back to Slade's body. He couldn't exactly take the old man back with him. Bob Jr. left the engine for a moment and scrambled forward. He flopped Slade over, got hold of the back of his belt and collar, and slung him onto the side of the boat, then rolled him over.

The corpse hung facedown in the swells, suspended in the sun-dappled greenish-blue water. For a second, Bob Jr. was afraid the old man might twitch and jerk his head out of the water, gasping for breath at the last moment. But he stayed down, legs drifting under him, arms splayed out. A thin haze of blood spread out slowly, clouding the water.

Good. It would draw sharks and anything else in the deeps that wanted a free meal. No one would ever know. As far as anyone else was concerned, Slade had died on the island.

Bob Jr. almost lost his balance as the boat rolled over the crest of a large wave. He shook his head. He didn't feel right. He looked back and saw that he was being driven back to the island again. Crawling back over to the engine, he cranked the throttle over again and headed in what he hoped was a southeasterly direction.

His stomach heaved and he almost threw up. Strangely, it didn't feel like he was seasick. Once the boat had moved away from the island, the ocean had been fairly calm, and besides, he had only been out there ten or fifteen minutes. This was something different, something connected to the goddamn head cold.

Thinking about the heaviness in his head made it worse, somehow. He slumped over, feeling all of his strength evaporate, bleached out by the Caribbean sun. It was all he could do to hold on to the tiller and keep the throttle twisted. He tried to reassure himself. It made sense. After all the adrenaline and shock from the morning, he was bound to feel exhausted once all the excitement was over.

He managed to turn his head to watch the island grow smaller and estimated it was at least a half mile behind him. The light from the flames was still plainly visible. He dropped his gaze to stare at his right hand, the one gripping the throttle.

A fat gray spider had nestled in the soft webbing between the knuckles of his fore and middle fingers. It didn't move. Bob Jr. wasn't sure if it was dead or simply content to rest there, motionless. He went to flick it away with his left thumb. The abdomen sac wobbled, but it remained rooted to the spot. A dozen or so irregular legs uncurled from the center.

Bob Jr. blinked and wondered what was wrong with him.

He hoped he was hallucinating.

Spiders didn't have that many legs. And these legs looked . . . wrong, as if they weren't spider legs at all. Some of them looked grotesquely disproportionate, as if they belonged on grasshoppers or crickets. Some were so tiny he didn't even realize they were legs at all until he squinted and got closer.

He wanted to whip his hand away, smash it against the side of the boat, drag it in the water and drown the damn bug, anything, but he didn't want to let go of the throttle. If just one of those choppers saw him, he was as good as dead. Truth be told, he wasn't sure if he could even move as fast as his panic wanted as it pleaded with his muscles.

What if it was poisonous? All kinds of nasty, poisonous insects lived in the tropics all around the world, creeping and crawling through the jungles. No. He'd come too far to let some goddamn spider poison him. He gritted his teeth and squeezed the bulbous body between his left thumb and forefinger, intending to pull it gently away from his skin and fling it into the water.

But as he applied just enough pressure to pick it up, the sac burst, dribbling a thick blackened soup over the back of his hand. The legs shivered furiously in mindless spasms. He pulled the body away from his skin, surprised that he couldn't see any head.

Then he saw the thin gray thread that trailed out of the center of the body and connected with the webbing between his fingers. He tugged gently and felt the gray tendril move under his skin.

The sensation made him cough again, gagging this time. He clutched at his throat with his left hand and gave a wracking cough. Black mucus spattered across the blood on the bottom of the boat. The fingers on his right hand fluttered of their own accord and released the throttle. The boat slowed and drifted in the swells.

Bob Jr. brought his hand closer to his face, willing his fingers to straighten, and watched in horror as they curled inward in an awkward fist instead, like some sick parody of a dead insect. They twitched and fluttered.

He struggled to breath and slumped even lower. He wanted to cry. The feeling of not being able to control his own hand filled him with a shaking terror that even eclipsed his growing unease over the stupid head cold. Deep down, he suspected it had something to do with breathing the same air as Dr. Deemer, but he refused to even entertain that possibility.

No. As soon as he could sit up, he was going to grab that throttle and get to dry land. He dimly realized his chin was wet; he'd been drooling. His ears felt like they had been stuffed with cotton. Everything was muffled, as if bass had been turned all the way up while everything else had been lowered on his headphones, the water lapping the rubber side of the boat, the distant droning of a helicopter, all sounding like he was inside an empty oil drum. He went to wipe the drool away and his hand came away coated in black, slimy spit.

The faint buzzing of a helicopter grew louder until he could hear the distinct thumping of the spinning blades. He tried to sit up and look back to the island, but could only manage to twist his head and look up at the engine. That's how he spotted a small black brick about the size of a satellite phone attached to the underside of the engine with a magnet.

He found that his thoughts were swimming away from him like skittish minnows, but he managed to grab hold of one and dimly realized that the Zodiac had a GPS tracker, an unwelcome stowaway. Then it was gone, slipping through his grasp.

He had forgotten all about the helicopter until its shadow covered the boat. Even then, he wasn't sure if it was really there or not. Very little oxygen was reaching his lungs. He was more concerned with the uncomfortable feeling that something was growing from the back of his throat, stretching up along his back teeth and climbing up into his nasal passages.

His thoughts grew slower and slower, drifting apart and settling like dead leaves sinking to the bottom of a pond. His last coherent image was a memory, of running across the vast lawn of home with his dog, while his mom hung laundry on the line over by the giant propane tank and his dad worked on one of the harvesters down in front of the largest barn and the sun burned over all the miles and miles of corn.

Then the missiles struck and Bob Jr., along with his thoughts, and the boat, vaporized into nothing but heat and ash.

CHAPTER 3

When the dispatcher called with a simple 10-21, Chief Sandy Chisel was standing on the front porch of the Einhorn farmhouse, arms crossed to keep her hand away from her pistol, listening to a load of bullshit.

Sandy clicked her radio and simply said, "Copy," then looked back down at Kurt Einhorn as he leaned back in the rocking chair.

"Don't know how many times I hafta explain things to you people," he said. "My wife, she's clumsy. Happens all the time. Don't see why you gotta come out here, wastin' taxpayer money just cause the stupid bitch fell down the basement stairs."

Kurt was known in the law enforcement business as a frequent flyer. Every few months, the neighbors across the highway called 911 when Kurt beat his wife so bad they could hear her screaming. Sandy's predecessor had warned her that arresting him and taking him to jail for the night wouldn't do any good. Just made things worse for Ingrid, the wife. The old chief had tried it a few times, hauling Kurt down to the police station in town, but inevitably, Ingrid would show up the next day, bruised and moving slowly and stiffly. She'd explain it was all a mistake, that she'd hit her face on the fridge door or dropped a hot pan on her foot. Calls and visits from spousal abuse counselors were ignored. Eventually, most people just figured if she didn't want out, then it was none of their business.

Nearly seven months into the job, this was Sandy's second visit as chief. She knew damn well the wife wouldn't say anything. Still, she went through the motions, taking her time as she walked Ingrid down the porch steps to the cruiser where they stood for a while under the summer night sky, listening to the occasional lonesome cricket. She explained in a low voice that Ingrid would never have to see him again, all she had to do was say the word. Ingrid, a thin wisp of a woman with short, frazzled hair, hugged herself and shrugged, looking everywhere but at Sandy.

After a while, Sandy gave up. It made her feel tense and irritable, like she'd been chewing on a ball of aluminum foil all day, but she knew damn well her words—her promises, attempts at shame, appeals for Ingrid's health—none of it made a bit of difference. Ingrid would suffer in silence until some night he'd hurt her bad enough to put her in the ground, or something would snap and she would up and leave. Then again, there was always that distant third possibility, and Sandy didn't think she'd be the only one not shedding any tears if Ingrid up and killed the son of a bitch.

Sandy led Ingrid back up to the porch. Kurt still sat in the rickety rocking chair and watched them with the sluggish, lidless eyes of a lizard. "Still waitin' for that beer," he told his wife. Ingrid didn't say a word, but she moved fast. The screen door slapped its frame behind her.

Kurt and Sandy regarded each other silently for a few long seconds. Moths beat against the bare bulb above. He reminded Sandy of a fat Gila monster, perched on a rock under the noon sun.

"Go ahead." When he smiled, his lips thinned and almost disappeared, revealing teeth the color of old tobacco. "Say something threatening. Tell me if she hurts herself again you'll make me sorry. Come on. Get me all nervous."

Sandy managed a tight grin right back. She kept her tone flat. "Not much point, I suppose. Looks like you got it all worked out."

"Do you well to remember that. Day I let some nigger-loving cooze tell me my business is the day I take a dirt nap."

This time, a wild mirth lit up her eyes and Sandy gave Kurt a chilling, genuine smile. "That dirt nap can be arranged. Easier than you think. Do you well to remember *that*." She headed back to the cruiser, hating the feeling that his eyes were following her ass and forced herself to walk slow, easy, unconcerned. Domestic disturbances were a cop's bread and butter, but she hadn't been on the job long enough to find that balance of shutting down her emotions but still caring enough to be an effective law enforcement officer.

She started the cruiser and pinned Kurt to the front of his farmhouse with the high beams. He stared back and didn't move. Sandy could see Ingrid watching from the kitchen window. The woman turned away from the window and left a blank rectangle of light.

Sandy followed the horseshoe driveway around past

the dark barn and back up to the highway. The Einhorn farm was set back off the road, but sound carried in the corn. The closest neighbors, the Johnsons, had called 911. Meredith Johnson, mother of twelve or thirteen children, Sandy never could quite remember, was standing on her front porch, watching and waiting.

Sandy sighed. She didn't doubt the Johnsons could hear the yelling from their front lawn. Their house was right across the highway from the Einhorns. The Johnsons were fundamentalist Christians and homeschooled all of their children, avoiding the pressures and temptations of public school and making sure their family knew the facts regarding topics such as evolution and global warming.

Meredith wore long dresses, a permanent frown, and kept her long brown hair pinned up in a severe bun that probably wouldn't come loose in a hurricane. She knew damn well Kurt wasn't in the backseat, and no doubt tomorrow she would be telling the rest of the sewing circle in the basement of their church all about how Sandy was such a disappointment as the town's police chief. Why, she couldn't even lock up an obvious sinner like Kurt Einhorn. Liz, the dispatcher, always referred to Meredith as "Sister Better-Than-You."

Sandy pulled up to the mouth of the driveway, working at putting it all out of her head. Nothing she could do about the armchair police in town. And it wasn't like that was a shock; she understood the scrutiny before she'd even publicly announced she'd run for the position. And in many ways, Meredith was easier to take than other folks. At least Meredith let you know exactly what she thought; the others were happy to smile in Sandy's face and tell her what a great job she was doing while calling her Chief Bitch when she was out of the room.

Albert came out onto the porch, holding his hand. Albert was a nice enough guy, but had the cognitive abilities of a bag of hammers. Sandy was close enough to hear Meredith yell at one of the kids inside, "Bring me a bandage. And some rubbing alcohol." Then, to her husband, "Quit your whining."

Sandy called out, "Everything okay?"

"Possum bit me!" Albert said.

"Shush," Meredith said. To Sandy, she called back, "He's fine. We certainly don't need help from the likes of someone like you." Meredith ushered her husband inside and shut the door.

Sandy wanted to remind them about the risks of rabies, but knew her effort would be wasted. So she pulled onto Highway 17 and rolled down the window for a deep breath of summer air. It was late enough that the heat had finally worn off, and a slight breeze tickled the corn that surrounded both farmhouses. She pulled up and stopped at the four-way stop at the intersection of Highway 17 and Road G and used her cell to call the office. A 10-21 code meant that the dispatcher had information that wasn't ready for the open frequency on the radio. Too many people got their kicks listening to the police scanner.

Liz answered it on the first ring, which didn't surprise Sandy. Parker's Mill wasn't exactly a hotbed of criminal activity. "Got a call from the Whistle Stop. Greg says Purcell Fitzgimmon's boys are awfully tuned up, causing a ruckus. Says he's heard your name mentioned a few times. Sounded like they were looking for a face-to-face. Thought you might like to hear about it first, before everybody else."

"Thanks, Liz."

"Thing is, it's all three. Guess the middle one is on leave or something. You want me to call Hendricks? He's still up north on 67, keeping an eye out for the drunks."

"Let Hendricks keep an eye on the drunks. Just finished at the Einhorns'. Heading over to the Whistle now."

Hendricks was a good cop, a guy who was good at talking folks out of heated moments. He went out of his way to avoid trouble when he was off-duty if at all possible, but had a knack for calming other folks down when he was on the clock. He had the patience to put up with hideous abuse from a drunk, then go and pick up the same guy on a Sunday morning for church service. Hendricks didn't care a whole lot which church he ended up at. They all told pretty much the same story anyway, he reasoned.

And despite lacking any discernible skill whatsoever, he was the kind of cop who truly believed riding a unicycle in the Fourth of July parade would help gain him a little more respect from the residents. At least he had eventually listened to her when Sandy had talked him out of juggling bowling pins, but he wasn't somebody she'd want backing her when she said howdy to hard cases like the Fitzgimmon brothers.

Sandy knew something like this would happen. Somebody was bound to test her. Somebody exactly like those boys. They had been raised not only to question every authority on earth except for their father, but to defy that authority as well, and thanks to Charlie's arrest, their grudge against Sandy and the rest of the Parker's Mill police department had gotten personal.

Back in November when she was only Deputy Chisel, Sandy had arrested Charlie Fitzgimmon for drunk driving and property destruction after he'd knocked over half of the stop signs in the county and was hauling them around in the back of his truck. This was the night before he was to report for basic training in either the Army or the Marines. She'd heard both versions.

Sandy had come upon his truck on the median, engine dead. Charlie was slumped over the wheel, snoring violently. She knocked on the roof.

Charlie blinked at her and eventually worked out that she was wearing a badge. He opened the door and got out all apologetic. "Thank you so much, Officer. I'm on my way, see, to an appointment with the government." He tried his damndest to walk a straight line over to her and instead stumbled and fell. He wound up on his back, shoulders and arms in the gutter, legs on the sidewalk, pissing on himself.

She hauled him in and didn't let him make a phone call until seven the next morning, making him almost late for his deployment. He'd never forgiven her.

A pair of headlights popped into view, way down the gentle curve to the west, moving fast. Sandy hesitated before pulling out. She squinted out of her window as the headlights grew brighter and brighter, eating up the darkness. The night was quiet enough that she could hear the diesel engine, straining and howling as the driver put the gas pedal on the floor and kept it there.

The truck blasted through the intersection as if the four stop signs never existed. The backwash rocked Sandy's cruiser. If the driver had seen her, he didn't react beyond pushing his vehicle as fast as possible. She automatically reached for the lights and siren, but stopped just short of clicking them on.

She recognized the truck. It was Bob Morton's. Latest model, all the bells and whistles. He was about the only one in the county that could afford a new truck, each and every year. He either owned or leased every damn cornfield in the county, and Sandy couldn't see any immediate reason why he would be driving so fast.

She knew she should go after him. The man deserved a ticket. He probably deserved a lot more than that. On the other hand, the Fitzgimmon boys were no doubt getting drunker and rowdier. Liz's tone suggested that things weren't out of hand yet, but serious trouble wasn't far off.

Behind her, Morton's taillights grew faint. At least he was heading east, where the roads dead-ended in yet more of his cornfields, so at least it wasn't likely he would hit anyone else.

Ahead, she knew the Fitzgimmons were waiting for her at the Whistle Stop. And the more time she gave them, the meaner they'd get. They'd been waiting seven months for something to happen.

She promised herself she'd have a talk with Bob the next day and headed to the Whistle Stop.

A year ago, if you asked people in Parker's Mill who they'd vote for in the upcoming Police Chief election, Sandy's name wouldn't even have been on the ballot.

They knew her name, certainly. Knew her mostly as that teen mom who fucked up her life. She was no more than an example that mothers would use to remind their daughters of the inevitable consequences of fooling around with boys.

For a while, Sandy was inclined to agree with them. Once Kevin had been born, she started applying for jobs and discovered how very few qualifications she actually possessed. Getting her G.E.D. was the first step. Then she saw an ad for earning her Basic Officer certification. The pay was worse than stripping, but the health insurance was better. She applied and was accepted. This news was met with less-than-enthusiastic applause within Manchester County. She graduated with honors, which made everything worse.

Amazingly enough, the earth did not crack, open up, and swallow Parker's Mill whole when the second woman in the history of the town joined the police force. She proved to be more than capable of arresting drunk drivers, nailing out-of-state cars for speeding, and giving talks on first aid to Boy Scout Troop 2957. The scout leaders wanted to put their scouts through a real threat, so they'd designed an elaborate scenario around the detonation of a nuclear suitcase bomb. The Church of Jesus Christ of Latter-day Saints sponsored the whole thing, and even provided Vietnam-era gas masks for the scouts as well.

They staged a real-life disaster scenario procedural drill; at least, that's what they called it. Hendricks put out blinking sawhorses to close off Third Street between Main Street and Franklin, but by that point, there were so many people crowding along the Main Street crosswalk taking pictures, it was clearly impassable.

The leaders parked a few cars at random between the new Walgreens and Vincent Smith's Butcher Shop and left the vehicle doors open. Everybody involved agreed that was a chilling touch. Somebody blew fog from dry ice down the street. Volunteers from the Springfield Drama Institute draped themselves across the street and Boy Scout leaders went around with red-colored Karo syrup and thawing chitterlings.

They fully expected her to fail. They wanted her to be overwhelmed, wanted to shock the boys, wanted to teach the town about chaos and the end of the world. So they kept the troop and Sandy in the firehouse where she reviewed the basics of first aid until the stage was set. They didn't tell the boys or Sandy, just pushed them out into the thick of things, while playing explosion sound effects from a scout leader's pickup sound system. Sandy took a moment to take it all in, then organized the twenty-six boys into five teams that spread out over the street, reminding the boys of the three categories of the triage triangle: 1. Those who are likely to live, regardless of what care they receive; 2. Those who are likely to die, regardless of what care they receive; and 3. Those for whom immediate care might make a positive difference in outcome.

She spoke low and reminded the boys that it was just a game. "Have fun." She sent them out into the late spring on Third Street to bandage to their hearts' content. Twenty-six scouts in gas masks ran through the street full of smoke and fake blood. She drifted around, making sure each team was organized and working, helping decide a few on-the-fence cases, all overacted with far too much screaming and moaning and groaning and thrashing around.

Sandy tried not to laugh while she stood with nine scouts watching two hapless, dying citizens who were not destined to survive got to act out their very own death scenes. They put on a show, Sandy had to give them that. Problem was, neither one of the actors wanted to be the first one to die. So they kept flopping around, trying to be the last to move. The Boy Scouts all saluted when they finally died and stayed still.

Eddie Hudson, the previous chief, knew she had been set up for failure and goaded the City Council to publicly recognize her achievements in the disaster scenario. After that, he noticed she had a head on her shoulders and took her under his wing. But even with her impeccable track record, nobody outside the Parker's Mill Police Department took her seriously as a law enforcement officer.

Then everybody in the country saw the video footage from her dashboard camera.

It is night. She is pulling over a weaving, possibly stolen, gray Lexus. When she goes up to the driver's window, a man pops up on the passenger side and shouts good-naturedly, "Hey there, sweet tits."

She takes three sideways steps toward her cruiser, following procedure, as if she were a basketball player on defense, creating a triangle between herself, the ball, and the basket. "Please get back in the vehicle, sir."

He laughs and says, "Aw, don't be hatin'. I got what you need, baby."

The driver starts to get out of the car as well, all slow and controlled, but then lunges at her like a Jack-in-the-box, arms outstretched.

Sandy draws her revolver. Back then she carried a Smith & Wesson Model 686 Plus with a four-inch barrel, loaded with seven standard .38 rounds. Since her attention was on the passenger, the driver is on her before she can bring the barrel up. The driver, nearly a foot and a half taller and at least one hundred and fifty pounds heavier, crashes into her.

Sandy fires the revolver as he drives her to the ground.

They fall out of sight in front of the cruiser with a howl of pain. Sandy rises back into sight, backing away, keeping the gun trained on the driver, still on the ground in front of the cruiser's grille. The mic can still hear him though, as he screams, "Oh *BEEEP* my knee, oh *BEEEEP* Jesus, my knee, my knee."

The passenger comes around the back of the Lexus and rushes at Sandy.

She plants her feet and pivots her hips and shoulders, smoothly tracking him. She yells, and even though you can hear her quite clearly, the TV stations always felt the need to stamp her words across the bottom of the screen in all capital yellow letters. "STOP. YOU WILL FREEZE OR I WILL SHOOT."

But the passenger is too full of rage and wildness to

listen. When he is less than ten feet away, Sandy pulls the trigger. Twice. Two sharp cracks, so close together they sound almost like one shot, and with the suddenness of a taxi clipping a pedestrian, the passenger drops.

For a moment, the only movement is from the spinning red and blue lights, fading away into the night as rendered by the stuttering pixels of the dashboard cam. The silence is broken by the driver howling, "My *BEEEEP* knee. You *BEEEEP*."

She slips off the screen and the mic picks her up, breathing hard, "Shots fired. Repeat. Shots fired. Officer needs ambulance. Two individuals in need of medical attention."

Cut back to the anchors and one of the newscasters would say something predictable like, "Truly incredible, breathtaking footage," in their special voice, a balance of solemnity and admiration, reserved for the stories that came after the daily tragedy and politics, before sports and weather.

Sandy's fifteen minutes of fame lasted long enough to get her elected as Police Chief of Parker's Mill. Eddie Hudson backed her, but it wasn't easy. Sandy had two strikes against her. One, she was a woman, and two, even worse, she was a single mom.

The sheriff of Manchester County, Erik Hoyt, never had seen eye to eye with Hudson and wanted one of his own troopers in the position. He thought it would be easy, but the residents had seen the video, of course, and felt that Parker's Mill boasted its very own genuine Annie Oakley. Some folks had private fantasies about their new police chief shooting all the goddamn illegal immigrants who were taking every job in the county. Others thought for sure she'd go down to the river and shoot anybody cooking meth. And still some in the town thought that if nothing else, she would at least keep those disrespectful teenagers in line.

Seven months later, the shock and awe of the video had worn off, and while Sandy was officially the chief of police in Parker's Mill, she was no longer the woman who had single-handedly taught two rich thugs a lesson they'd never forget, let alone the new law officer who rode in on a white horse and straightened out the town.

She was back to being a woman, a single mom, and a pain in the ass.

CHAPTER 4

Bob Morton Sr. had promised himself he wouldn't cry.

At least, not until he reached his son's cornfield.

He didn't think he was going to make it.

Sobs kept threatening to erupt out of his chest like something alive struggling to get out into the open air. He gritted his teeth and a low keening sound seeped out. Through blurry tears gathering on his lower eyelids, he could see that he was doing at least eighty miles an hour. He had to slow down. If he crashed, then where would that leave Belinda? He couldn't do that to her, taking away both her son and husband on the same day.

He forced himself to pull his toes back, easing off the gas. The big diesel engine's whine dropped to a low hum in relief. At least he could see in the high beams that the field was coming up soon. He pulled over and turned down a dirt road, mostly used by the tractors and harvesters, and followed it to the end.

The tears were flowing now. But that was okay. He was here. He had bitten back a cry that almost escaped, because he wanted—no, *needed*—to wait until he was

kneeling in the rows of corn to properly grieve for his
son. He tried to tell himself that it was completely different from when he was a boy, running up the long
driveway from the bus for the bathroom at home and
failing every time, pissing his pants every time he had
to come home from school and face that empty house.

He knew he was lying to himself.

It was exactly the same.

If he could just hold on to his control, hold on to his
dignity, his manhood, then everything would be okay.
His son would still be gone, true, but at least he would
have shown the universe that Bob Morton Sr. was a man.
A man who took care of his business.

Crying before he gave himself permission would
make him weak.

He hit the brakes when the road ended in a T-intersection,
knowing that he was too late. He was openly weeping
now, tears and snot running down his face, and there was
no hiding it. He barely managed to twist the key, killing
the engine, before stumbling out into the humid summer
air, wind alive in the cornstalks. He plowed forward into
the rows, boots crunching across the countless caterpil-
lar husks that carpeted the soil, before sinking to his
knees, and finally, finally let out the scream that had
been building ever since he had talked with the man
from Allagro.

The Whistle Stop was way down on Highway 67 but
was located just inside the town by a technicality, a
strange quirk in the city limits. Chicago had its O'Hare
Airport, and Parker's Mill had its Whistle Stop. When it
was built, the owner had bribed the town council to

stretch the border of Parker's Mill so it just barely included
the roadhouse. During prohibition, it was easier and
cheaper to pay off the town rather than the county sheriff.
Subsequent town councils had condemned the corrup-
tion, but they weren't stupid. Prohibition or not, the
Whistle Stop brought in a lot of money as taxes or fines
or special levies or whatever they wanted to call it.

The city limits had never been altered since.

It was Saturday night, and the place was packed.
Sandy pulled in and parked right in front, one of the
perks of being chief. She got out and spent a moment
trying to decide if she should wear the hat or not. In the
end, she decided it couldn't hurt. At twenty-six years
old, she stood only five foot, three inches, and weighed
maybe 110 pounds. She was going to need all the help
she could get.

She settled the hat on her head and squared her
equipment, checking everything with a light touch. She
now used a Glock Model 22, with fifteen .40 caliber
rounds. These days, it didn't seem right to carry a pistol
that she'd used to kill a man, her being a peace officer
and all. The Glock was locked and loaded, safety on.
Radio on her right shoulder. Flashlight behind her
pistol, next to the Mace. Two full clips heavy on her left
hip. And a special new surprise tucked away behind the
clips, riding lightly against her left butt cheek.

Godawful crappy modern country music spilled out
from inside. The music was shit, loud as always, but the
crowd noise was low. For a bar like this on a Saturday
night, the place should have been roaring. Sandy made
one last scan of the parking lot, looking for the father's
truck. As far as she knew, the only person to own a vehicle in that family was the father, Purcell. She couldn't

see it; either they parked around back or they had found a different car.

The front two doors were open. The bouncer was gone.

The song ended, and in the brief silence, Sandy could only hear some murmuring and faint laughter. Sandy went inside and immediately stepped sideways, slinking back against the wall. She didn't want to linger in the open backlight of the doorway.

The Whistle Stop smelled of sweat and stale beer. It was built like a barn, or maybe a church. The middle was open, with a high ceiling. Long bars on both sides were chock-full of female bartenders in tight denim shorts and western shirts unbuttoned down to the centers of their chests. There was a stage up front, for when they could get live music. It wasn't often. A digital jukebox served as backup. It was right up front, and pulled even more attention to the empty stage, which gaped like a missing tooth. And even that didn't work right half the time, so the management just threw in seven CDs on shuffle. Most were country hits, of course, your Garth Brooks, your Rascal Flatts, your Shania Twain, your Toby Keith. And once in a while, just to keep everybody happy, they'd include an actual rock *and* roll album.

The next song kicked in. Heavy-duty guitars. The oldest brother, Edgar, sat alone on the stage, bouncing his head slightly to the only noncountry music recognizable down to the bone of every man, woman, and child inside that building. Power chords that struck a vibration throughout the entire universe. Sandy always gave a silent thanks whenever she heard something from the obligatory soundtrack to bars around the world, AC/DC's *Back in Black*.

Most everybody else was clustered along the two bars, waiting for the situation to be sorted out. Nobody moved around a whole lot, except for the youngest brother. Axel Hillstrom Fitzgimmon. He was nineteen, a mean, arrogant little punk. Technically, he was under-age and shouldn't have been even allowed inside the Whistle Stop. He lived in a shack with Edgar they'd built themselves up the hill from their father's house. Axel worked for an auto-repair garage in town, getting paid to carry heavy shit around all day and drive the tow truck once in a while. Tonight, he was putting on a show, having himself one hell of a good time all over the dance floor that stretched from the stage almost to the front door. He'd chased everyone off the dance floor by treating it as his own private mosh pit and jumped around as if the floor had an electric current.

She couldn't see Charlie.

Fredriquo Guiterrez, the bouncer, better known as Freddy G, was over by the bar, holding a bloody bar rag against his mouth. Freddy G was over forty, balding hair pulled back into a ponytail, still finding work as a bouncer thanks to genetics. Stories floated around town that he had once lifted two full-grown men by their belts and thrown them in the mud. Nobody knew if it was true or not, but he was nearly seven feet tall with a foot-ball lineman's gut and arms.

He knew she was here, but wouldn't meet her eyes.

Charlie was the worry. Back from some sand coun-try, full of pep, ready to rock and roll right along with the music. He was always deliberately vague about his deployment, and wanted folks to believe he was in-volved in some hardcore Black Ops, Company-style CIA-type shit.

She made herself a target. Stepped onto the dance floor.

Axel kept on flailing around. Edgar ignored her and bobbed his shaved head in stuttering, jerking movements along with the beat. He was the shy brother, and except for a nervous tic that made him giggle uncontrollably whenever he touched a firearm, she ignored him. Her presence had been noticed by the rest of the bar, though, and everybody else whispered and nodded. The minimal crowd noise faded away, until only the music filled the roadhouse.

Sandy knew the Fitzgimmon brothers couldn't have made Freddy G bleed without being sneaky, so she was more than ready when Charlie tried to slip his forearm around her neck. She dropped her chin into her chest and stomped down with her boot, crushing his toes. His left forearm slipped off her forehead while his right fumbled for her handgun and couldn't unsnap the leather.

She brought her right elbow back and caught him in the solar plexus. Air chuffed out of his lungs, whistling past her right ear. Her left hand found the second holster on her left hip and whipped out the Taser X26P, a handy little compact plastic *fuck you*.

From there, it was simply a matter of twisting out of his grasp and squeezing the trigger. Two vicious barbs, each connected to the weapon with coiled wire, jumped out and dug themselves deep into Charlie's abdomen like fishing lures out for vengeance. Over 13,000 volts sparked through him, effectively shutting down any kind of control Charlie had hoped to exert over his own body. He involuntarily groaned, twitching like a cattle prod had been shoved up his ass.

Axel was already rushing at her. Sandy grabbed her canister of Mace clipped to her belt with her right hand and brought it up, blasting him directly in the face. To Axel's credit, he didn't slow down. He just couldn't see anything anymore.

Sandy sidestepped his pinwheeling arms and let him crash into his brother. The two of them went down like two trees in a monsoon. Her hand went to her third and last weapon, the Glock. She gave Edgar a meaningful look.

He sat still on the stage. His head wasn't bouncing anymore.

Sandy left the Glock in its holster, replaced the cartridge in the Taser, and turned back to the younger brothers.

Axel kept trying to stand up, but couldn't find his balance with his eyes screwed tight, as clear mucus gushed out his nose and filled his bottom lip, his entire face the color of homemade hot sauce. He crawled away, managed to find his feet, and struck out in a random direction until he banged against the front doorframe and staggered outside.

The charge only lasted five seconds, and Charlie regained control. He sat up and glared at her. "You fucking—"

Sandy wasn't in the mood and shot him again with the Taser.

Charlie writhed on the dance floor for another five long seconds. At the end of it, he went limp. Sandy knelt among the Anti-Felon Identification confetti that had sprayed out of the Taser when it had been fired. She gathered all four wires and snipped them off with a Leatherman. Keeping his shoulder pinned down, she used her right hand to rip the barbs out of his torso with as much of a ninety-degree angle as she could manage.

She decided he could live without the sterilizing swabs and Band-Aids and stood, using her boot to roll Charlie over onto his stomach. He groaned. She ignored this and crossed his hands in the small of his back. She snapped plastic zip ties around his wrists and left him facedown on the dance floor. She decided to leave Axel for now and pointed at Edgar. "You. Facedown on the floor. Fingers laced on the back of your neck. Now."

"I didn't do nothing," Edgar said. "You got no right."

"I'll give your lawyer a call later. At the moment, I will cuff you one way or another. You can either climb into my vehicle under your own power or I will be forced to persuade you. The choice is entirely yours."

Edgar didn't like it, but he got on the floor and interlaced his fingers at the back of his head. He glared sideways up at the bar patrons as Sandy handcuffed him. "Fuck all y'all. Buncha bitches and pussies." She left him facedown on the floor. He continued to yell at everybody as Sandy went out the front. "Bitches and pussies. Fuck you. Fuck all of you. I know who you are."

Sandy found Axel punching her squad car. She kicked his legs out from under him and put him on the asphalt. He tried to push off the ground but Sandy jammed her knee deep in the center of his back to remind him to be still. She wrenched his arms back and zip tied his wrists as if she'd just roped a calf in a rodeo.

Folks spilled out of the doorway to watch.

Sandy threw Axel in the back of the cruiser and went back inside. She found Freddy G standing over Charlie, giving serious thought to stomping on Charlie's head.

Edgar was still cussing at anybody in his line of sight. Charlie was smart enough to stay quiet and pretend to be nearly unconscious.

Sandy looked up at Freddy G. "What's the damage?"

He peeled back his bloody lips in a grimace. One of his top incisors was gone. "Keeping it in a shot glass over there," he explained.

"I'm no dentist," Sandy said. "But crushing his skull won't grow you a new tooth."

"It'd make me happy," Freddy G said.

Sandy couldn't argue with that.

Edgar rolled over and saw the bouncer looming over them like Paul Bunyan. "Hey man, this is your job, ain't it? What you get paid for. You gonna whine like a bitch all night?"

Sandy stepped in front of Freddy G and helped Edgar to his feet. "Let's get you to the car before any accidents happen."

Freddy G shook a pudgy finger at Edgar. "Y'all are not welcome in here anymore. I see you in here again, I'll put you in the fucking hospital."

Edgar started to say something back, but Sandy gave his arms a swift, savage tug straight up, torqueing the hell out of his shoulders. He gave a squeal of pain and they were out the door.

Edgar went in the backseat with Axel. Charlie took longer, mostly because he couldn't walk on his own worth a damn. Sandy tipped her hat at Freddy G, who was settling back into his spot on a bar stool outside the front door. He spit blood into the parking lot and didn't wave back.

* * *

When the phone rang, the Mortons had just finished dinner. Belinda was in the kitchen, washing up, and Bob was settling into his chair with the paper and the remote.

Belinda knew better than to answer. Even though it was almost always for her, she would wait until her husband picked up the cordless phone they kept between his chair and the couch, and if it was for her, she would wait for him to call her name before she picked up the handset in the kitchen.

Bob said, "Hello?"

The voice on the other end was no one he had heard before. "Mr. Morton?"

"Who is this?"

"Mr. Morton, this is Paul Cochran. I am the acting Vice President of Affairs for Allagro and I am afraid that it is my duty to call with unfortunate news." Cochran waited a moment, giving Bob a moment to ask the obvious question.

Bob said, "What are you talking about?"

A sad, heavy sigh. "I wish I could be there in person to tell you. However, certain safety protocols are preventing any of us to travel at the moment. I will be there shortly. Tomorrow night at the latest."

Bob repeated, "What are you talking about?"

"At approximately eleven-thirty a.m. local time, our Caribbean facility was targeted by an extremist environmental terrorist organization. Everyone on the island was killed, including your son." The voice softened. "My deepest sympathies."

Bob felt as if he was tipping forward into an impossible abyss and almost dropped the phone.

Cochran seemed to sense this and waited for a moment before resuming. "Of course, we will do everything within our power to find those responsible and bring them to justice. Your son was a valued member of the Allagro team. I hope that the knowledge that your son died defending his deepest beliefs makes this burden easier to bear."

Bob did not know what to say. His involuntary Midwestern compulsion for politeness kicked in and he mumbled something like, "Thank you for letting us know."

"Our thoughts and prayers are with you at this difficult time. As I said, I will be flying out at the earliest possible window . . . and I will be accompanying your son's remains. This information, at the moment at least, is still classified. I trust that it will remain so until Allagro is able to present the facts at a press conference tomorrow. Please, for the sake of your son, and the company he had devoted his life to, please do not speak to anyone from the media until I am there to assist you."

"Of course not," Bob said. His voice, his living room, everything, seemed very far away.

"I will be in touch shortly. If you need anything, call your son's office. They will put you in contact with me. I know this is terrible news, but your son would want all of us to remain strong and hunt down those responsible. Again, please do not speak about this with anyone. Can I count on your cooperation?" Cochran asked.

Bob managed a noise that sounded almost like a "Yes."

Cochran said, "I will see you soon," and the line went dead.

Bob let the phone fall in his lap, working at piecing together what he had just heard. The only thing he knew for certain was that his son was dead. Why he believed the man on the other end of the phone, he couldn't say. He believed the news nonetheless. His son was dead. He pushed his way past the questioning eyes of Belinda and stumbled out the back door, heading for his truck. He needed some time to process this, and he'd be damned if he was going to cry in front of his wife.

Now, surrounded by his son's corn, he finally succumbed completely to the anguish that had been struggling to explode since he dropped the phone. He screamed at the night sky. His howls echoed up and down the rows of corn that his son had promised would change everything. He could still hear Bob Jr.'s voice, saying, "Dad, trust me, these seeds, they're gonna revolutionize how the world farms. This corn, it's special. Really special. Get it in the ground. You'll see."

Bob believed that genetically modified seeds would save the world. He believed this even more than he believed in his Lord and Savior, Jesus Christ. And both were absolute truths. God had given Man the tools to feed himself. This was a fact.

Bob had no doubts. None.

Genetically modified seeds would save us all.

So Bob couldn't get his son's seeds in the ground fast enough. He'd watched the corn as it grew, nurtured it, handling everything personally, from the irrigation duties to spreading fertilizer. Getting close to being ripe, it didn't look any different from the regular corn he knew. Same ears. Same leaves. Same stalks. Kernels near bursting with a deep neon yellow.

Maybe that was the point. Maybe there was no difference. And right now, he didn't know, he didn't understand, and he didn't care. His son was dead. He rocked back and forth, until toppling over, face on the ground, dirt spilling into his open mouth. He sobbed. Gasped. He grabbed at the soil, let it run through his fingers.

He was not aware that when he sucked in yet one more gust of air to scream into the dirt, he inhaled a small number of microscopic fungus spores, which stuck to every wet surface they encountered. The inside of his mouth. His throat. His lungs.

They went to work, sending tiny, hairlike filaments deep into the tissue.

And started to grow.

When Bob's outpouring of agony had passed, when he could regain control, when he could gather all the strings of his pain and pull them even closer for a while, he swallowed, spit out some of the soil that had found its way into his mouth, and went back to his truck to drive back home and tell his wife their son was dead.

CHAPTER 5

"He pukes back there, both of you are cleaning it up," Sandy told Edgar and Charlie.

Axel had been trying to get the Mace out of his nose and throat the whole ride into town while Sandy followed Highway 100 north as it wound along the Mississippi River. He'd been using his T-shirt as a snot rag, and for a while it looked like he had everything under control, but the guttural retching sounds he made while trying to take a deep breath worried everybody in the car.

Edgar and Charlie hated Sandy and being stuck in the backseat with a vomiting Axel made it worse. Charlie was still pretending to be dazed and confused from the Taser, but Edgar was taking out his anger on his youngest brother. "You fucking puke in here, Axe, I'm gonna kick the living shit out of you. Swear to fucking Christ."

Axel didn't act like he'd heard anything. He sat in the center, leaning over, one arm flat out against the clear, bulletproof partition, eyes screwed tight.

Sandy pulled to a stop at Parker's Mill's only stoplight, at the intersection of Highway 100 and Main Street. At this time of night, the intersection was utterly empty.

Located fifty miles east of Springfield, Parker's Mill had around a thousand citizens. Not too many of them were Bible-thumping evangelists like the Johnsons; they were mostly decent folks who sometimes got out of line. Some were more prone to finding trouble than others.

Main Street marched east for three blocks, with a few banks, a church, a car wash, a couple of gas stations, a combination video store and karate studio. The police station was two blocks down. The few other commercial buildings clustered a block or two along Main Street included a Moose Lodge, more churches, a library, a volunteer fire department, a Stop 'n Save grocery store, an empty hardware store. Every building and light post was covered in red, white, and blue bunting in preparation for the big Fourth of July Sweet Corn Jubilation.

It went without saying that Parker's Mill lived and died with the corn.

Only Edgar noticed that instead of turning right and heading to the police station, Sandy kept going north along Highway 67. He tried to get his brothers' attention. They ignored him. A mile later, she turned left on Highway 104 and they crossed over the river.

Edgar couldn't hold it in anymore and said, "I don't know what you think you're pullin'. It ain't gonna work."

Sandy didn't answer, and turned off immediately after crossing the river, into the Fitzgimmon driveway. This was a long dirt road that wandered through the scrub along the river.

Edgar said in delight, "Oh, I get it. It's that time of the

month, right? You're on the rag. Making you all screwy. Cause you, you have no idea what your fuckin' doing, do you?"

When the road abruptly turned into the foothills, the cruiser's headlights found a gate in the middle of the road. Beyond it lay the Fitzgimmon farmhouse. It was set back from the gate about fifty yards, surrounded by a dozen or so oak trees at least a hundred years old.

Sandy got out and found the gate locked. It didn't surprise her. Purcell didn't trust anybody outside of his own family. She waited a moment, knowing he'd damn well seen the headlights and was watching her, probably through a scope.

The porch light flicked on, and in the glow, the house didn't look like it had been painted or repaired since it had first been built, right around the time the trees had been planted. Purcell's rail-thin silhouette appeared in the doorway.

At least it wasn't obvious if he was carrying a firearm.

Sandy took that as a good sign.

Purcell was something of a dark legend in town. Everybody had heard about him, but few had seen him. He didn't like to leave his farm unless it was an emergency. He coaxed corn and soy out of the thin soil that covered the slanted creek beds and rolling hills. He lived off his own well, grew his own food, and crapped in his own septic tank. He sent his wife to the Costco once a month for staples like flour, coffee, and Pop-Tarts.

Everybody in town had their own stories. The only thing they agreed was that Purcell had done time. The stories ranged anywhere from six years in the easy-going county jail or ten years in nasty San Quentin.

Beyond that, they said he was a gunrunner. He used his farm as a hideout for drug shipments. He'd found Jesus. He was in the witness-protection program. He was plotting something evil with Charlie Manson. He was ex-CIA.

To Sandy, it sounded like a small town with too much time.

She had checked one night, feeling that as the chief she should know as much as possible about any known lawbreakers in town. Purcell wasn't the only problem child, not by a long shot, but he was one of the most colorful, and in some ways he was downright alarming.

He had been part of a crew in St. Louis, taking down a Brink's armored car outside of the last grocery store stop of the day. They got five miles and it all ended in a roadblock. No shots were fired. Purcell served five years in the Chillicothe Correctional Center for armed robbery. Moved back to his parents' homestead when he got out. His parents were long gone. The house was barely habitable. He married a woman from Finland. Nobody knew a damn thing about her and either she didn't speak English or pretended not to when she came to town.

Nobody saw him or heard from him for years. That's why folks weren't sure about him. Until all three of his boys were the right age, and Purcell sprung them on the Parker's Mill public school district at the same time. Edgar went into the third grade, but was eventually moved down to the first grade so he could learn the basics of reading and arithmetic. He eventually caught up when he was in the fifth grade, but forever suffered being adrift, and never had any friends. Axel unleashed holy hell on the kindergarten and was eventually expelled in the first grade. His education came in the form of homeschooling until he was fifteen. Charlie's academic career began smoothly enough, until he managed to scandalize the entire town when he was arrested for releasing all of the animals tethered to the lawn of the First Baptist Church's nativity scene. Sheep, goats, and a blind mule went wandering through Parker's Mill in the early morning hours, while Charlie took the baby Jesus doll and sent him down the Mississippi River, much like Moses.

"Evenin'" said Purcell as he approached the gate.

"Evenin'" Sandy said. "How you doing?"

"Aw hell, you know. Can't complain. Well, I could, you know, but nobody'd listen," Purcell laughed. "How's the new job working out for ya?"

"Not exactly what I expected."

"I'll bet."

"Heard you were working on an organic certification."

"Yeah, yeah. They're makin' me jump through more hoops than a goddamn circus freak." He rested his forearms on the gate and shook his head. "They got people crawling all over my farm, taking samples of everything, the soil, the water, the corn. Surprised they didn't want a sample of my piss."

Neither Purcell nor Sandy acted as if the three brothers in the backseat of the cruiser even existed. They might have been two old friends shooting the shit on a slow Sunday afternoon.

"Still, it's worth it," Purcell continued. "Seems to me

it's maybe the last act of freedom we have left, not being forced to put all these asshole chemicals in our food."

Sandy got a better look at the man. It looked like his wife had been keeping his hair short with the sheep shears. Ropy muscles slid and rolled under leathery skin. His eyes sparkled in the glow of the headlights. Purcell was getting old, but he was still tougher than tree bark.

"Well, best of luck to you," Sandy said. "Suppose it's time we get down to the reason I'm out here."

"Thought you might, sooner or later."

"Your boys, they were causing the Whistle Stop some problems. Gave the bouncer a hard time. Now, he's a good guy. Not the kind of bouncer that picks on folks 'cause he gets bored."

"Can't say I'm surprised. They been awful jumpy these past few days. Thought they might blow off some steam somewhere. So . . . why'd you bring 'em back here? Seems to me, folks like you think they belong in jail for a night or two, they cause that kind of ruckus. Ain't that what usually happens?"

"Usually."

"Yeah, and you brought 'em back here. Why's that?"

Sandy shrugged. "You helped my dad out once. Figured I owed you one for my family." Her family car's tire had blown out on the way for an Easter Sunday church service in 1994. Purcell, who had clearly spent the night in his pickup, was on his way home from a night out. He pulled over and helped Sandy's dad pull off the tire and even donated the spare tire when he discovered Sandy's dad didn't have one.

"Shit. I'll take your word for it." He grinned in the headlights. "Don't remember much. That was what, twenty some-odd years ago? You been waiting all this time to say thanks? Coulda sent a thank-you card."

Sandy didn't answer. It was difficult to explain. She just knew she would never forget the image of this man as he loped across the highway twenty years ago, long hair in his face, carrying the tire over his shoulder, hair sticking to both the tire and his tongue. He took the jack from Sandy's dad without a word and crawled under the car. Sandy and her mom waited way, way back, damn near in the freshly plowed field. It was still a little close for Sandy's mom, who wasn't sure if they should break into a run, fleeing to the nearest farmhouse, or offer the man some freshly baked cookies as a thank-you. Sandy didn't know why her mom was so nervous; she understood just fine that the man was helping them.

This wild man, this force of nature, this was her first real encounter with a human who had endured unthinkable violence as well as inflicted severe pain on others. At eight, she had listened keenly to her parents' private conversations and had heard of Purcell Fitzgimmon. He supposedly put a poor mail carrier in intensive care due to the unacceptable condition of a package.

And yet here he was, calm and collected and kind as Mr. Rogers. She would never forget his languid wave as he got back in his truck and pulled back onto the highway. She wasn't around when her dad returned the spare, but she didn't need to be. Purcell had already made a long-lasting impact. He taught her that the world could be gentle and beautiful and wild and vicious all at the same time.

The Chisels were on their way in less than ten minutes and even made it to church on time.

Sandy finally just said, "If your boys get out of line again, they will face some serious problems." She wasn't kidding. If Charlie got arrested, he could get kicked out of the armed forces, or whatever the hell he was doing. Edgar and Axel had enough combined charges to put them in the state pen for a long time if they were unlucky enough to face a pissed-off judge who wanted to prove he was tough on crime.

"And I appreciate that," Purcell said. "What happens next?"

"Up to you. They're your problem now." Sandy went to the back door and pulled out the boys, one by one. They stood, a little too meek and mild, like they were trying not to laugh. Sandy unlocked the cuffs from Edgar and snipped through the zip ties on Charlie and Axel with her Leatherman.

Purcell never opened the gate. "Well then. It's gonna be like this. You three. You look at me. You too, Charlie. You ain't so big, boy. You get caught doing dumb shit and you're out with my vehicle, thought you were smarter'n that. We gonna have a *talk* when you get back."

They flinched as if he'd thrown a punch.

Purcell's polite, civilized veneer was gone. His features had shifted slightly, eyebrows lowered, eyes narrowed, lips pulled back, as the headlights lit his face from below, giving him a feral, savage look; Sandy understood she was looking at the real Purcell. The transformation unnerved her.

For a moment, she worried she had made a terrible mistake. If the Fitzgimmons wanted, they could be on her before she could reach her weapons, let alone her radio. And she was the one that had let them loose.

But Purcell never looked at her. His rage was aimed at his sons, every word a razor wrapped in barbed wire. "Right now, you gonna march on back down to the Whistle Stop and bring my truck back." Sandy now understood why the brothers had reacted as if each word was a physical blow. God knew what this man had done to them as they grew up.

"The walk will sober you up and make you think," Purcell said and gave Sandy a challenging look. She didn't object. It was a hell of a walk. The Whistle Stop was over twelve miles south. "And if there is one dent, one single hint of a scratch, when you get back here you will beat the living shit out of each other for my amusement." It was not an idle threat.

They didn't argue, didn't glare at their old man— nothing. They waited silently, like cowed dogs that had the shit stomped out of them.

It was time to go. "Gentlemen." Sandy nodded at them and their father and got back in the car. She backed up into a wide space, pulled around, and drove back down the driveway.

The spiders crept out of the darkness of the far southern edge of Bob Morton's private cornfield, drawn toward the movement and soft sounds inside the Einhorn henhouse. The sagging structure was built out of leftover scraps of lumber that Kurt had scavenged from construction sites. He'd thrown it together down at the edge of the huge backyard, where the grass ran up against the rows of crops. He sank a few fence posts, surrounded them with old chicken wire to encircle a ten-foot rectangular pen, and built a little house that sat unsteadily on stilts at the end. Thirteen hens called it home. There used to be a rooster, but when it wouldn't shut up early one dawn, Kurt, fighting a brutal hangover, trudged down the lawn, grabbed the rooster by the neck, and whipped the body around until its neck had snapped.

Under a perfectly curved sliver of a nearly blackened moon, the creatures scuttled into the cool grass and passed easily through the chicken wire. At first glance, they might have been mistaken for fat spiders. Spiders didn't quite move like these organisms, though. These blobs lurched along unsteadily on mismatched legs. They moved slowly.

The spider-things gathered around all four of the support posts and swarmed up into the henhouse. As they climbed, the blobs hung unnaturally, as if they weren't connected to the legs by any kind of bones, either internal or external. They swayed, plump and gray as death, as their too-many legs clumsily worked their way up all of the four-by-ten posts.

They left nothing but silence behind them.

As the nearly invisible moon passed through the long night, the spiderlike creatures laboriously crawled up into the henhouse. Dozens. Then hundreds. At first, there were a few mildly startled clucks, a few investigative pecks, as the chickens tasted the new creatures. The insects tasted sour, and the texture of the flesh was even softer than worms. The chickens snapped at the spiders in irritation, but even that slowed and stopped as the spiders overwhelmed the birds.

Silence descended upon the henhouse.

SUNDAY,
JULY 1st

CHAPTER 6

When the sun rose, Sandy was out in the garage, beating the shit out of a punching bag while an old boom box blasted Ramones tunes.

She had learned long ago not to think about her job when she was punching and elbowing and kicking and kneeing and head-butting the bag. When she had started out as a deputy, she would come home and try and relieve her stress by gathering a mental image of some asshole she'd encountered on the job, then dump as much aggression and anger as possible on the bag, unleashing all that steam in one forty-five-minute eruption.

It worked fine, until one night on the job she almost put her fist through some drunk dipshit's face thanks to her new muscle memory. Since then, while working out, she found it was better to disassociate from the worst images of humanity and focus solely on the movement of muscles as they drove her skeleton.

She would have preferred to hang the bag outside, but she had to be conscious about how she was viewed in the community. It was bad enough that some of her fellow cops teased her, saying that she must have been picturing the father of her boy when she was attacking the bag. She'd laugh, too, and say, "Sometimes." For her, though, it was more about taking out her frustration about everything that she couldn't control, wringing stress out of her body, simple and complicated at the same time.

Her ex, Kevin's father, would probably say that she couldn't make up her mind about a damn thing. The irritating thing was that he was probably right.

She stepped back a moment, gathering herself for another flurry of punches, and looked back to the door to the house. Kevin liked to get up late on Sundays, so she let him. She used to take him to church, but finally stopped when he asked her about her own beliefs, specifically what she thought happened when somebody died. She thought this might be one of those Hallmark or Lifetime moments where the parent sits down with their child for a life-changing talk, a moment they would both remember forever. She had also decided long ago that honesty was the only policy, with the exception of Santa Claus. She told him, "I took you to church not because I was worried about your immortal soul. I took you because . . . it was expected of me. I thought it was the right thing to do. I never worried about any of the stuff they told us. Life is beyond all of us. It's up to you to find what you believe."

Kevin nodded. Said, "Cool." And ran off to play with his rocket ship models.

So much for the Hallmark moment.

Sunday mornings now, she let him sleep in and play video games if he wanted. He was old enough to pour his own milk into a bowl of cereal and had proved more than capable of feeding himself. It wasn't always appropriate, such as Cheese Doodles at six a.m., but he never went hungry.

Last Sandy had heard, Kevin's father was in southern Indiana, wiping down windshields while the other worker drained oil from cars in a Quik-Change. There was no paternity test. They both knew, without a doubt, he was the father, even if he never admitted it.

The other problem was that Barry, Bar to his buddies, had tried to disappear two or three times now.

The last time Sandy had caught up to her dear old ex, he was working at a big box superstore as the guy who collected the shopping carts. The confrontation in the middle of the massive parking lot was brief, painful, and embarrassing for both. Disgusted, Sandy got back in her car. She told him to get in touch when he was a man, and until then, well he could fuck right off.

Bar assured her he was getting his life together, and he would send her money.

They both knew this was a lie.

It was easier to pretend it wasn't.

She usually spent Sunday mornings in the garage, then went back and made a big breakfast. If nothing important happened, like a car wreck or robbery or, God forbid, a murder, Sundays were her days off. The town, for the most part, complied. Nothing much happened and since things stayed quiet, Sandy could enjoy a full day at home with her son.

But lately something wasn't working with Kevin. Most times, they got along fine. He understood the rules, he did his chores and homework without complaining too much, and was happy to once in a while put down his books or tablet and join her for dinner. The past few months, though, the timing was off, they weren't connecting, and Sandy couldn't figure out what she was doing differently, and wondered what problems her son was facing alone.

Whatever it was, she'd bet that it was probably related to the town, channeled through the school. She hoped it wasn't a girl. He hadn't exactly discovered sex yet and it took a backseat to his TV shows and books. She knew it wasn't the most comfortable thing for him, being the son of the police chief, but they'd had long talks about bullying and how to respond, and she felt he would open up if that was the situation.

She headed in for some breakfast. And maybe a nap.

Ingrid always enjoyed these calm mornings after Kurt's storms. She hurt, make no mistake. After the cop left, he'd trapped her in the bathroom and gone after her with one of her pots. Ingrid wedged herself in the corner between the toilet and the wall, tucking her fingers into her armpits, knees into her chest while he went to town on the backs of her shoulders and the back of her head whenever he made a particular point, hissing that it wasn't his fault she was too dumb to understand, reminding her it wasn't any fun having to make all the tough decisions.

When he was too tired to beat on her anymore, he straightened, threw the dented pot in the bathtub, said, "You want to hide next to the toilet, you face the consequences, stupid bitch." He unzipped his jeans and pissed on her.

Ingrid didn't see the beatings as much different from

sex. Sometimes it hurt, really awful, but when it was over, Kurt was spent and tired. He kept his distance. Sometimes for days. He'd gotten whatever it was out of his system and would leave her alone for a couple of days while she healed up. He ate in front of the television, as always, but she got to eat dinner in the kitchen by herself. It was a relief, not worrying if her eating was annoying him. The rest of the time, he spent in the front room, watching TV, drinking beer, or in the bathroom, with the paper. She knew he hid pornographic magazines in the paper and sometimes she could hear him masturbating in there.

Again, it was actually a relief. It meant he wouldn't expect anything that night and it certainly smelled better in there when he was finished.

She made her way down the lawn, letting gravity guide her. Her entire face was swollen, leaving just slits for her eyes, and she couldn't see much. She carried a basket for eggs. He might be leaving her alone for now, but he still damn sure expected breakfast.

Ingrid peered through the wire. It looked like the hens were still inside the coop. Maybe something had spooked them in the night. Usually, once the sun was peeking over the corn, they were out scratching at the dirt. She would have to remember to feed them later. She only trusted herself to carry one thing at a time, and since she had to get Kurt's breakfast started, she would bring the seeds down later.

She brushed the new cobwebs out of the way and opened the back of the henhouse. The hens were still in their nests, strangely quiet. They moved slowly away from her searching fingers, if they moved at all. Her aches and pains pushed any puzzlement out of her head until it was all she could do to shove her fingers under the closest hens and find the eggs in the straw. She collected four eggs, still warm, and deposited them in the basket. She latched the henhouse door, and shuffled back up the lawn.

The chickens never made a sound.

Bob couldn't sleep.

He parked himself in his chair with a pint of Jim Beam and waited for the news to report what he already knew. Belinda had spent the night in their bed, sobbing into pillows. Bob tried not to listen. It was important to them that they each grieve in their own way, independent of the other. Bob, having let all of his anguish out in Junior's cornfield, sat silent and motionless in his La-Z-Boy. He felt his gaze bounce ever so slowly from Fox News to Junior's high school portrait on the mantel and back to the TV, all night long.

He rarely drank anything stronger than lemonade, and the Jim Beam went straight to his head. It didn't help.

Especially when the aerial footage of the smoking island hit the news networks. Bob felt lost within the blurry, shaky images, and only a few key phrases penetrated his fog of mourning. "Total annihilation . . . one hundred and sixty-four confirmed dead . . . quite possibly a result of ecological terrorism . . . the State Department is pledging full cooperation with Haitian authorities . . . Allagro stock has fallen significantly, following rumors of a failed new seed launch . . ."

Bob was never one to sit still and wait, but now, there was nothing else he could accomplish. He wanted to go out and smash something, but he needed to listen for any breaking news. There was still a part of him that wanted to hope, hope that his son had somehow made it off the island in time, and was drifting in the ocean somewhere, just waiting to be picked up. He fought against this hope, fought against it like white blood cells fighting off an infection. Still, the hope swelled inside him like an abscess, even though he knew it was poison.

He coughed and felt around for the bottle of Jim Beam on the floor next to the La-Z-Boy. He hoped he was wrong about its being empty. But he needed something to soften the blow. He knew his son was dead. He just needed the confirmation to kill the hope that he was wrong. And until then, he was a fish caught on a hook; doomed, but still alive, still allowed to struggle.

Kurt was still in the bathroom.

Ingrid thanked the Lord for small favors and set the basket of eggs on the kitchen counter. She pulled milk and bacon out of the fridge, deftly sliced a hunk of butter from the stick, and flicked it into the frying pan on the stove. She turned the heat down low, just enough to melt the butter. Her hands found a clean bowl next to the sink and set it next to the eggs. Despite being so injured that she couldn't walk without pain, she found peace in the kitchen. Her body seemed to glide around by itself, pulling out ingredients, collecting utensils, all while an internal clock kept track of the heat and time on the stove.

She reached out, grabbed an egg from the basket. Cracked it with a precise, practiced motion.

Tiny black centipedes scurried out of the broken shell and crawled over her hand.

Ingrid didn't see them at first. She only felt a vague sensation that the weight of the egg was off, that the yolk should be spilling out into the bowl. A whiff of something foul and rotten invaded her nose, and the long black insects spread across the back of her right hand and slithered up her arm.

She uttered a deep cry of disgust and whipped her hand at the floor, trying to fling the bugs away. Her left hand knocked the basket off the counter, and the rest of the eggs smashed on the floor. Hundreds of long, black insects erupted from the shattered shells and weaved and seethed across the tiles. They looked as if ropy black tissue had stolen dozens and dozens of spindly legs from other insects and was now blindly searching for more warm flesh.

Ingrid slapped at her arm, trying to brush the string-like bugs away. Her fingers left dark gray streaks where she had crushed clusters of the centipedes, spattering them across her skin like thick droplets of oily rain. She cried out again and fell back into the fridge, clawing at her arm with her fingernails, ripping at the writhing horrors. They moved in S patterns, like tiny, frantic snakes, surging up her arm, wriggling under her shirt, and crawling up her neck.

Ingrid went berserk, spinning and flailing. Her shoes spun in the wreckage of the infected eggs, crushing bugs, creating a blackened slime on the kitchen floor. She slipped in the mess and fell, smacking her head into the stove as she went down. One wild arm struck the edge of the frying pan and sent it crashing against the back of the stove.

On the floor, Ingrid whipped her head back and forth as the centipede things crept over her jawbone and forced their way into any hole they could find, worming into her skull through her mouth, her nose, her ears, slipping between her eyelids and eyeballs.

Her body flopped and thrummed against the tiles as if she were having an epileptic fit. Eventually, her legs stopped shaking. Her arms slowed and stopped. The insects on the floor swarmed across her body and disappeared under her clothes.

For a full five minutes, Ingrid did not move.

Her right hand fluttered and curled into a soft fist. Her head twitched. Her eyes, which had never closed, gazed dully at the ceiling. She managed to roll over to her stomach and draw her knees under her. She rocked back and forth for a while, as if getting used to how gravity worked. Moving like a toddler, she crawled toward the back door.

Kurt's voice boomed through the thin slats of the bathroom door, echoing throughout the empty farmhouse, "Better not be burnin' the fuckin' bacon again."

CHAPTER 7

Bob hadn't moved in hours. He couldn't even remember the last time he'd been in the bathroom. The news was still maddeningly vague. Nobody knew anything, only that the island had suffered a massive, severe fire, and it was feared that there were no survivors. But that didn't stop all the speculating.

Bob couldn't even muster the indignation that the White House had not even held a press conference yet to express their sorrow and condemn those responsible. He couldn't understand why it was so difficult to simply provide a list of the known fatalities. A brief phone call from his son's employer was not enough. He needed the power of television to make the death of his son final. Then he could move on. Until then, he was stuck in a sort of formless limbo, caught between knowing deep in his guts that Bob Jr. was dead, and the irrational hope that refused to let him sleep, to rest, to even blink.

Around nine in the morning, a white van turned off the highway and cautiously trundled down the long driveway slowly, as if it wasn't sure it was in the right place. From his chair, Bob watched through the front windows as it approached the house. It got close enough for Bob to see the logo, WGON in bright blue letters, tilted slightly to suggest movement and urgency, and the words ACTION NEWS underneath. This was a TV station out of Springfield.

For the first time since the phone call, Bob worried he might throw up.

He didn't want to face reporters. Especially TV reporters. With cameras. He'd chew his own testicles off before he sent his wife outside, so he focused, planted his feet on the wool rug, and stood. The room wobbled a bit but straightened out, and for the first time in twelve hours, he felt almost strong. He suffered a moment of intense dizziness when he bent over to grab the remote, but it passed and he turned off the TV. Belinda had been quiet for a while now, and he closed the bedroom door, then went outside, hammered down the wide concrete back steps, trying to contain the rage and sorrow as he went to greet the unwelcome visitors.

He wished he had more bourbon.

The white van circled around the great oak in the center of the farm, taking its time, tires rolling over the smooth gravel. Bob got the feeling they were already filming and wondered how they would portray his life in the shape of the long equipment sheds full of irrigation and harvesting machines. It stopped and the young, hot reporter got out of the passenger seat while another person got out of the side.

Bob had been to enough political and business public displays of friendliness in the form of godawful free hot dogs, bags and bags of potato chips, and endless carbonated soft drinks. All as if the public was nothing but voracious cattle, lining up to feed at the trough when dinner is called. All free. *Free*. That magic word. Even if only half of the people that flocked to these garish campaign events voted, and even then, even if only half of those votes went to Bob's guy, it was all worth it.

During these grand openings and political rallies the media had not only been invited, but required. Bob had dealt with enough PR people to know that the girl reporter was a puppet, controlled by the guy next to her. He was the producer. He had on a Chicago Cubs hat. Bob hated him immediately. This was Cardinals country, and everybody else could get the hell out.

Bob had been used to being on their side. Today was different. He knew that the third guy to get out always had the camera. He didn't want to be onscreen and held up his hand.

This camera guy already had the soft light mounted on the camera lit when he climbed out behind the producer. The producer started talking fast. "Mr. Morton, Mr. Morton. I'm Allen Wilson, and WGON needs to know, sir, what have you heard about your son?"

"No. No. This is not the time for you to be here." He shook his head. "Stop filming. Now."

Allen was a go-getter. "Mr. Morton, please." He knew when he was closest to big news and got to be first on the scene. "The American people deserve to know!"

Bob knew they'd edit out anything they said to make it look like he was shouting nonsense. He'd seen it happen dozens of times to political rivals, and now that it was happening to him, it made him tongue-tied and he couldn't even manage a simple "No comment."

"Please leave," was the best he could get out.

The WGON crew got closer. The producer gestured

at the reporter and let her take over. She spoke in deep, sympathetic tones. "You have no doubt heard, Mr. Morton, that your son has been reported lost in what some are calling the West Island Massacre. What do you say to this news, tonight?"

"I . . . I . . . do . . . not wish to speak at this time . . ." Bob saw, out of the corner of his eye, another vehicle coming up the driveway. This one was a rental car, small, sleek, and gray, like a seal splitting through a green sea of corn.

The car didn't take the scenic route like the van. It aimed for the news crew and slid to a stop uncomfortably close, leaving a few feet of skid marks in the gravel. The man who jumped out wore a deep black suit and no tie. Sunglasses. Mid-thirties maybe, but there was some bad, bad years in there. Thinning hair swept back in perpetual irritation.

The man ignored Bob and targeted the news crew. "I'll ask you once. Leave. Now. I'll even be polite and say please. Just this once. Mr. Morton has just lost a son. When he is good and ready he will invite you to a press conference. Until then, understand that you are trespassing on private property and Mr. Morton has every legal right to defend his property. You have three seconds to get back in that van and leave immediately. One."

"I'm sorry, who are you?" Allen asked as the cameraman swiveled to take in the newcomer.

"Two," the man said, pulling out a thin, short-barreled 1911 handgun from a shoulder holster inside the suit. He racked the slide back and faced them.

Allen stood his ground. "If you think you're gonna

stick a gun in our face and chase us off, you got another—"

The man put a bullet into the oak tree in the center of the driveway. The gunshot hit the quiet farm like a nuclear bomb. Even Bob jumped. The cameraman jumped as if he'd been pinched by a pair of pliers and dumped his camera into the backseat. The reporter didn't waste any time hopping into the passenger seat and locking the door. Allen wouldn't meet anybody's eye as he mumbled something about the First Amendment, but he scrambled into the van with the other two. The van pulled around, accelerating back down the driveway.

The man put the pistol back in its holster and turned to Bob. He extended his hand. "Mr. Morton. Paul Cochran. First of all, let me extend my deepest condolences on the loss of your son."

"Thank you," Bob said and shook Cochran's hand. His head felt numb.

"Forgive me, but I have to ask. Did you say anything about your son, anything at all?"

"No . . . no. I don't think I said . . . they just showed up."

"Good. If am going to be able to help you, I need total and complete honesty. When was the last time you spoke with your son?"

"I . . ." Bob fought off a wave of grief so strong he thought he might start crying in front of Cochran. He bit it back and swallowed. "Last week. Maybe. I don't know. He was excited about his trip."

"Okay. Did he say anything about any new products?"

"Just that they were about to announce something . . . something big."

Cochran waited a moment, watching Bob closely. He

tilted his head, and Bob could only see twin reflections of the blazing sun in the lenses. "Did he ever send you anything? Anything related to his work?"

Bob said, "No . . . no," before he realized he had just lied. He didn't know why. It just seemed important to protect his son. So he didn't mention the seeds he had planted and the two acres of corn he had visited last night. "No. What is all this about?"

"Precautions. Nothing more."

His time outside, in the sunlight, allowed Bob to focus. He remembered this was his farm and decided to act like it. "You said on the phone you were the Vice President of . . ."

"I am one of several acting Vice Presidents of Affairs, yes."

Bob gestured at Cochran's side, indicating the gun. "And what all does your job description entail?"

Cochran gave an easy, empty smile. "Well, my duties vary. Let's just say I'm involved in whatever myself and my employers deem necessary."

Bob nodded. "You're a fixer."

Cochran shrugged slightly. "If there is a situation that I believe can be fixed, then yes. It depends. Right now, however, my job is to guide you through a difficult period. Look at it this way, Mr. Morton. I am your new best friend."

"You're a lawyer?"

"I have a law degree, yes. And I will be happy to answer any other questions you and your wife may have. However, at the moment, decorum prevents me from continuing. I am afraid I have pressing business we must attend to first." He went back to the car and withdrew a leather case from the backseat. He set it on the hood and popped the latches.

Then, with all the solemn dignity the situation required, he turned, holding up a silver urn.

The back door slammed. They both looked over to the house. Belinda stood at the top of the steps, one hand clasping her robe across her chest, the other holding a fistful of Kleenex up to her face. When she saw the urn, her eyes widened, then rolled back. She uttered a short cry, her legs gave out, and she tumbled down the back steps.

Kurt finally emerged from the bathroom, bowels empty, paper read, and hollered that he was ready for his breakfast. No one answered. He poked his head around the corner and started to get mad when he found the burner still on and Ingrid gone. The kitchen was a fucking mess. It looked and smelled like his wife had waded through pig shit and tracked it all over the tiles. He didn't want to step in the congealed remains of raw eggs and whatever else was on the floor, so he leaned over to turn off the burner. He opened the fridge as if she were hiding inside. Almost disappointed, he shut the fridge door and stood for a while looking at all the shit smeared across the floor.

Then he grabbed the hot frying pan and went looking for his wife.

First, he went upstairs, going through each room, under the bed, in the closets. All empty. Next was the basement. He had to go outside and kick open the warped doors that sloped down at an angle from the house to the overgrown lawn. Stomped down the cement steps.

He hollered her name again. Still nothing. He went through the first floor again, in case he had missed something. He ended up at the front door and threw the frying pan at the fridge.

Kurt kept his .12 gauge Remington in his truck, his last refuge. This was where he would retreat from all the women in his life. He could live out of his truck, if necessary.

He got the Remington out and pumped it. Yelled, "I know you can hear me. You got one chance, right now, to come crawling back to me. You do that, and I forgot this all happened, just this once. You go back inside, we're okay. You don't come out right fucking now, I will cripple you, so help me Christ. I will break your fucking hip with the stock of this shotgun. This is it." His words faded into the silent corn. "Last chance. Okay. Okay. I find you, I am gonna fuck you up so bad." Kurt started out the driveway toward Highway 17. He didn't think things had gotten too far out of hand with Ingrid last night.

But then again, he hadn't taken a very good look at her. Come to think of it, he hadn't even seen her this morning. Most times, after he'd just fucking had it and unloaded all his anger and stress and frustration, that next day, he didn't want to be in the same room as her. He didn't like to be reminded of what he'd done, and it was easier to deal with everything if she kept her distance for a while. Until she healed up enough to talk without a lisp from a fat lip and swollen jaw. Eventually, things would go back to normal, but until then, he was happy for her to be in the next room.

He walked out onto the highway and paced around the hot asphalt for a while until he heard a vehicle. He faded back into the corn and watched, in case Ingrid came out of hiding and tried to flag down the driver. The pickup never even slowed down and Kurt never saw anything else move.

He started back to the house. His anger was starting to dissipate in the unflinching daylight, slowly, insidiously replaced by something else. Unease. He would never admit it. Not to anyone, not to Ingrid, especially not himself, but the fear that always lurked around the edges of his consciousness was flaring up and consuming his thoughts. The absolute one thing he could control, his wife, was gone. Not just out of the house, not just at the store, not just at her mother's, but *gone*. And without that central anchor, that one element in his life that he could keep his thumb on, everything else in his life was becoming unhinged and floating away untethered.

He was lost without Ingrid.

He checked the barn. He had no idea why. Ingrid had not stepped inside the barn in years. He may have forbidden her, back when he kept his skin magazines out there, but he couldn't remember now. It didn't matter. She wasn't inside. He found nothing but rotting hay, sagging timbers, and cobwebs.

He stepped back into the sunlight, clutching his Remington, holding it as tightly as a child seizing its favorite blanket in the throes of a nightmare. He screamed, "Ingrid! Ingrid!"

The cornfields were silent. Not even the insects answered.

MONDAY,
JULY 2nd

CHAPTER 8

A fuzzy green patch of mold was growing on the bottom corner of the bread. Sandy eyeballed it through the plastic wrapper and swore. Why the hell was it so hard for her to manage to make Kevin's lunch the night before? She never could get it done, and yet, every damn morning, she rushed to throw together something halfway healthy and fill in his lunch box. They were running so late she would have to put his bike in the back of the cruiser and drop him off at school. There wasn't enough time for him to ride.

Kevin sat at the table, listlessly pushing his spoon around his cereal bowl. It didn't look like he'd eaten anything.

"You gotta help me keep an eye on this stuff, too, okay? I can't keep track of everything in the fridge. You're in here more than I am."

She found herself wondering if it would be safe to eat if she cut away the mold. Surely a little penicillin wouldn't hurt. Then she shook her head and threw the half loaf of bread in the trash in case she changed her mind later. Back in the fridge, she dug around and found a few slices of leftover pizza. Perfect. She didn't want to think about how long they had been in there.

Still buried in the fridge, Sandy said, "Okay, you win. No whole wheat bread today. How's pizza sound?"

Kevin shrugged.

She drew back and looked at him. Kevin could happily live off cold pizza and nothing else. Maybe Doritos on the side. Aware she was watching, he stuck a spoonful of cereal in his mouth. She slipped the slice into a gallon Baggie, sealed it, and put it in his lunch box, mashing down the grapes and chocolate milk. "You don't seem too thrilled." She zipped the lunch box shut.

Kevin shrugged again. "It's great, Mom. Thanks."

Sandy didn't want to push it. Tonight. Tonight, she promised herself, she was going to get to the bottom of whatever was happening with her son. Hopefully, her job wouldn't keep her out too late. "Come straight home after school. Mrs. Kobritz will be here. She'll feed you dinner and stay with you until I get home. Homework first, okay? No games until the homework is done." She caught him rolling his eyes. "What? You want to spend next summer in math class too?"

She couldn't understand how her son, a kid who lived to toss dice around a table full of other sweet-natured dorks yelling about casting spells and killing orcs, could have failed his math class. She loved him dearly, and understood that his heart did not belong on a ball field or hockey rink. Kevin forever had his head buried in some book or was playing some space shoot-'em-up game that was far too complicated for her. Math should be easy for him. Maybe he just wasn't getting it, it was that simple. Maybe she was letting her own impressions of middle school cloud her reasoning. Back then, it seemed like if you were a smart kid, you were smart in every subject.

Sandy hadn't been one of the smart kids.

The phone rang. Kevin sensed a chance to escape and left his cereal and disappeared upstairs to find his shoes. She stood at the kitchen counter and watched him go. Tonight, she promised herself again. She answered the phone and immediately wished she hadn't. "Hello?"

"They told me you hadn't managed to make it into the office yet."

Sandy recognized that flat drawl, that condescending tone, forever insinuating that she could never measure up as a genuine law enforcement officer. "Sheriff Hoyt." His call was about as welcome as a fart at the dinner table.

"You heard about this mess down in Haiti? Fire wiped out a goddamn island." His words sounded like a jackhammer driving a railroad spike into old concrete.

"I, maybe, I don't know. Haven't been watching the news much this morning."

"Ain't surprised. Keeping up on current events does tend to get in the way of you gals' soap operas and reality television, don't it?"

Sandy started to ask, "What can I do for you, Sheriff?"

Sheriff Hoyt interrupted. "If you'd been paying attention, you'd know that one of our own lost somebody down there." He told Sandy all about Bob Morton Jr. and how the Allagro facility had been destroyed by eco-terrorists. "Bob Morton. He's one of us. One of the good guys. We're going to give him our full support. Least we can do as Americans. His boy's funeral and memorial is scheduled for tomorrow. Gonna need you there, to help with all the overflow traffic. Media, tragedy groupies, fuck knows. Think you can handle that?"

"You're asking me if I think I can direct traffic?"

"Yep."

"I think I can handle traffic."

"Good. Funeral is at the First Baptist. Starts at nine sharp. Gonna need you out there early. Take Main and Third. I want you out there right in the middle of the street. Don't be shy now. You and that half-wit deputy steer ever-body over to the parking lot at the Stop 'n Save. Citizens'll have to walk to the service. My boys'll be there, case you need help, positioned all down Third, watching ever-body. State Department's worried there might be follow-up attacks. Need you on your toes for this one. You send any troublemakers our way. We'll take care of any tree huggers looking for a fight."

Sandy said slowly, "Okay, Sheriff."

"That is, whenever you get into the office. No rush." A high cackle. "This job may not be clocked, Chief Chisel. However, taxpayers do expect you to show up once in a while."

Bob tried not to grunt as he strained against the toilet in the only bathroom. The house was damned quiet, and he didn't want to embarrass himself or his new house-guest. Most days, he was regular as clockwork. This morning, though, his body wasn't responding. Funny thing was, it felt like he had a basketball jammed up in there, but apparently it wasn't in any mood to cut loose.

Maybe it was the booze.

Maybe it was the thought of the ashes of his son in the front room on the mantel.

He zipped up and flushed the empty toilet. It wouldn't look right to spend all morning on the commode. He had things to do. Cochran had explained that, as a leader of the community, Bob had a responsibility. An obligation. The terrorist attack on the island had created a lot of turmoil and suspicion. It was up to Bob to set things straight in the town.

He washed his hands and was comforted at the thought that Cochran was in his house, looking out for him and Belinda, like a lawyer from hell. They hadn't had any more visitors from the media since Cochran had run those parasites from WGON off his farm. Bob was secretly thrilled that his very own attack dog was armed.

Cochran answered the phone now.

Belinda never really ventured from their bedroom anymore, poor thing. She was taking the death of their only child awfully hard. A few women from the church had stopped by, and after Bob told Cochran they were okay, they had all trooped upstairs to sit with his wife. Bob hoped that might have helped to snap his wife out of her darkness, maybe get her back in the kitchen, but no luck. She still wouldn't come out. Bob and Cochran had been forced to make sandwiches to feed themselves.

At least they would get a decent breakfast this morning.

It was time to visit the Korner Kafe.

The Korner Kafe had been nestled at the intersection of Highway 67 and Main Street as far back as Bob could remember. Some of his first memories were gobbling down chili dogs for lunch there with his father. Somewhere along the years, maybe from the very beginning, a few unwritten rules had been established regarding each of the meals for the Korner Kafe's diners. Lunch was reserved for the farmers to bring their children. The adults were silent, leaving the kids to chatter. Dinner was for the wives. But breakfast?

Breakfast was reserved for the men. The farmers.

Business was conducted at breakfast.

And in Parker's Mill, the Korner Kafe was the only place to take care of business. Handshakes sealed the deal. Paperwork was signed on the Formica countertops. The rest of it, such as filing paperwork with city hall, was pure formality. If you expected the rest of the men to take you seriously, you damn well showed up no later than six a.m., at least five days a week. The place was closed on Sundays.

Bob and Cochran stepped through the door at seven-thirty. Protocol permitted Bob to show up late; he'd lost his son, after all. Cochran followed behind; he was trying to blend in, at least a little. He'd left his suit and tie back at the farm and now wore a New Holland cap and plaid shirt with jeans and work boots.

Esther, the only waitress in the place, turned down the volume on the TV, perpetually tuned to Fox News, in deference to Bob's mourning. Somewhere on the far side of forty, Esther favored bras that had been hammered into torpedo shapes in the fifties, and sported a platinum blond dye job that looked like it might have been achieved using the same bleach the busboy splashed on the floor at the end of each day.

Bob always sat in the most enviable spot in the diner, the red stool at the end of the counter. The spot was

reserved exclusively for him; he wasn't only the richest
farmer in the valley, he was also the farmer with the
most acreage under his control. The Korner Kafe was
shaped like a large L; those with the most power sat
closest to the ninety-degree corner where the cash register resided. If you weren't a farmer, and instead some
nameless trucker passing through on his way to Chicago
or St. Louis, you sat in one of the booths. Only local
farmers had the right to sit at the counter.

Cochran settled onto one of the stools next to him.
He was with Bob, so nobody said anything about where
he sat.

Esther took Bob's hand, said, "So sorry to hear about
your boy. We all know he had a hell of a future with that
company."

Bob nodded and pretended to study the menu. He
could feel Cochran surreptitiously checking out the rest
of the diners. The place was half full of men who
dressed the same, but Bob knew there were key differ-
ences. Two of the nearest men, Perkins and Crews, wore
hats emblazoned with the Allagro logo. The three along
on the short, bottom end of the L-shaped counter wore
caps stitched with competitor brands, like Monsanto
and Syngenta. Bob wasn't sure if they would concern
Cochran more than the shiftless farmers down at the far
end that wore either caps with baseball or hockey logos
or nothing at all. They were the men who had no alle-
giance, no stake in the seed wars currently raging across
the nation. They were the ones who caused problems.

Bob didn't have to knock on the counter to get their
attention. Everybody had stopped talking once he
and Cochran had come inside. He said loudly, "I know

there've been a lot of rumors flying around these past couple days."

Nobody moved. Even the cook in the back held off on cracking any new eggs over the griddle.

Bob didn't look at anyone in particular. "This is what happened. Yes. My son was one of the men killed on that island two days ago. You all know he worked for Allagro. He died a hero, protecting our freedom. The memorial will be held tomorrow, at the Baptist church, at ten in the morning. Me and Belinda would be honored if you could make it."

Silence reigned. One by one, the men climbed off their stools and came forward to shake Bob's hand and offer their condolences. The movement of the men along the counter was as slow and solemn as Good Friday in the Catholic church over in Jacksonville.

Forget the Internet and that social media bullshit. Hell, forget the damn phones. This was how news spread in Parker's Mill. By noon, everyone in town would know that Bob was as stoic and tough as the weathered visages at the top of Mount Rushmore, facing the death of his son with a firm resoluteness.

Bob's reputation would be stronger than ever.

The decision to confirm his son's death in the Korner Kafe was no accident.

Then some asswipe down at the far end of the counter had to pipe up with, "Have you heard then, how it, uh, exactly happened on that island?"

Cochran took a sip from his coffee mug to give Bob a chance to answer.

Bob didn't call out the asswipe by name, but he knew who'd asked the question. Buck Walsh, who farmed a piddly little sixty acres. He'd asked it just to drag up some bad decisions that Allagro had made, just to ruin the moment, just to be an asshole.

Bob repeated, in the same questioning tone, "What happened to that island?" He shook his head, looked around the counter at everybody. "I'll tell you exactly what happened. My son, and one hundred and sixty-three other souls, died. Murdered. In cold blood. Attacked without provocation. Attacked without warning, without . . . reason." He paused, but not long enough to give the smartass a chance to say anything else, "Everyone on that island died a tragic, unnecessary death."

Cochran had put the cup down and had his cell phone out. He tapped it on the counter, slowly, absentmindedly fidgeting with it, until the tiny black eye of the camera was facing down the end of the counter, waiting to catch a glimpse of the heckler.

Bob folded his hands. "Now, as best as I understand it, those responsible have been identified, and are now the subject of a manhunt the likes of which you have never seen. I'm talking Osama bin Laden level searching here. I have been personally guaranteed that forces on our side will erase those killers off the face of the earth." Bob's eyes held the guarantee. "Our dead will be honored."

"Yeah, but who were they? The terrorists?" Walsh asked.

Cochran got the question on video.

Bob thought it was obvious and talked like he was explaining the sunrise to a toddler. "The same sonsabitches that blow up medical testing centers. The same ones who hide railroad spikes in logging trees. The same godless bastards that think plants and bugs and dirt are worth more than human life."

He turned to address Walsh directly. Enough was enough. "What do you want from me? My son is dead."

Walsh shrugged. "I know. And if it was me, I'd want to know exactly who killed him. Who told you it was eco-terrorists? Allagro?"

"Aw, give it a rest, Buck," Perkins said. He was an overweight farmer a few seats down from Cochran and hid his baldness with his Allagro cap. "Nobody wants to hear you rant and rave this morning."

Walsh put his elbows on the counter, raised his eyebrows. "Nobody's ranting and raving, Doug. Just asking a few questions. Not my fault nobody wants to think about these things. Seem like you all are happy to swallow any bullshit that Allagro feeds you. Everybody's happy to repeat the company press release, to point fingers and holler for retaliation, but where's the evidence?"

Cochran touched Bob's elbow lightly, and when Bob glanced down, Cochran flattened his hand out, gently patting the air under the counter. The meaning was clear. Be quiet. Let this play out.

Perkins slammed his fist on the Formica. "That ain't the issue here. Point I was making was that you needed to be more respectful. It's the wrong morning to spout that nonsense."

"Respectful? Hell, seems to me real respect is digging to get at the real truth of what happened to Bob Junior. That's respect."

"Admit it," Perkins waggled a thick finger at Walsh. "Allagro could release actual video surveillance of these terrorists killing everybody and it still wouldn't be enough."

"Come to think of it, that's a damn good idea," Walsh

said. "Fact is, we haven't seen a whole lot more than a lot of smoke. Where's the pictures on the ground? You all are taking Allagro's word that these eco-terrorists, a bunch of hippie dipshits at the best of times, managed to firebomb an entire goddamn island in the middle of the ocean. Does that not strike anyone else as being tough to swallow?"

"Listening to your paranoid fantasies is hard to swallow," another farmer on the Allagro row said.

Walsh continued, "I mean, you don't think that Allagro, one of the most secretive, most powerful corporations in the entire world, wouldn't keep an eye on one of their most valuable laboratories? You don't think that they would have every inch of that island under video surveillance?"

"Christ, here we go again." Perkins looked heavenward for help. "You just answered your own goddamn question. What is it about the term 'total destruction' that you don't understand?"

"I think you are underestimating the level of technology involved here. I think—"

"I think," Perkins interrupted loudly, "that you like the attention. It's predictable. Next you're gonna accuse us all of being drug dealers again."

"Hey, you want to grow that cheap Frankencorn just so they can turn it into sweet garbage, be my guest. Just don't expect me to pretend that your shit smells like roses."

"There you go again, pissing on the GMOs. Guess you don't have a problem with the world starving to death."

"Gentlemen," Cochran spoke up suddenly. "I can appreciate and respect your views. However, I believe we have lost the true goal as to why Mr. Morton stopped by this morning. He was merely extending an invitation to join him, and his wife, in honoring the memory of his only son."

The Korner Kafe fell silent.

Walsh asked, "Who are you?"

Cochran fixed the full force of his stare on Walsh. "My name, Mr. Walsh, is Paul Cochran. I am an attorney. I have been retained by Mr. Morton during this difficult time. If you have an issue with an organization such as Allagro, I suggest you take it up with that particular corporation. In the meantime, in the interest of behaving like a decent, humane neighbor, I highly suggest you keep your personal opinions to yourself and show Mr. Morton all due respect in his time of mourning." Cochran addressed the rest of the diner. "I know that Mr. Morton would appreciate it if public discourse regarding his son's death remained civil and polite, and I would like to personally thank each and every one of you for observing this request."

Cochran surreptitiously tapped Bob's elbow, indicating that Bob should stand first. Bob put his coffee down and stood, somewhat disappointed they wouldn't be having breakfast.

Cochran stood as well, saying, "Thank you, gentlemen. We hope to see you all at the memorial service tomorrow. I certainly hope you take my advice to heart. If we are forced to meet under different circumstances, if you choose to ignore Mr. Morton's request, I can assure you that you will regret it."

CHAPTER 9

Kevin didn't tell his mom that Jeremy Glover had taken a shit in his lunch box.

He shouldered his backpack, heavier today, took his bike from his mother as she lifted it out of the trunk, and endured a good-bye kiss on the cheek. As she pulled out of the parking lot in the cruiser, he locked his bike in the rack and stood in the shade of one of the elm trees that lined the schoolyard.

That was about the only good thing about summer school. Cover. If you stepped back a little, you could hide behind the trees, and become invisible to the second floor. You could still hear, though. Could tell if they were up there.

In the winter, there was nowhere to hide outside. You couldn't wear white-and-gray camouflage fatigues, like in video games. You couldn't sneak away from anybody.

However, at least during the regular school year, you could disappear inside the school, in the mess of students, just another coat and hat in the throng of students that filled the hallways.

In the summer, Kevin stuck out.

Jeremy wanted his buddies to call him Jerm for short. He liked that. Capital *JAY-EE-AR-EM*, baby.

Jerm and his buddies were looking for Kevin. Always.

At least they weren't in the same class, unlike in the spring, when they all shared a math class. Kevin had spent too many classes worrying about them and couldn't remember a damn thing. That's how he ended up in summer school. Jerm and the two other assholes had been placed in some other summer program entirely. It was some kind of remedial thing, supposed to help them catch up to the rest of their peers. Shared periods in gym and lunch were the worst. Kevin had nowhere to go. The teachers protected him some of the time. Sometimes, he got caught and was lucky if they just tripped him, called him a few names.

Sometimes, it was worse.

Like when Jerm and the assholes surprised Kevin out behind the school. Jerm grabbed Kevin's backpack, pulled the notebook and binder out, and dumped the food on the ground. Stepped on it. Put the empty lunch box on the ground, pulled his pants down to his knees, and squatted.

Even the other two assholes, Javier and Morgan, had been seriously disturbed by their friend. They hid it though, with maniacal laughter and frantically swiping the air in front of them to wave the smell away. Jerm wiped his ass with the lid, zipped the lunch box up, put it in Kevin's backpack, and handed the backpack to Kevin.

Kevin took it.

He'd replayed that particular moment in his head a million times. Couldn't change it. Wished he'd done anything, *anything*, except take his backpack like a fucking pussy. He'd taken it and stood there while they whooped it up and went upstairs.

He'd spent hours and six gallons of bleach trying to erase the memory. It was never clean enough. Never would be. He could never bring himself to tell his mother he would never eat out of that lunch box ever again. The Baggies and food inside would get tossed into the first garbage can or Dumpster he passed.

They'd since been waiting every morning at his locker since summer school had begun. "There's the fucker. Smelled you comin'. Fuckin' pussy-ass mother-fucker. Your mommy around now? Huh? She gonna arrest me? Huh? Chief Bitch? Huh? Chief Cunt?"

Some days, Kevin hid by the bike racks, out of sight from his locker and the second floor, in the shade of the trees, and went in late. He got used to waiting, got used to being lectured on tardiness, and simply blamed it on his mother, knowing she felt bad about getting him there late, and if anybody ever talked to her about it, she would assume it was her fault. Better than running into them at his locker.

It couldn't last forever. Kevin was cracking. He had nightmares of his fingers breaking off when he went to grab things. Sometimes he would look around and real-ize he had no memory of getting there. He spent hours in the bathroom, both at school and at home, either suf-fering through horrible diarrhea or puking his guts out. His mom hadn't noticed his weight loss yet, but it was only a matter of time. He saw himself as the earth itself, cool on the crust, but deep inside, nothing but burning, bubbling, molten lava.

Until one morning, hunched over the toilet at home,

dry-heaving at the thought of going to school, something inside him decided, quite simply, *enough*. There would be no more fear. He would end this, one way or another, and to hell with the consequences. Anything was better than *this*.

He knew where she kept her old revolver, the one she'd used in the Incident.

Cochran walked slowly out to the edge of the yard, and stood near the antique tractor, waiting for the men upstairs to answer the phone. Flowerpots had been spaced out across the top of the tractor, while vines grew around the wheels. There was no place private enough inside, so he had gone outside to make his call.

"Go ahead." Only one voice spoke, but Cochran knew the others were listening.

"The announcement was made and the service will be tomorrow," Cochran said. Breakfast at the diner hadn't gone as well as he had hoped, but it hadn't been a total disaster, either.

"Good. Get it over with, sweep it out of sight."

"Yes, sir."

"Any signs of further infection?"

They knew the idiot son had mailed some package to his father three and a half months ago, but nobody knew what the hell was inside. It could have been anything. A book, a letter, a contract, pictures, anything. It also could have been a packet of seeds.

On paper, Cochran's primary goal was to accompany Bob Morton Jr.'s remains back to his parents and oversee the memorial service. He was also supposed to protect the brand, make sure that no reporter tried to grab some easy ratings by dragging Allagro's name through the mud. Unofficially, he was to keep his eyes open and make sure that none of the infected corn seeds had made it back to the Morton farm. The last thing the men upstairs needed was another containment breach. It would halt their research for decades.

Cochran surveyed the cornfields and looked back at the house. "No. I have not seen any evidence yet."

Truth was, Cochran wasn't entirely sure what he was looking for. Before leaving for Illinois, they'd sat him down in a windowless room with a couple of scientists who couldn't give him a straight answer even if he'd put a gun to their heads. The company undoubtedly had their heads in a vise, and he figured that was the real reason they were so goddamn nervous. They knew damn well if they couldn't figure it all out and provide adequate answers, they might wind up in one of the fertilizer tanks.

"We're years away from understanding this," the mycologist had said, stabbing his cigarette into an overflowing ashtray. "Years." He was Asian, Korean maybe, and wouldn't stop smoking no matter how many times the other scientist asked.

The other scientist, a plump little microbiologist, couldn't sit still and paced the entire time. "You people built a bridge across evolution, jumped millions of years, just like that." He snapped his fingers. Sweat had soaked through the armpits of his shirt and his eyes looked like a couple of hardboiled eggs bulging out of dark hollows. "You need to tell your bosses that we tried to warn you when the tests started coming in. We tried. Make sure you tell them that. You can't just release something like that and expect it to behave."

Cochran didn't say anything.

The mycologist lit a new cigarette. "Some basic facts that you need to understand." He held up his hands and tapped his nicotine-stained fingers as he went. "Fungi is neither plant nor animal. Yet it shares characteristics of both. The scientific community continually debates how to classify these organisms." He spit a fleck of tobacco on the floor and shook his head. "In the last thirty years, the taxonomy classifications have changed more often than a map of Eastern Europe. But it has been on earth since the beginning. It was almost the first conscious life-form, but never quite made it, and God cursed it to clean up after the rest of the species."

Cochran thought the man needed some rest and checked his watch to politely remind him to get to the point.

The mycologist ignored Cochran's body language and ticked off another finger. "We've identified over 80,000 species. However, there are undoubtedly more. Many, many more. At least 1.5 million. Maybe even 5 million."

"Who gives a shit," the microbiologist snapped, waving at the smoke. "None of them have ever, ever acted like this. This stuff, it gets in you, it grows like cancer on crack."

This, the mycologist agreed with. He nodded. "And God help you if you are close when it is ready to reproduce."

The security footage taken from the conference room on the island made this quite clear. They'd watched in silence as Dr. Deemer's head had cracked open and the eyes had popped, releasing the spores.

The mycologist told him that the fungus had somehow made the jump from one species to another with surprising ease, and that it was controlling the infected insects on the island to a limited extent before liquefying the abdomen and the head, then repurposing the legs somehow. Nobody was still quite sure how it worked, and the company wasn't in any hurry to replicate it under controlled conditions. That island had been one of their top research centers, complete with some of the most secure laboratories in the world, and now it was nothing but a charred slab of rock in the middle of the ocean, thanks to the fungus.

While the microbiologist paced, the mycologist fired up yet another cigarette. He sucked in a lungful of smoke, blew it out his nose while staring at the table. He looked up, met Cochran's eyes. "We think it can infect you two ways. One, when the fruiting body is large enough, it will burst, spreading microscopic spores into the air. These spores will infect anything they come into contact with. That's like most fungus. But," he paused to take another drag, "there's something else going on too. You ever catch athlete's foot?" He didn't wait for an answer. "All you have to do is touch it. That's all. A simple touch under the right conditions."

He'd pointed to the footage from the security cameras from Greenhouse #6, where the two executives had broken in and tried to escape using the Zodiac tied up in the tidal pools. "They had already been infected, back in the boardroom, but here," he pointed to the cobwebs. "Here, they picked up some of the infected insects. Of course, they were not insects any longer, not really. They were simply vehicles for the fungus to expand, to search out more flesh. See, traditionally, normal fungus will 'move' to food by growing toward it, but this species has figured out a way to actively use its victims to carry the fungus to new food. It has become a predator."

The microbiologist stopped pacing and wagged his finger. "We don't know that yet. We don't know anything yet."

The mycologist shook a sheaf of papers at his colleague. "We know damn well they used *Ophiocordyceps unilateralis* as a foundation for the DNA sequence." He looked back at Cochran. "This is a fungus that controls ants. It latches onto the brain stem of a rainforest ant and controls their behavior, compels them to climb up to an optimum height, clamp on the underside of a leaf with their mandibles, and stays there until a large enough fruiting body grows from within the ant, until it explodes, raining spores down below, and the whole process starts all over again."

Cochran almost felt sorry for the ants.

The mycologist threw the paper on the table and talked without looking at the other scientist. "So don't tell me we don't know anything. We know too damn much. That's how we got into this mess in the first place. We know just enough to go tampering with building blocks of life, but act surprised when life doesn't react the way we hope it will. Besides," he looked back at Cochran, "this isn't the first time something like this has happened. Look at the Permian-Triassic extinction, 250 million years ago. Sixty percent of all scientific *families*, more than eighty percent of *genera*. That's ninety-six percent of all species in the ocean. All gone. We think that fungus had something to do with it. You want something more recent? Look at the plagues of Egypt. They all have a strong possibility of a fungal origin. They—"

"Oh, give it a rest," the microbiologist said. "If I have to listen to any more of your superstitious nonsense I'm going to shoot myself. Dragging us back to the Dark Ages will not help us solve anything."

"Man's hubris is what brought us to the brink of extinction in the first place."

The microbiologist leaned over and yelled in the mycologist's face, "Spare me your platitudes, you fucking moron." He went back to his pacing, and mimicked the mycologist's accent, pretending to smoke with fluttering, exaggerated gestures. "Because, you know, you can't spell fungus without *fun*!"

The mycologist had merely shrugged and lit another cigarette.

Cochran hung up the phone and listened to wind rustle the corn leaves. That meeting had been utterly useless. And now he still had no idea what the fungus looked like. How the hell was he supposed to be aware of microscopic spores in the air? The company had supplied him with emergency gear in the trunk of the rental car, but gave him explicit instructions not to use it unless he encountered irrevocable evidence of the fungus itself. Allagro wanted everything quiet and controlled.

He took one last look around the yard and trudged back up to the house to sit by himself in the living room, staring at a muted TV while Belinda sobbed in the bedroom and Bob locked himself in the bathroom.

Kevin had seen the footage from the Incident. Over and over. He'd watched videos of his mom arriving at the courthouse as reported by various networks on YouTube. He'd marveled at her coolness as people shouted questions and chanted slogans. Remembered how he'd heard her crying in the shower a couple times late at night. She would be furious if she knew he'd watched them again. Kevin knew the faces of everyone involved, especially the complainant. Knew how the asshole tried to get up out of his wheelchair and lurch over to the podium to speak to the press against his lawyer's overly theatrical advice, like it was some kind of professional wrestling match. Knew too well how the asshole's knee now worked like one of those wacky inflatable doofuses out in front of used car lots, forever flopping in random directions.

Kevin stood in the cool shade of the elm trees and felt the heaviness of the backpack. Reached inside. Curled his fingers around the solid holster, Velcro scratching against his palm. He knew exactly what his mom's gun had done. As they supposedly used to say in the old west, *God may have created all men, but Samuel Colt made them all equal.*

He was going to kill Jerm and the other two assholes with it if they fucked with him again.

CHAPTER 10

"Such a horrible racket, all night long."

Sandy was listening patiently to a couple of old women complain about the speeding, reckless drivers who had turned Fifth Street into a drag-race strip. Sandy had a feeling that anything that happened after seven p.m. instantly translated into "all night long," for the two women, but she made sympathetic noises and made sure they noticed how she was writing everything down in her notebook.

Actually, she was writing a grocery list. Started with *bread*.

She said, "Well, I thank you ladies. You have taken the first, most important step in letting us know. Now, the next thing I need from you is to give us a call whenever something like this happens again. That way, we can catch the perpetrators in the act." Sandy tried not to smile. She couldn't remember the last time she'd actually used the term "perpetrators." Still, it filled the old women with joy. They were regular crime-fighters now.

She was getting back into the cruiser when Liz broke

over the radio with a couple of missing person reports. The first was Mrs. Ferguson saying her husband hadn't come home from the fields yet.

She waved good-bye at her new deputies, started the car, and got on the radio. "I'm betting he stopped off at the bar. Still, have Hendricks go on out and get her statement."

The second was from the Einhorn residence.

"What, again? Already?"

"This one's different. It wasn't the neighbors that called," Liz said. "Sounded like Kurt himself. Told me his wife was missing. Been missing for almost twenty-four hours now."

"You're kidding."

"Wish I was."

"Ten seventy-six." Sandy replaced the radio. She sped through the town, wondering if Ingrid had finally escaped after all these years. Then another, darker suspicion arose, and it sounded much, much more plausible. Kurt wouldn't be the first abusive husband who killed his wife, hid the body, then called the cops and claimed she had run off.

When she got there, though, she found Kurt sitting on the front steps, cradling his shotgun and surrounded by empty beer bottles. He didn't look calm and composed, ready for the authorities to grill him. The arrogant asshole from the other night was gone. In his place was a haunted shell. Raw, red-rimmed eyes stared blankly at the cruiser as Sandy pulled up to the house.

Even if it didn't look like he saw her at all, he spoke

first. "Didn't do nothin' to her. Nothin'. I know what you're thinkin'. I know how it looks."

"How does it look, Mr. Einhorn?" Sandy took it easy, keeping an eye on the shotgun.

"I know damn well how it looks. I mean, I had to teach her some manners once in a while, but it was for her own good. I didn't do anything real bad. Shit. Didn't even see her yesterday morning, so whatever happened, it wasn't me."

"When was the last time you saw her?"

"I dunno. Late that night. Two nights ago, I guess."

"Is it possible she went missing earlier? In the middle of the night, maybe?"

He shook his head. "Heard her making breakfast. Then nothing. She's gone. Been looking for her. All gone. I don't know where." His breathing hitched, and Sandy realized he was starting to cry.

"You mind if I look around?"

"Be my fucking guest. She ain't here, though. Wastin' your time."

"I'd feel better if you put your shotgun down."

"I need it."

"Not asking you to put it away. Maybe just lean it against the porch over there."

Kurt grumbled about it, but he did what she asked. He flopped back down and tried to find a bottle with a little beer left.

"Thank you." Sandy stepped past him and over all the bottles and went inside. She stopped for a moment and simply listened. The house was still. She checked around the front room, but it didn't look any different since the last time she was here. A bitter, slightly rotten smell pulled her to the kitchen.

She noted the bacon on the counter. It looked a little green and was probably responsible for at least part of the odor. The egg basket and frying pan on the floor. The dark substance on the floor was crusty, almost like some kind of clay. It was dry now, but Sandy could see the skid marks in the swirls and spatters. She took her pen and gave the stuff an experimental poke. It crumbled under the touch of the pen.

Sandy went upstairs. Nothing in the two bedrooms. In the bathroom, she found a little smear of dried blood on the wall next to the toilet. Maybe it was time to give Mike, the county forensics investigator, a call.

She heard engines. Recognized them. They sounded just like her own cruiser. She went to the window, and saw three county squad cars pulling into the wide area between the house and the barn. "Shit," she breathed. Somebody in the sheriff's department must have been listening in on the Parker's Mill radio communication. Their arrival was like dumping gasoline on a child holding a sparkler.

She watched through the window just long enough to see Sheriff Hoyt step out of his cruiser and hold a bull-horn up to his mouth. A goddamn bullhorn. Like his voice wouldn't carry twenty feet. Typical overkill from the sheriff's department.

Sheriff Hoyt's amplified voice boomed around the farmyard. "STEP AWAY FROM THAT SHOTGUN. NOW."

Kurt's voice yelled back. "Fuck. You."

Sandy bolted from the bathroom. She knew, with a cold certainty, this was about to get worse. There was no time to radio Sheriff Hoyt, no time to get his attention, no chance to calm everybody down.

More yelling, back and forth, as she crashed down the narrow stairs. She had hit the first floor and started to turn from the kitchen to the front room when gunfire erupted. She crouched, filled her hand with the Glock, and waited. The barrage continued. She could not hear a shotgun's flat booms, only sharp cracks from handguns, over and over and over.

Sandy edged back around into the kitchen and waited. Made sure she wasn't touching any of the crap on the floor. The shooting slowed and trickled away, like popcorn still defiantly bursting in an air-popper even after the power had been cut.

She rose and went through the front room, called out the front screen. "Clear! Officer inside."

Sheriff Hoyt answered her through the bullhorn. "CLEAR."

Sandy stepped through the front door, onto a front porch riddled with bullet holes, and found Kurt face-down at the bottom of the steps. His stained white T-shirt was now solid red. He'd been shot at least ten or twelve times. His shotgun rested against the porch railing, in the same spot where he'd left it when she went inside. Gun smoke hung in the farmyard like smog. She looked out at the five county deputies, still crouching behind their squad cars, still aiming at the porch, as if Kurt might get up like the goddamn Terminator or something and start shooting.

She put her Glock in its holster.

Called out, "I think you got him."

The hallway was empty. The path to his locker was clear. Kevin walked slowly into the school and couldn't stop shaking. His backpack suddenly weighed a thousand pounds. He swallowed, but saliva kept filling his mouth, and he was afraid he might throw up, right there in the hall.

He couldn't tell if he was relieved or disappointed that Jerm wasn't waiting for him. He'd played the scene out in his head, over and over, where Jerm would smirk at him and say something about his mom. Kevin had decided he wasn't going to say anything anyway. He wanted to keep it as simple as possible. As soon as Jerm said something, anything, Kevin would reach into his backpack, rip open the Velcro, and pull out the Smith & Wesson.

He imagined the stunned look of terror on their faces when they finally realized that they had pushed around the wrong kid. That was the part he lingered on, every night since he had made his decision to steal his mom's revolver. The gun wasn't only for show; he wasn't going to use it just to scare them. If the Incident had taught him nothing else, it taught him that you never draw your weapon unless you are fully prepared to use it. When he pulled it out, he was going to aim square at Jerm and the assholes' chests and start squeezing the trigger as fast as possible. He wanted to put giant holes in them; they deserved it.

Kevin was still lost in the images of their faces as the realization hit them that they were about to die, when the door to the boys' bathroom banged open behind him and he heard Morgan say, "No fucking way she let you touch her tits."

A pause. Then, "Thought something smelled like shit out here." Jerm.

Kevin almost dropped his backpack. He couldn't breathe. Couldn't turn around.

They came up behind him. Jerm said, "Did Chief Mommy pack you a nice lunch today?"

Kevin felt his backpack yanked violently to the side, dragging him with it. He slammed into the lockers. As they passed, Morgan said, "You stink, bitch. Tell your mommy to give you a bath."

They continued down the hallway, Javier protesting. "Fuck you guys if you don't believe me. She let me feel her up. Swear to God. Next time, you watch, I'm gonna get her to suck my dick."

Jerm shook his head. "Is that what you tell yourself when you jerk off, dude?"

"Touching your cousin is kinda gross, dude," Morgan said.

"I told you, she's a fucking second cousin, man. Like, we're hardly even related."

"And you're gonna see her, when, next fucking family reunion? When's that? Ten fucking years?"

"Fuck you guys. Y'all are just jealous."

Kevin watched them as they sauntered away, without giving him so much as a backward glance. He thought about how easy it would be to pull out the Model 686, shout, "Hey!" and when they turned around, start shooting.

The thought almost made him smile.

And that was enough. Simply knowing that he had the power of life and death over the bullies made everything okay. He waited until they had turned the corner, heading upstairs, before he took a shivering, shaking breath. He slumped against the lockers, marveling at how much his hands were shaking. He didn't know whether he was going to laugh or cry.

In the end, he put his backpack in his locker, took out his math book and binder, then slammed the door. He double-checked it was locked and went to class.

Sheriff Hoyt was a little guy with a big hat and a bigger gun. He was seriously fucking irritated that Sandy was already at the scene of the crime when he and his boys had taken down a goddamn cold-blooded murderer. There hadn't been a murder in Manchester County in over three years. Without an occasional murder, the absence of serious crime skewed the books, made it look like they were slacking off. That their law-enforcement presence wasn't absolutely necessary.

Sheriff Hoyt firmly believed it didn't hurt the people in Manchester County to be reminded once in a while to appreciate just how much they needed their sheriff.

A scared populace was a compliant populace.

But here was Sandy, fucking up the works again, just by doing her job.

She knew all this, knew it before she even walked out onto the porch, and wasn't surprised at all to see Kurt's body at the bottom of the steps. She wouldn't particularly miss Kurt; the man was a cockroach and should have been made to pay long ago for all the pain he had inflicted on his wife.

Nevertheless, the law was supposed to obey the rules. They weren't supposed to just go around shooting people because they felt it was justified and nobody would cause a ruckus over whoever ended up dead. Her report could complicate things for the sheriff.

While his deputies stood over Kurt's corpse making jokes, one of them took Kurt's shotgun and casually laid it on the grass near the body. Sandy pretended not to notice as she leaned against the side of Sheriff Hoyt's cruiser.

He paced around the driveway, looking back at her every once in a while. "All I'm askin' is that you back me up here. Save me a lot of bullshit red tape." He spread his arms wide. "Ain't nothing for you to mention in your report that he was in an agitated state of mind, and wouldn't relinquish his shotgun. Simple as that."

He got closer and stopped pacing. Looked straight into her eyes. He was one of the few cops that stood at her height, and it chafed him something godawful. He dropped his voice, became her best pal. "Look. I know it ain't easy for you. Lord knows, I know. And we both know that I can make things easier for you. Didn't work out that my boy was elected. Fine. I am a man who can accept defeat gracefully. However, I do expect everyone under me to accept my authority."

"I'm not under your authority, Sheriff. Thought we understood each other."

"Maybe, maybe not. Doesn't matter. What does matter is that the law enforcement agencies in this county understand each other. This son of a bitch murdered his wife. Let's not kid ourselves. We took care of this particular problem. No tears will be shed. We'll find the wife's body, and case closed."

"Find the body, and the DA decides whether the case is closed or not. No body, and we don't know for sure if there was a murder or if Ingrid finally had enough and ran away. Technically speaking, Sheriff, if you don't have a body, you have a missing person."

Sheriff Hoyt looked like he wanted to punch her. "Gonna stand there and tell me this son of a bitch didn't pound his wife into fucking hamburger on a regular basis?"

Part of Sandy, deep down, the tired part, wanted to simply say, "Okay. Sure. Whatever." It would be so much *easier* if she simply submitted to Hoyt.

She couldn't. She had met plenty of men like Sheriff Hoyt. Men who took their rarefied positions for granted and expected everybody else to do the same. These were the men that ruled their little kingdoms. If you stuck out, you or members of your family could be isolated and subdued, simply if you didn't fit within Sheriff Hoyt's narrow definition of normal and decent and law-abiding. When Kevin came along, his birth was met with outright hostility from the town, as if Sandy and her son had been set ablaze with the sin of green hellfire.

"Yeah. He beat her. But where is she?"

"Then what's the problem? He killed her. We'll find her," Sheriff Hoyt said. "Seems to me, we took care of a menace to our society. It's what communities do when they are threatened. They elect men like me to take out the trash. In the end, it don't matter two shits what you think or say. You go ahead and put your concerns in the report. Fact is, now that I think about it, you didn't see jack shit. You were inside, and couldn't see what was actually happening. Fine. I'll deal with the extra headaches. It won't matter in the end. But you, you don't wanna support me or my men, fine and dandy. You're not gonna like the shitstorm that'll follow."

"I'll keep my umbrella handy," Sandy said.

Sheriff Hoyt laughed. "You're a regular comedian. Yessir. Oughta get your own reality show. Pretty soon, though, you're gonna find out the hard way nobody else is laughing. Now get the fuck out of my face and let real men do their jobs." He walked over to Kurt's body, calling out, "Knock it off. Rick, you get Paulie on the radio. Tell him to get out here, take some pictures, collect casings. We got ourselves one uptight, by-the-book police chief on the scene here, so I will expect everything in triplicate."

Everybody gave Sandy a sideways glare.

Sheriff Hoyt continued. "If in doubt, bag it, catalog it, report it. C.Y.A. gentlemen, C.Y.A. Somebody get hold of Chirchirillo. Tell him I expect a coroner's report on my desk no later than six p.m. this evening. Rest of you, spread out. We got a body to locate."

Sandy decided to wander around the property herself. She didn't think Ingrid was in the house. Not unless Kurt had stuffed her somewhere, and she didn't think that was likely. She supposed he could have tried to hide her body in the barn, but again, her gut reaction after seeing Kurt like that on the front steps, she didn't think he had anything to do with her disappearance.

She also didn't think that Ingrid had finally run off. It wasn't in her nature. Sandy started to wonder if maybe Ingrid had had some kind of accident, and Kurt had missed her during his search. It still didn't sound right, but it sounded like more of a possibility than Kurt throwing her in the wood chipper.

Since she'd already been through the house, she thought maybe it couldn't hurt to take a glance in the basement. She drifted around to the back, waited until no one was looking her way, and lifted up one of the cellar doors. There was a chain attached to a lightbulb at the bottom of the steps, but the bulb was broken. She flicked her Maglite around but only saw some old lumber, a rusty water heater, a pile of old cabinets, some gas and oil cans, and a tangle of rakes and shovels leaning against the corner. Cobwebs cloaked everything.

Over in the corner, there was a three-foot square of two-by-fours that had been nailed together. At first Sandy thought it was a cover or hatch that had been tossed on the floor. She saw scuff marks around it where the dust and cobwebs had been disturbed recently, and she realized that it was the cover to the septic tank. Kurt must have been having problems with the plumbing. She nudged it aside with the tip of her boot and tried to breathe through her mouth as the stench crawled out and burned her eyes. She quickly aimed the beam of her Maglite down there, but saw only murky, chunky liquid. The rest of the tank stretched out of sight under the wall of the house. If Ingrid's body was down there, then Sandy was happy to let the sheriff's men find her.

Sandy pushed the cover back over the access hatch and left the basement. It felt damn good to get out in the fresh air again. She walked down to the henhouse and looked inside. Empty. The hens were quiet, still in their nests.

Sheriff Hoyt's voice came barreling down the lawn. "You still here?" He stood in the open back door, hands on his hips. "What part of leave this fucking crime scene did you not understand?"

Sandy gave him a wave and walked back up the sloping lawn, heading for her cruiser.

Sheriff Hoyt wasn't finished. "Listen. You are not welcome here. Go write some parking tickets or show some Boy Scouts how to wipe their ass. If you aren't

gone in sixty seconds, I will cite you for obstruction." He
ducked back inside and let the screen slam behind him.

Halfway to her car, she decided a quick check in the
barn couldn't hurt. If Ingrid was hiding out in there,
Sandy thought it might be best if she was the one that
found her, not those assholes in the house. There was
also a chance that Ingrid would remain hiding from any
men, but she might come out for Sandy.

Sandy stepped into the stifling heat of the barn, stood
still for a moment to let her eyes adjust. "Ingrid?" she
called softly. The only response was a few weird insect
noises in the shadows in the back, as if a couple of
crickets were trying to woo a whole colony of sick
cicadas. "Ingrid? This is Chief Chisel. I can help you.
Ingrid?" She took another step inside.

A few moths fluttered through the angled shafts of
sunlight that speared through the roof. Something rustled in the dry straw to the left, near the livestock stalls.
The uneven calls of the crickets or whatever they were
got louder. Sandy looked up into the gloom. Some kind
of insect was making a clicking, scratching sound up
there, as if it was crawling over the rafters and along the
galvanized steel roof.

The skin on the back of Sandy's neck started to itch
and she took a step backward toward the sliding door.
Now it sounded as if the barn was alive with movement.
The insect calls grew even higher pitched, even more insistent. They sounded frantic, hungry.

She had a sudden, overwhelming sense of being
stalked and surrounded and let her fear pull her from
the barn. Once out in the full sunlight, she tried to slow
her breathing, slow her racing heart, and tell herself to
stop being such a wuss. There was nothing dangerous in

the barn. Maybe all the bullshit with Sheriff Hoyt was affecting her instincts.

It didn't work. She could feel the sweat coating her back, still chilly despite the sun. Could still hear those strange insects, that rustling in the straw, the skittering across the roof. She walked quickly to her cruiser and kept her eyes down. She didn't want any of the sheriff's men to see her nervous and unsettled. She opened the driver's door and was about to get in when she noticed something else.

In the barn, the insects had been loud and boisterous. Now, outside, she couldn't hear anything but the wind. No insects at all. The farmhouse and the surrounding cornfields were unnaturally silent.

CHAPTER 11

"Like a fucking BOSS!" Elliot shouted into a cloud-less sky.

Elliot was a string bean who sported maybe five or six actual muscles and had a face that was perpetually sun-burned year round. He was Kevin's best friend. When Mrs. Kobritz visited her daughter in Green Bay, Kevin practically lived at Elliot's house. It was hard to tell who was happier to have a best friend.

Elliot was probably the smartest kid in town. His parents had sent him off to build robots in Bloomington for two weeks earlier that summer. Once he got back, he waited across the street for Kevin every day after summer school.

Today, Kevin hadn't said a word. He hit the street, pedaling hard, and blew right past Elliot. Instead of rolling toward his house where Mrs. Kobritz was wait-ing, he headed north, to Highway 100. Elliot struggled to keep up. He didn't press his friend, content to wait until Kevin told him what was up.

Elliot followed Kevin all the way to the town dump,

way out on Route 59. There, they'd slipped under the chain that prohibited anyone from dumping anything unless it was a weekend, followed the dirt road as it twisted through the mountains of garbage and junk until they found a cul-de-sac, complete with an irresistible target. The old TV was sitting out all by itself, begging to be destroyed.

Kevin squeezed his fingers around the checkered grips of the Smith & Wesson, fighting against the sweat that wanted the gun to slip. He couldn't bring himself to place his index finger against the trigger. Not yet. He sucked in a shallow breath, fighting to let it out smoothly through his nose. He wasn't worried about crying in front of Elliot. Crying wasn't a big deal. They'd cried in front of each other plenty of times.

Elliot knew all about Jerm and Morgan and Javier, of course. He was a target himself. Knew exactly what Kevin had endured. Of course, it was worse for Kevin, since his mom was the chief of police and all that. When Kevin had told him what he had been planning, Elliot had listened in awe.

So when Kevin had pulled the Model 686 out of his backpack and aimed it at the TV, Elliot had yelled, "Like a fucking BOSS!"

That had been the first time Kevin had smiled all day. Maybe all week.

He focused on the TV. To pull the trigger meant that all of this was real. It meant that he had actually stolen the gun from his mother, which seemed worse in so many ways than planning on murdering the school bullies. If he torched off a round, then he had crossed a boundary. If he didn't fire the gun, and replaced it without ever firing a shot, then it never happened.

Kevin couldn't do that, though. He had decided that shooting Jerm and the other two assholes wasn't worth it, but he couldn't bring himself to simply put the gun back. He had to fire it, to make it all significant. All of it, all of the panic, all of the dread, would continue as if nothing had changed, if he couldn't pull the trigger.

He had no idea what would happen if he fired a bullet through the TV.

He knew that he would probably put a big damn hole in the TV, of course, but he didn't know what would happen to him inside. Would anything change? Would he still suffer silently from the bullying until he cracked? Or would he find strength and know that he could endure anything? He hoped it was the latter, but he wasn't sure.

And he wouldn't know until he squeezed the trigger and let the hammer fall on a primer, sparking that special contained explosion that blasted a cone-shaped hunk of lead into the cathode ray tube.

So he steadied himself, planted both feet shoulder-width apart, grasped the wooden grips with both hands, and filled the notch in the back sights with the white dot on the foresight, and slowly, ever so slowly, settled his forefinger on the smooth trigger.

"Holy fucking shit," came a voice over one of the hills of garbage.

Kevin flinched and almost jerked the trigger. He and Elliot spun to find Jerm and the other two clambering down a pile of old cement pylons and tangled rebar. Morgan and Javier approached cautiously, like they were sneaking up on a yard where a mean dog might be home. Jerm, though, he never hesitated, never took his eyes from the gun. He ambled forward with all the confidence of a drunk climbing behind the wheel and insisting that, hell yes, he could drive.

"Don't fucking tell me you had this at school," he said. "You did, didn't you?"

Kevin couldn't move, couldn't blink. He felt encased in ice. Jerm was on top of him before he realized what was happening. Jerm got close enough that Kevin could see how tight the Miami Heat jersey clung to Jerm's pudgy frame. Saw how acne had destroyed the round face, decimated by fresh craters like the surface of the moon. Noticed how a fresh galaxy of ripe pimples had spread across the low forehead and the double chins.

Elliot froze as well, like a possum hoping nobody would notice was still there.

Jerm grinned. "Wow. I mean, holy fucking shit." He whistled at the beauty of the handgun. "Your mom's?"

"Yeah," Kevin croaked.

"And what exactly did you have a gun at school for, huh?" He squinted in mock confusion. "For us? Shit. For us, right? Gonna teach us a lesson, huh? Damn. Didn't think you had the balls. Guess you showed me, huh?"

Kevin swallowed helplessly. He'd forgotten all about what the revolver could do, what damage it could inflict. He might as well have been holding onto a hunk of cast iron he'd picked up in the dump.

"Good thing you didn't shoot us, right? Woulda caused a hell of a mess." Jerm eyeballed the TV. "Easier to shoot that, I guess. Hey, tell you what. You let me shoot that TV a couple times, then we're outta here, leave you guys alone. We'll let it go this time. You say no . . . man, we're gonna hafta go tell Harrison." Mr. Harrison was the vice principal. "Then your mom'll know what you did." Jerm crossed his arms, looked down at Kevin. "Just let me shoot the TV once. It's the least you can do, you know? Then I'll give it back and we all go on our way like nothing happened. Promise."

And there it was. An opening. A way out of this awful mess. Kevin looked to Elliot for help, some kind of guidance, but Elliot kept his eyes on his shoes.

"Just one shot," Kevin said, hoping his voice wouldn't crack. He took the handgun in his left hand, grasping it by the barrel, then held it out to Jerm. "Just one. I gotta get it back."

"Sure, sure. I hear ya," Jerm said and took the handgun. He hefted it and whistled again. When he looked back at Kevin, those dull brown eyes had gone cold, as if tiny pinpricks of light were all that was allowed to reflect despite the summer sun in the cloudless sky. "I cannot believe how fucking dumb you are."

He turned to his buddies. "I mean, holy shit. Can you believe this? How fucking stupid can you get?"

Elliot's eyes had gotten impossibly huge and flicked back and forth from Jerm to Kevin. He looked like he wanted to crawl into a hole, pull dirt and garbage over his head, and hide for a few weeks.

The full realization of what he had just done hadn't yet hit Kevin. At first, he merely felt the familiar shame of being mocked by Jerm, a reflex action that happened automatically, but when the scope of what had just happened finally sank in, he felt it with an almost physical blow, as if Jerm had kicked him in the solar plexus. He thought he might throw up again.

His first coherent thought was of his mother. What would he tell her?

Then he had more immediate concerns, because

Jerm had gotten over his own initial shock over being
handed a loaded gun and was now aiming it at Kevin's
face.

"Motherfucker." Spit flew through the gaps in Jerm's
teeth. Then, just for emphasis in case everybody hadn't
heard him, "Motherfucker!"

He stepped closer and jammed the barrel against
Kevin's forehead. "Gonna bring a gun to school and
shoot me, motherfucker? Really? I mean, fuckin' really?
I oughta blow your fucking brains out. You should've
shot me when you had the chance. How's it feel now,
huh, being on the wrong end? Your mommy ain't around
to help you. How do you think that'll sound to her? That
you went and got your brains blown out by her own
fucking gun. Fucking hilarious."

He dropped his voice to a whisper. "Think that's what
I'm gonna do. Blow your fucking brains out and kill
your little faggy friend too. Let your mommy find you all
the way out here, dead in a fucking dump." His breath
smelled of hard-boiled eggs and onions.

Morgan and Javier took a page from Elliot's play-
book and froze as well. They'd been around Jerm
enough to know that he was needlessly cruel and unpredictable. It was beyond just possible he might shoot
Kevin. In fact, they thought there might be a damn good
chance he might just snap and shoot the kid in the head.
Neither of them wanted to admit it, but they were
scared. Terrified down to their bones. They thought
Kevin was a sniveling little shit, and had no problem
fucking with him day in and day out, but this, this was
something altogether different. This was something they
could never take back.

Javier was the only one who could say anything. "Jerm, man. I think you made your point, you know?"

Jerm didn't look like he'd heard. He kept moving the end of the barrel, still strangely cool in the heat and dust, in tight circles against Kevin's forehead. "Yeah. I'd laugh my fucking ass off, waiting for that cunt to find you here, head all gone. And if they did find me, shit, I could just claim self-defense, with it being your gun and all." His face went slack, and his eyes bored a hole somewhere above Kevin's hairline, lost in his own fantasy world.

Kevin didn't dare to breathe. The barrel drifted over his forehead in looping figure eights, like a nearsighted cobra deciding whether or not to strike. He wanted to squeeze his eyes shut tight, and pray that he would never hear the gunshot, but he was still frozen, and couldn't tear his eyes away from Jerm's slack, masklike face.

For a full minute, no one moved in the dump. The only sound was the dry, snapping sound of the wind flipping a few pages of an open discarded encyclopedia near Elliot.

Jerm's eyes found Kevin's. Kevin saw something spark, saw the blackhead-riddled eyebrows rise. Jerm let his jaw fall open and tilted his head, as if awe had overtaken him and he was about to witness something divine. He pushed the barrel firmly into the center of Kevin's forehead.

Kevin tried to say, "Please," but it came out as a breath, soundless.

Jerm didn't so much as move his arm as pivot his entire upper body, sliding the barrel off Kevin's forehead. His gaze settled on the TV beyond Kevin, and he squeezed the trigger.

The blast ruptured Kevin's left eardrum. The pain was sudden and excruciating.

The TV screen exploded.

"Fucking that's right!" Jerm hollered in delight. He turned back to his buddies, wide-eyed and open-mouthed. "You see that?"

Kevin slapped his left hand to his ear and was dimly aware of blood pooling around his palm and trickling down his wrist. He might have cried out but he wasn't sure. He didn't think he could hear anything. He tripped and fell over Elliot's bike.

Jerm squeezed off two more shots without warning, blowing the shit out of the TV. He wandered down to the fatally wounded television, surveyed the destruction for a moment, then, as if he hadn't caused enough damage, kicked the shattered remains of the screen.

Kevin tried not to cry out. He got up and staggered away, clamping his hand to his left ear. The pain blasted through his brain and ricocheted throughout his body, always ending back up in the side of his head. His entire universe had shrunken to the flames of agony burning brightly in his left ear. It was so bad he had forgotten completely about Elliot, about the gun, about Jerm and the assholes. He moved his jaw and almost screamed at the fresh, oozing anguish.

When Jerm had finished kicking out all the glass in the TV set, he looked back at Kevin. "Fuck him, let's go." They climbed back up the hill to their bikes. Jerm still carried the Smith & Wesson revolver. He studied the gun for a moment, popped the cylinder out, and made a big deal out of plucking out the spent shells and counting the three live rounds left.

He shouted down at Kevin and Elliot, "See you

pussies at school." It seemed more for Elliot's benefit, since Kevin was hunched over, holding his head. Elliot's eyes never left Jerm.

Jerm felt a silly grin climb across his face and couldn't wipe it off. He stuck the handgun in his shorts and they pedaled off through the heat and cornfields.

The cursor blinked at Sandy. Halfway through her report, right when she'd gotten to the discharge of multiple weapons, her fingers froze over the keys and she glared at the screen as the flat slash of black pixels flashed like an accusatory wink. *Sure,* it seemed to signal, *we all know what happened, and if you don't want to say anything, it's okay. I won't say anything, either.*

Sandy pushed back from her desk and went looking for a cup of halfway warm coffee. The police station was quiet. There was a stack of new missing person reports, but they were all outside the town limits, out beyond the Einhorn place, and therefore in Sheriff Hoyt's jurisdiction. Nobody was in any of the three cells. Hendricks was back out on Highway 67, watching for speeders and drunks. Liz was in the call center, doing her nails.

Sandy gave the coffeepot an exploratory swirl, tentatively touching the glass. Room temperature at best. She poured it in the sink and pulled out the container of ground coffee to start a new pot.

If she wrote down what she had heard, implying that the Manchester County deputies had shot and killed an unarmed man, Sheriff Hoyt and the union would make sure that she never worked again in law enforcement.

She'd be lucky to find work as a security guard in some second-rate mall. Instead, if she gave his version of events, essentially saying that the deputies had fired out of self-defense, then she didn't know if she could live with herself.

As the water hissed and bubbled, Sandy thought of Kevin. What would help him the most? She wanted to go out and ask Liz for advice.

Liz had six kids and fourteen grandchildren. She'd married a cheerful empty-headed bartender who had blown an artery in his head in the middle of mixing a highball and dropped dead, right there behind the bar, six years ago. Liz might have been pushing sixty, with a bald patch on the crown of her head bigger than the mirrors in all the compact cases she kept in her desk, but she had the brightest, most outrageous fingernails in Manchester County. Today Liz was concentrating on gluing tiny little stars across her red, white, and blue nails, getting into the patriotic spirit for the big Fourth of July celebration. Each nail was at least two inches long.

Sandy knew the answer even without asking the question out loud. Liz would say, "Honey, you want to know what I would do for my kids? You try to tell me what I wouldn't do. Whatever you say, you'd be wrong."

CHAPTER 12

They both thought it was a good idea to go to Elliot's house first.

For one thing, Elliot's parents were both at work and the house was empty. Elliot was supposed to be at the town library. That's where they were headed next, so they could claim that they'd been there all afternoon.

The second thing, and maybe the most important, was that neither of Elliot's parents were cops.

Elliot led Kevin to the upstairs master bedroom. Kevin was impressed. He'd never been in that bedroom before. Elliot had made it clear it was off-limits. He was also intrigued with how neat and orderly everything was; the bed was made, no dirty clothes on the floor. It wasn't like that at his house. Housekeeping wasn't high on Sandy's list of priorities.

He followed Elliot into the bathroom. The light passing through the frosted glass window made everything blue and cold. Elliot found a bottle of ibuprofen and took a few minutes to read the label. "Six to eight hours. Okay." He shook out eight pills, gave two to Kevin, and wrapped the other six in toilet paper. "For later," he explained.

Kevin winced when he swallowed the two pills, but it didn't hurt as bad as back at the dump.

Elliot's eyes went wide and still behind his glasses. "I've never seen anybody take drugs before."

They soaked a washcloth in hot water and wiped the trickle of dried blood away from Kevin's ear. After that they looked over themselves in the mirror, trying to gauge if anyone else would be able to see the terror. Kevin felt that his mom would sense the screaming panic just behind his eyes, but at least the blood was gone. If he kept his eyes down, and didn't talk much, he might be able to escape to his room before she suspected anything.

Elliot asked the question that had been chasing them since the dump, like a slow but inevitable freight train. "What are you going to do?"

Kevin stared at himself and tentatively touched his left earlobe. "I don't know."

Elliot buried the washcloth in the dirty laundry bin and locked the door behind them. They retrieved their bikes and rode off, making plans to meet tomorrow at the library after school if things didn't fall apart in the meantime.

Kevin rode home. He had to give Mrs. Kobritz some story, something boring so she wouldn't mention it to his mom. When he got there though, the house was locked. Mrs. Kobritz usually parked her little Toyota at the curb. The space was empty. The house was silent when he let himself in. Perfect. He wasn't expecting it, and it had never happened before, but he wasn't going to complain.

He surprised himself and found that he was starving. He threw a few turkey corn dogs in the microwave and took them up to his room in the attic. After leaving his math homework on the bed, he settled in front of his giant, ancient television. The thing was so old and heavy it had taken both him and his mom to carry it up to his room. He dunked his corndog in ketchup and powered up the used game system he'd gotten for Christmas last year.

He kept the volume low so he could hear the front door when his mom got home. That way, he could try and claim he'd been working on homework. His mom would know better, but he figured it was better to get caught for a minor infraction, instead of raising her suspicion.

All he knew was that he had to get the gun back into the hiding place before she noticed it was gone.

Bob was in the bathroom again. He strained. He pushed. He gritted his teeth.

Still nothing.

He thought his announcement at the Korner Kafe had been a disaster, since that cheap prick Walsh had decided to pick that particular morning to be even more of an asshole than usual. But Cochran had surprised him by saying that the whole thing had been fine.

In the pickup on the ride back, Cochran smiled and patted Bob's shoulder. "Hell, I've been to press conferences that were a hundred times worse. You did great. The farmer throwing his weight around, Walsh, is it? He was going to ask questions no matter what you told him. He just needed a chance to show everybody that he's still a tough guy. Don't worry about it. No, the important thing is that everyone saw your strength. That's what will last." Cochran squeezed Bob's shoulder one last time, then looked out the window at the rows of corn that flashed past in hypnotic bursts. "That cocksucker wants to push things, he'll find out the hard way that the people in charge don't take kindly to troublemakers."

Bob had been reassured at the time.

Back at home, back in the bathroom, he just wanted to feel better. He hadn't eaten anything in at least fourteen hours yet still couldn't pass anything. He'd thrown up his wife's prune juice that she kept in the back of the refrigerator. He'd swallowed a couple of Dulcolax as soon as they'd got home. So far, nothing.

It wouldn't have been so bad if his stomach had been still. But he felt constant mounting pressure inside, as if something was pushing his stomach and guts into his spine. No matter how hard he forced and squeezed, it felt like he'd swallowed foam insulation that had settled and expanded.

He got up, disgusted with himself, zipped. Washed his hands. Saw that his skin was starting to break out. Weird little blackheads were clustered around his frown lines. Perfect. Just what he needed. He spent some time scraping his tongue against his teeth and spitting into the sink. The spit was black and foul. He ran water for a while to wash it all down the drain so he wouldn't have to look at it anymore.

He checked his watch. He'd been in the bathroom ten minutes. It was past time to get out, to get back to Cochran. Bob didn't want to leave his guest for too long.

It was bad enough his wife would not leave their master bedroom.

There was another reason as well. Cochran had asked to look over his records, just to make sure there wasn't anything that the press could get hold of and make things embarrassing for the Morton family. Cochran had been awfully convincing, and Bob had opened up everything, spreading it all out on his antique rolltop desk. He'd expected Cochran to glance at everything and declare it all up to snuff. Instead, Cochran rolled up his sleeves, asked for a cup of coffee, and spent hours poring over Bob's records, seed receipts, fuel usage, acreage and yield estimates, and every other damn thing.

Bob was starting to regret giving the man so much access to his private business and didn't want Cochran to uncover anything unpleasant, least of all the two acres out by the expressway where he'd planted Junior's seeds.

He dried his face, made sure his shirt was tucked into his jeans, and stepped into the living room. His rolltop desk was over by the big windows. Reports, graphs, and receipts were strewn about as if a tornado had hit the desk and sprayed everything inside out onto the floor.

Cochran looked up and smiled. "Feeling okay?" he asked. "I can get a doctor out here in the hour, if you need."

Bob shook his head. "Feel fine. Besides, I got any problems, I can always call Mike Castle. He's been taking care of me and Belinda for years, hell, decades now, I suppose."

"Of course, of course." Cochran nodded. "I just meant if you wanted to discuss anything that maybe you wouldn't want to talk about with your family doc, then I know some folks, experts in their field, that might help, that's all. Anything different, unusual. That's all."

Bob drew himself up to his full height. "I feel fine. I am tired. I miss my son."

Cochran nodded solemnly. "And God bless you for having the strength to carry on." He nodded more briskly. "Just wanted to let you know that any other care you might want is available. You need anything, anything at all, you let me know."

"I appreciate that. Anything changes, you'll be the first to know."

Cochran studied his face. Bob couldn't tell if the lawyer's gaze lingered on the weird blackheads near his mouth. Then the moment was gone, and Cochran turned back to his paperwork. "Why don't you go upstairs and rest. The memorial service is tomorrow, after all. Might be a good idea for you and your wife to get some sleep. I would imagine the media will be out in full force; we'd like to have you looking your best."

Bob didn't want to admit it, but Cochran had a point. Bob was feeling awfully tired. He wouldn't dare disrupt his wife in their bedroom, but there was always the bed in the guest bedroom. It was made and empty; Cochran had been sleeping on the couch in the living room. A lie down in a nice, dark, cool room might be just what Bob needed. He said, "Okay," and started up the stairs.

Cochran called to him as Bob started up to the second floor. "Oh, you know anything offhand about this little bit of land you've got, a skinny patch down by I-72? Your records are somewhat confusing."

Bob had sense enough to keep climbing the stairs. "No idea. I'll look everything over later. Right now, I need some rest."

It had been a hell of a day. Sandy promised herself that once she had paid Mrs. Kobritz, she was going to step into the garage and beat the shit out of the bag for a while. Then, after a hot bath and a large glass of red wine, it was time to sit down with Kevin and find out, once and for all, what was happening with her son.

Back at the office, she had ultimately sat back at her desk and typed out a report so vague and sloppy it would have made her instructors crumple it up and throw it in the trash. It certainly wouldn't stand up to any kind of scrutiny from Illinois Internal Affairs. She hoped it would never come to that.

For today, it was enough to simply get through the report and not piss off Sheriff Hoyt.

Mrs. Kobritz's car was not out front. Sandy pulled into the driveway and collected her thoughts. In the past five years, Mrs. Kobritz had never missed a day or night looking after Kevin. It was possible the old lady had forgotten, but something in Sandy's gut, the same feeling that told her that Kurt hadn't killed Ingrid, was now telling her that Mrs. Kobritz wasn't the kind of woman who would forget to look after a child.

Sandy went inside and called out, "Kevin? Mrs. Kobritz?"

Kevin appeared at the top of his stairs. "Hey, Mom. What's up?"

"Where's Mrs. Kobritz?"

He shrugged. "I dunno. She wasn't here when I got home."

"That's . . . different."

He shrugged again.

"She never called, anything?"

He shook his head.

"What are you up to?"

"Uh . . . homework?"

"Sure," Sandy said, nodding as if she believed him. "No more games until your homework is done. I mean it."

"Okay, Mom." He rubbed his left jaw as if it hurt, but she couldn't worry about that now. Maybe his molars were coming in or something.

Sandy dug out her cell phone and called Mrs. Kobritz. Mrs. Kobritz lived by herself in an old farmhouse south of town, not too far from the Einhorns. Sandy listened to the phone ring and started to realize that if Mrs. Kobritz didn't answer, she would have to drive out to Mrs. Kobritz's house. That meant she would have to drive past the Einhorn place, something she wasn't looking forward to. The phone continued to ring. She didn't expect an answer. Mrs. Kobritz didn't own a cell phone. She didn't even have an answering machine.

As Sandy listened to one ring after another in Mrs. Kobritz's empty house, a tight ball of apprehension began to grow in her chest. Mrs. Kobritz and her late husband never had any children of their own. The old widow would never simply not answer her phone, no more than she would ever leave a child alone. The more the phone rang, the more Sandy became convinced that something had happened.

Sandy was just about to hang up when the connection

clicked and opened, and Mrs. Kobritz was on the other end, all breathless and frantic.

"Hello, hello?"

"Mrs. Kobritz? This is Sandy. I—"

"Oh thank God it's you. Please, you have to come help me."

"Are you okay? I—"

"Please, please come help me look for him. I don't know what happened."

"Look for who?"

"Puffing Bill, of course. He's gone. Please, I have to find him." Puffing Bill was the pit bull Mrs. Kobritz had picked up from the animal shelter a few months after her husband had died. Cops had found the dog at the end of some country road. Mrs. Kobritz had instantly named the dog after her father's favorite train engine. Her father was a huge train buff. The entire second floor of Mrs. Kobritz's childhood home was taken over by a massive model train layout. She knew her father had seen some awful things after landing in France during D-Day, and although he never spoke of his experiences, he'd found a release for all that stress by playing with his trains. He favored the trains of the Wild West, mostly the Jupiter trains, but his absolute favorite had been the very first steam locomotive ever built, Puffing Billy, from England.

That's where the name originated. It was better to tell people the story of the name, instead of where the dog himself had come from. He'd survived the life of a fighter and had gotten loose somehow, instead of being shot, clubbed to death, or used as bait to stoke a stronger dog's bloodlust. When he'd been found, he'd been all chewed up and damn near dead. The vets donated their time and patched him up, but ultimately had to amputate his front right leg.

Once it healed, it didn't slow him down much at all. He got used to a quick hopping motion to move around, and before long, he could move quicker than any human. It didn't look like he felt his past wounds at all. Savage scars from ripping teeth had been torn across his body. Most of his lower lip was gone. His harsh, whistling way of breathing had also contributed to the name of Puffing Bill.

Mrs. Kobritz loved that dog like the child she'd never had.

Sandy tried again. "Mrs. Kobritz, I don't—"

"He's been gone since I let him out this morning! You have to help me." It came out plaintive, stripped of any pretense, straight down to the naked need, pleading with Sandy to make everything all right and bring her dog home.

"This is really a job for the animal control officer, let me call him—"

"That man would not know his own ass from a hole in the ground." For Mrs. Kobritz, this was pure blasphemy, worse than if a demon had possessed her and proclaimed to the town that Satan fucked her in the ass every Sunday morning before church and she was enjoying the living hell out of it. "And you know it."

Sandy didn't know what to say. She certainly couldn't argue with Mrs. Kobritz. The animal control officer, Mark Higgins, was a sloppy drunk who was more than happy to catch neighborhood dogs and exterminate them to pump up his quota and justify his salary. She sighed. "Fine," she said eventually. "I'll be out as soon as I can."

She hung up and dialed Elliot's parents, Randy and Patty, and asked if she could drop Kevin off. They were over the moon that their son had a friend, and would do anything to help. Sandy called up the stairs to Kevin. "Grab your toothbrush and pj's and anything else you need. This might take a while."

Technically, she was off the clock. Despite Sheriff Hoyt's insinuation that she was rarely on duty, she'd spent too much time at work this week already, and that made the union and the folks at OSHA nervous. And technically, she shouldn't have been driving the cruiser. She shouldn't have still been in her uniform.

But Sandy figured being chief superseded all that and besides, no civilian was going to complain. Instead, she worried if she was pushing her luck by slowing as she approached the Einhorn place. She wanted to see the circus firsthand but knew she shouldn't risk being seen. She should be going so fast that if somebody happened to glance down the driveway, she would be nothing but a blink of headlights in the last faint glimmer of summer light.

Being on duty a few hours too many could be over-looked. Spying on cops working a crime scene was another thing. She chewed this over and kept the needle at sixty miles per hour as the cruiser passed County Road E and knew she had just over thirty seconds until she passed the Einhorn place. She took her foot off the gas.

Even though she'd decided to sidestep this particular hurricane, she was still curious. She flicked off the lights and coasted in darkness.

As she got closer, Sandy knew they hadn't found Ingrid. If they had, the place would be quiet. Now, it was ablaze with raised lights. Stuttering sparks of camera flashes drilled into the night as Mike, the county forensics investigator, did his best to document everything. Lots of lights. But no sirens.

The cruiser slowed until it almost rolled to a complete stop. She got a good look up the driveway. There was no question. Sheriff Hoyt and his boys were still looking for a body.

Lights flashed on the Johnson's front porch and made Sandy jump. The front door opened and slammed. A young girl, maybe twelve or thirteen, which would have made her one of the older children, ran out into the front lawn. A split second later, Meredith's stern silhouette filled the doorway. "You get back in here right now." Her voice was like a steel bear trap, and with each word, it snapped shut. "You know very well you are not allowed outside this late. Get back in here and say goodnight to your father."

The girl turned, clenched her fists, and stamped her foot. "He's sick. I won't touch him."

"You will give him a kiss good night or you and I will visit the shed. Is that what you want?" It was too much for the girl to resist any longer. She lowered her head and started back to the house. Meredith suddenly noticed Sandy's cruiser, sitting motionless on the highway. She called out, louder. "What are you doing out there, sitting in the dark?"

Sandy didn't have much of an answer.

Meredith wasn't listening anyway. "You don't fool me, Chief Chisel. You mind your own business." With that, she swept the girl inside and slammed the door.

Sandy feathered the gas and passed the driveway, still keeping the headlights turned off. She followed the road by starlight.

Mrs. Kobritz's house was a half mile down. It was a relatively new house for the area, meaning it had been built in the last fifty years or so. The front yard was full of flowers and rainbow-colored wind wheels. They hung motionless in the headlights as Sandy parked the cruiser next to Mrs. Kobritz's Toyota.

It looked like every light in the house was on, spilling golden light into the deepening shadows. Sandy kept her headlights on and walked up to the front door. She knocked. Rang the doorbell. Sandy called out, "Mrs. Kobritz?"

No answer.

She tried the front door. It opened. "Mrs. Kobritz?"

Silence.

"Shit," Sandy breathed. Why couldn't anything be simple? She called out again, but knew the house was empty. If Mrs. Kobritz or Puffing Bill had heard, they would be at the front door in a heartbeat. Still, she couldn't leave the house without checking. So she made a quick sweep. No surprises. It was empty.

The house was built at the crest of a low hill, surrounded by a typically expansive lawn. Flower beds and wind wheels bordered the grass. Attached garage. No barn. No outbuildings at all. A low fence of cross-hatched railroad ties separated the back lawn from the cornfields. She flicked her Maglite around the immediate property, just in case Mrs. Kobritz had fallen and was hurt, but Sandy knew it was useless.

No one was around.

Sandy went back to the cruiser. She turned in a long,

slow circle under a darkening sky. It didn't make any sense. Mrs. Kobritz had answered the phone maybe fifteen, twenty minutes ago. Her car was still in the driveway. She couldn't be far.

Sandy turned on the spinning red and blue lights at the top of the cruiser and hit the horn a few times. She thought about turning on the sirens, but it felt wrong. She thought of her son and wondered how long she should spend out at Mrs. Kobritz's. She saw herself explaining the twenty-four-hour guideline if someone came into the police station and reported a missing person.

Missing for twenty minutes didn't exactly inspire panic.

Still, there was no denying that, in her heart, she knew damn well something was wrong. Mrs. Kobritz wasn't the type who tended to flee to Vegas on a whim. Mrs. Kobritz wasn't someone who slipped away in the dead of night to escape child support payments.

Mrs. Kobritz was someone who gave the closest neighbor a seven-page list of detailed instructions on how to water the flowers if she left on an overnight trip.

And Mrs. Kobritz would never abandon her dog.

Sandy hit the horn a few more times and kept the lights flashing. Nothing. No hearty welcomes. No invitations to join her for dinner. No shouts of recognition. Nothing. She decided she would take one more walk around the perimeter of the property and wound her way through the little orchard and garden, into the backyard.

She saw something moving in the corn.

Sandy tensed and waited. The corn rustled.

She heard something wheezing. Puffing Bill came out of the rows, trying to sniff the air with his ruined nose. He saw her, momentarily forgot whatever had been on his mind, and bounded over to her with his own peculiar hopping gait, lost in a frenzy of dog happiness, his stump of a tail wriggling furiously.

She didn't realize she had been reaching for her sidearm until she unsnapped the holster and felt foolish.

Sandy waited, hoping to see Mrs. Kobritz follow her dog up the back lawn. She never appeared. Puffing Bill banged his head into her knee, demanding affection. Sandy gave his head a quick, perfunctory pat. He settled onto his haunches, tucked his one leg across his chest, reared back, and looked up at her. Cocked his head, clearly not satisfied. When she didn't respond, he gave up, disgusted, and took a leak near the roses in the backyard.

It was so quiet she realized she could hear the dull rush of traffic on I-72 two miles away.

She called out, "Mrs. Kobritz? Hello? Mrs. Kobritz?"

Nothing. Not even crickets.

Puffing Bill froze when he heard Sandy's voice. He looked back to the corn and there was a suggestion of a distant rumble in his throat. He had remembered that something was wrong.

She'd never seen the dog scared. She'd once seen him take a slow walk around one of the big rigs rumbling in the vacant lot next to the Korner Kafe, as if the dog had been sizing up the truck, looking for a weakness. Nothing scared him.

She flicked her Maglite at the corn, swept it back and forth. The frantic movements of the light created lurching, fragmented shadows that leapt away at the flick of her wrist. She slowed the light at odd moments, trying to catch someone unaware. But her meager light could only illuminate five or six rows deep. Sandy knew that out there, out in the deep darkness, the fields went on for miles and miles, broken only by the occasional dirt track or highway. It was a vast, wild ocean, rolling on and on under a hazy bubble of stars.

Sandy turned off the Maglite and left the backyard, going around to the front, wishing she hadn't left the flashers going on the roof of the cruiser. The spinning red and blue lights gave Mrs. Kobritz's front yard and driveway a tense, jittery feel, and even if nothing was wrong, she couldn't help but feel the lights were making the situation worse.

Puffing Bill joined her, sticking close. He remained at her side as she crossed the front lawn to the cruiser. His ears were up, and he kept his eyes moving.

She opened the driver's door and switched off the lights. Puffing Bill slipped past her and hopped nimbly into the front passenger seat. He put his one paw on the dashboard and swiveled his wide head, surveying everything from behind the windshield.

"Great. Thanks." She called the office on her cell, wanting to keep the news of her old babysitter quiet. "Liz. I need to report a missing person." She went down the list, giving Mrs. Kobritz's vitals, promising she'd find a picture soon, and told Liz to get the word out.

Sandy didn't want to, but she got in the car and went next door to ask the sheriff if he'd seen or heard from the Einhorns' neighbor.

CHAPTER 13

Earlier, Sandy had missed Jerm entirely.

He'd been pedaling up Highway 17, handgun tucked safely in the front of his shorts. He'd seen the headlights crest over the horizon a mile or so distant and knew he had a few minutes to slip into the corn and let the car pass. But the lights had disappeared, and he figured he'd missed them turning into a farm or home. He kept pedaling.

His cousin had once told him that all cop cars had square headlights. It was like a law, or something. So Jerm kept an eye out for square-shaped headlights as he pedaled along the highway, past endless rows of corn. His lungs burned and his legs ached, but the cold, heavy metal of the pistol pressing into his belly gave him strength to keep going. He couldn't wait to show it off at school tomorrow.

When the cruiser came gliding out of the darkness of the highway with no lights and a nearly silent purring engine, Jerm damn near had a heart attack. If she'd had her headlights on, Sandy would have spotted him in an instant.

Jerm saw a ditch and yanked his handlebars to the left. He bounced down an embankment into the nearly empty irrigation ditch, jumped off, and swiftly rolled his bike into the concrete culvert that ran under the highway.

Above, he heard that crazy church lady yelling at somebody. At first he thought it might be him, but relaxed when he realized it was one of her kids.

The water was ankle-deep, and in the stifling heat of an Illinois summer, Jerm barely felt the tepid water. He leaned his bike against the wall and moved deeper into the large pipe.

Ten feet in, the light from the stars faded. Except for a flash of reflection on the surface of the water once in a while, the light had vanished. The air became palpable, as if it were a black, impenetrable liquid. The culvert was nearly four feet in diameter, and Jerm found he could move forward fairly quickly through the utter darkness, as long as he hunched over and kept his head down. He stopped when he thought he was halfway through the tunnel and froze, listening.

The engine fluttered above and the cruiser sped away. Jerm grunted in relief.

Something sloshed in the water down at the other end. The sound echoed down the closed space of the pipe and reverberated past Jerm.

A shape broke the circle of light. It fluttered one moment, went still the next.

He pulled out the cell phone he'd stolen from his brother, knowing full well that his brother had plucked it out of some tween's backpack at the mall. He couldn't

make any calls, couldn't even break the code to get into
the phone, but when he turned it on, it gave off a soft
glow, and he used that light to guide him farther down
the tunnel.

He got close enough to see that it was an old woman.
She was turned away, huddled against the side of the
cement pipe, knees drawn to her chest, skinny arms
hugging herself. Frizzy, gray hair hung over her face.

Jerm got closer.

Recognized her as that old bitch, Mrs. Kobritz. She
had some sort of growths popping out of the wrinkled
skin around her mouth and nose; they looked like little
torpedo-shaped mushrooms. When she turned her head
and opened her mouth, she didn't make a sound, but he
could see even more of the mushroom things erupting out
of the inside of her cheeks and across her tongue. One
arm reached out for him. The fingers twitched, and she
vomited a thick black paste over her distended stomach.

He scrabbled backward, slipping in the algae that
coated the bottom of the tunnel. Strangely, he found it
was hard to break eye contact. Her eyes pleaded with
him. They seemed horribly aware of her situation, and
she silently begged him for help, for relief, for something he could not understand.

Jerm finally broke the contact and twisted around
and looked back down the tunnel to his bike. His feet
found purchase on the slime-covered concrete and propelled him down the pipe. His fingers clawed at the
cement as he splashed along. He got close to his end and
risked a look back.

The shape of the woman was still there. She hadn't

moved. His heart slowed, and he found he could take a breath. He turned back, took a deep breath, and prepared to scurry the last ten feet to his bike.

A new sound reached his ears, echoing and distorted as it spiraled down the pipe to him. It was soft and sinister. He aimed the phone back down the tunnel. After a few seconds, the light faded and he had to hit the button again to wake the phone up. At first, he couldn't see anything. He whipped the phone back and forth, sending the shadows in the tunnel reeling and swaying like drunk yo-yos.

He gradually realized the scattered movements along the curved walls of the concrete pipe were truly crawling toward him, and it wasn't just the frantic sweeping of the faint light. The sudden knowledge made him drop the stolen phone, and he lunged for his bike with both hands. He pushed the bike backward out of the culvert. It toppled over sideways in the weeds. He clambered out, and even though his bike had fallen over, he felt triumph as he emerged from the darkness into the starlight.

Then he felt something crawling up his calf.

It was almost like a cluster of tiny cactuses moving across his skin, as dozens of the spindly creatures crawled up his legs. More dropped on him from the top of the culvert. They swarmed across his body, moving in snakelike motions, slithering up his legs, scurrying down through his hair, crawling under the collar of his Motörhead T-shirt, squirming underneath his cargo shorts.

Thousands of insect legs overwhelmed Jerm, crawling across every inch of his flesh. He stumbled and fell forward, clawing at the centipede-looking things that crisscrossed his face. He rolled over, splashing through the wet weeds, kicking wildly. He staggered back up, ripping and grabbing them. He ignored his bike and simply started running.

He could still feel them, though, as his feet slapped the pavement. Felt the smooth worms with stolen legs that had no head and no tail. Felt the tiny legs grip and latch his skin.

He kept slapping and pulling them off as he ran off down the dark highway.

TUESDAY,
JULY 3rd

CHAPTER 14

Everybody wanted to see the urn but nobody knew whether to call it a funeral or memorial or service or wake or what. Sheriff Hoyt finally had to run out to Bob Morton's farm and ask the farmer's new best buddy, Cochran. Of course, who the hell that guy actually was was a whole other question. Cochran himself was awfully vague on the subject, but you didn't have to be a goddamn rocket scientist to figure out that he was an Allagro company man, through and through.

Cochran said the morning service was open to the public, and therefore was to be referred to as a memorial to Bob Morton Jr. It certainly was not to be called a funeral. Not under any circumstance today. Cochran was awfully particular about that. He made sure that everyone in earshot understood that that particular solemn event would certainly not be open to the gawking eyes of the public. Absolutely not. That would be a different ceremony entirely, an utterly private affair, between Bob Jr.'s parents, the local reverend, and Bob Jr.'s employers.

Sheriff Hoyt relayed the information over the radio as he drove back through town, followed by Bob Morton's black sedan, the car Bob used when dealing with the bank or going to church. Cochran drove. Another state trooper police escort brought up the rear as Sheriff Hoyt led the small procession through town.

At least that obstinate chief and her dipshit deputy were stationed out on Main Street like he'd asked, directing traffic into the Stop 'n Save parking lot. He gave her a casual salute. She responded with an even more casual salute of her own and a mysterious half-smile as he rolled past. He couldn't figure out what she was thinking. That bothered him.

Sheriff Hoyt was a man who liked to know what everybody was thinking. In a place like Manchester County, it was pretty obvious damn near most of the time. If somebody was pissed, they didn't hold back. Same thing if they were happy. There wasn't a whole lot of psychology involved. Most everybody came out and said what was on their mind.

But this new chief of Parker's Mill, she wasn't somebody who played along, made her thoughts obvious. He couldn't figure her out. And wasn't it just like a woman to make simple things complicated? Shit, he'd kept her involved, hadn't he? He could've sent her out to keep on eye on speeders on 67 but since this little shindig was in her town, he'd thrown her a bone, kept her close to the action.

That little smirk chewed the shit out of him.

Last night hadn't helped. As if it wasn't bad enough that they couldn't find the stupid Einhorn wife's body, perky little Chief Chisel had to pop back up and ask if they'd seen the friggin' neighbor. She knew damn well they hadn't.

That made it . . . He ticked the names off in his head. Seven goddamned missing persons in less than twenty-four hours.

That kind of thing wasn't good for paperwork.

He'd worry about that later. This morning, at least he'd kept her clear of the memoriam or memorial or whatever the hell Cochran wanted to call it. He didn't give a shit what she was thinking. She wouldn't interfere with Bob Morton's affairs, that much was guaranteed.

Sandy was in the middle of Main Street trying to explain to Mrs. Perkins why this was not a good morning for shopping at the Stop 'n Save when Liz's steady, calm voice came out of her radio.

"Code ten-ten. Individual is calling from his cell phone. Says it is an emergency. Says he is being threatened with bodily harm. He is apparently unable to leave the vicinity of lower Access Road Fourteen. Requesting immediate assistance."

Mrs. Perkins didn't give a damn about the call and said so. She was furious because she couldn't find any parking in the parking lot. Incredulous, she had driven back out to Main Street, straight to Sandy to complain. "Are you telling me that I, a taxpaying figure in this community, cannot shop in peace at her own grocery store?"

Mrs. Perkins was perhaps the fattest human being Sandy had ever seen in person. Sandy always saw the car in the drive-through lane at the fast food places

around town. Mrs. Perkins was perhaps the target con-
sumer of the town's only export, the cheap, starchy corn
combined with fructose for a sweet syrup that the indus-
try added to anything they could. Maybe Mrs. Perkins
was angry because she had eaten out her entire supply
and needed more. Today. Now.

Sandy said, "This'll all clear out before noon. I can't
imagine you'll starve to death by then," and winced in-
wardly as soon as the words escaped.

Mrs. Perkins rolled her eyes. Shook her chins. "You
didn't . . ." She lowered her voice. "I don't know what
kind of dirty shit you think you're pulling here, you
bitch, but you better believe you will be hearing about
this later. Oh, so help me God. You *will* hear about this."
Mrs. Perkins stomped on the gas for a block and then
had to jolt to a stop for the town stoplight.

Sandy ignored her and got into her cruiser, clicking
her radio. "Copy. This the place I think it is?"

"'Fraid so. Want me to contact the county boys?"

Liz got loud and jumped around a lot over things like
the Rams' football games and margarita hour at the bar
at the Parker's Mill Inn, but when it came to her job, she
grew emotionless, stone-cold solid. Sandy could gauge
the seriousness of the situation over how much feeling
Liz removed from her voice. This time, she sounded like
a damn robot.

"Not right now. Let them take care of the situation at
the church. Let me get a feel for the situation first."

"Ten-four." The radio clicked off.

Sandy started the car, cranked up the lights and siren
and tore off, heading west, toward the river. Access

Road Fourteen was the location call for the Fitzgimmon farm. She shook her head. "Son of a *bitch*."

One damn thing after another today.

Sheriff Hoyt turned right on Third Street and went south for a few blocks until they came to the First Baptist Church of Parker's Mill.

He'd put his best three men in charge of handling the media, and they'd corralled all the reporters and riffraff out on the southwest corner. He knew they wouldn't screw up and answer the wrong questions because they simply didn't know a damn thing. He slowly eased his cruiser through the knots of people and parked in the alley.

Ordinarily, he would have had a field day clearing out all the onlookers from the middle of the streets, but Cochran had made sure that everybody involved truly understood the enormous significance of the occasion. When Cochran explained it to him, it made Sheriff Hoyt's blood boil.

The terrorists had killed nothing less than one of America's very own farmers.

And Sheriff Hoyt would not stand for that kind of shit. From providing a dignified atmosphere to honor dead Americans to whatever else was required, Sheriff Hoyt was a man who would get the job done. He was a man the country could count on.

He removed his hat when he entered the church and took a seat near the back.

That way, he could keep an eye on everybody.

The reverend started things off with no surprises.

"Ladies and gentlemen. Brothers and sisters. Let us be reflective in the presence of thine Lord and Savior." Everybody had to straighten or shuffle into a different position for some reason before they became still and quiet.

After ten or fifteen seconds the reverend couldn't take not hearing the sound of his own voice anymore and started in about the eternal God and Father so Sheriff Hoyt tuned him out and scanned the faces of the men in the church instead. Cochran sat up front, in the pew behind Bob Morton. Every so often, he would lean forward and give Bob's shoulder a squeeze.

Sheriff Hoyt didn't trust the man. He was a lawyer, for one thing, which was more than enough, but there was something else, something hidden. Sheriff Hoyt had interrogated enough suspects to know when something else was going on behind their eyes. Cochran had a whole lot of something else going on in his head, that much was clear.

Eventually, the reverend turned the pulpit over to the mayor, who seized the opportunity to give his own speech, get his face in front of the cameras. As he was winding down, other men saw their own opportunity appear. They started lining up under the sun-dappled stained-glass windows in the east wall of the church.

Everybody used the pulpit as a platform, starting out talking about how great Bob Jr. was, and then they'd pitch their particular skill or cause. A high school buddy said, "I remember goofing off in class with him. Seemed like a good guy. Happy to see him get so far. We all go our different directions, I guess. Bob Jr. went his way. I went mine. Helping my dad out at the barbershop these days. Happy to see any of you fellas in there if you want to talk."

Somebody else wrestled the mike away. "Thanks very much. As you can see, Bob Jr. had nothing but friends. And friends, let me tell you, whenever Bob Jr. was in town, he made sure to eat one hell of a dinner at my steakhouse. You come on by, tell that pretty little gal up front you're a friend of me and Bob Jr.'s, you get ten percent off your total bill."

And on and on.

Eventually, Cochran took the mike. If anything, the line of men waiting to speak had gotten even longer. "I'm sure Bob and Belinda appreciate all these fine sentiments, and they know how much their son was loved by this community."

That was his cue. Sheriff Hoyt stood, put his hat back on, and left the church as the reverend reclaimed his pulpit and started another prayer. Sheriff Hoyt propped the doors open and cleared a way down the crowded steps. He went out to the sedan and stood by the back door, waiting for Bob and Belinda to appear at the church doors. Everybody out on the street with a camera got ready.

When the Mortons did appear, it wasn't quite the impression Cochran was striving for. Sheriff Hoyt figured Cochran would want Bob Jr.'s parents stoic and dignified in the face of tragedy. Instead, they weaved and lurched down the steps, and Sheriff Hoyt thought it was almost embarrassing. Bob Sr. damn near had to carry his wife down the stone steps. Bob himself looked . . . bad. He kept a handkerchief up to his face and kept wiping at the corners of his mouth. He looked like he should be home in bed; he looked truly sick and

moved like he'd been kicked in the nuts a few times. He
had no business being out in public.

Maybe that wasn't fair. Sheriff Hoyt had never lost a
son. He didn't even have a family, so he had no clear
idea how it would feel. He looked at the concrete, a little
ashamed. The man had just lost his son. Bob was having
a hard enough time holding up his wife, who was clearly
here under the influence of a bottle of wine and three or
four Xanax. A little compassion was probably called for
in this situation.

Sheriff Hoyt opened the back door of the sedan and
waited patiently.

The radio on his shoulder erupted in a shrill squawk.
"Attention, all units. Attention, all units. Multiple re-
ports of shots fired, Pleasant Prairie Trailer Haven.
Repeat, multiple reports of gunfire. Please respond."

Kevin crawled through the tall weeds on his hands
and knees until he saw Jerm's trailer. He could occasionally catch the faint squealing of a mindless, ex-
citable studio audience for some daytime talk show
coming from a TV inside, but he couldn't see anything
moving, either inside or out. It looked like sheets or
something had been hung over the windows.

He'd gotten up early, surprising the hell out of his
mom, and played with Puffing Bill in the backyard for
a while. Before he went outside, he had secretly swallowed another two ibuprofens. Any more, and Elliot
would have been severely disappointed in him. Out in
the backyard, part of him was worried about Mrs.
Kobritz; she'd always been like a grandmother to him,
but he was always thrilled to see her pit bull. Making the

dog happy was almost enough to smooth away the churning in his guts. Pretty soon, it was time to gather his backpack and pretend to ride off to school. If he left any later, his mom would insist on giving him a ride.

Kevin had no intention of getting close to school this morning.

He'd ridden through town toward school, though, just in case his mom decided to follow him or something. He didn't think that would happen; he knew she had to help out with some big funeral or something in town. She'd said there would be a lot of news reporters around, so maybe they'd watch the news later tonight, see if she was on TV.

He hid out under the bleachers that overlooked the high school baseball field, watching the shadow of the old water tower crawl across the infield. It was quiet out there, and it gave him a chance to sort out his thoughts. He'd tried thinking things through last night, but the fears had crowded out everything else, making it impossible to think clearly, until he finally passed out from exhaustion. Now it was possible to lay everything out.

Kevin didn't think Jerm would take the gun to school. Jerm had to consider the possibility that Kevin had told his mom, and she would be waiting for him at school. If Jerm didn't have the gun on him, he would allow himself to be searched, then he could deny everything. At least, that's what Kevin would do.

He realized he had no idea what Jerm would actually do.

Jerm might be stupid enough to take the gun to school, just to show it off.

Of course, there was always the possibility he might bring the gun just to shoot Kevin. But Kevin didn't think that would happen. If Jerm had wanted, he could have shot Kevin back in the town dump, then claimed it was self-defense. No, Jerm was dumber than a bag of hammers when it came to most stuff related to school, but he was awfully cunning when it came to slipping out of trouble.

Kevin also knew that Jerm couldn't afford to miss many classes of summer school. Jerm sure as hell didn't want to get held back another year. That would mean he would be taken out of the regular school system and forced instead to take classes in the special education building out near the school district offices, where he would be sitting alongside the developmentally disabled students. Kevin figured Jerm had too much of a sense of pride to let that happen.

So that meant that Jerm would likely hide the gun while he was in school, then retrieve it later. And the most obvious choice was somewhere safe, somewhere close to home.

When the shadow of the water tower had reached the pitcher's mound, Kevin hopped on his bike and pedaled out to the southern edge of town. Along the way, the houses went from colorful two-story Victorian ladies down to cheap ranch-style homes decaying behind dead lawns.

Jerm lived with his mother and older brother in the trailer park. The place was full of empty double-wides, high weeds, and garbage cans that always seemed full. The owner had worked at the big tractor factory in Peoria until he was laid off or fired, nobody knew exactly which. Now he sat out on his deck that over-looked the algae-choked pond at the front of the property, drinking beer and fishing. Fishing, in this case, consisted of watching a faded red bobber float listlessly in the green water all day and listening to the Cards games on the radio.

Kevin knew that Jerm lived here because he had once ridden along after his mom had picked him up from school. The owner had been trying to deliver an eviction notice, but Jerm's brother had threatened the man. Sandy had gone over to smooth things out, to try and work out a deal. She got the owner to give the family another month to pull together enough money, but it had never sat well with Jerm. He saw Chief Chisel as the one who wanted to evict the family. It didn't matter that Sandy had been trying to help the family out; Jerm was convinced that Sandy was responsible. Kevin had been left waiting in the front seat of the cruiser, and been in plain view when Jerm came storming out of the trailer. From then on, Kevin had been marked.

Kevin walked his bike along the fence line, ducking out of the owner's line of sight. He left his bike behind when he got close to Jerm's trailer and waited for any movement. There was still a chance that Jerm hadn't gone to school; he may not have been able to resist the temptation to stay home and play with his new toy.

After watching the trailer for a while, Kevin was satisfied that Jerm probably wasn't home. He ran across the little blacktop road and flattened himself next to the front steps. He waited a few seconds, hoping his heart would stop hammering in his chest just a little, then climbed the warped wooden steps, keeping his knees flexed and bent.

He saw that the front door was open, with only the screen door shut. The screen was full of rips that had been repaired at some point with gray duct tape. Now, the duct tape was curling up off the mesh from the summer heat, leaving gaps big enough that Kevin could stick his fist through. It didn't look like it did a very good job of keeping the mosquitoes out.

The breathless audience inside erupted in orgasmic applause yet again.

Kevin slowly twisted the screen-door handle, cranking the lever down. It clicked, and he eased it open, dreading squeaks and squeals. It swung open fairly silently, and he stuck his head inside the stifling heat of the trailer. It took his eyes a moment to adjust.

The noise from the TV came from off to the right, the front of the trailer. The kitchen was directly ahead of him, which meant the bedrooms waited to the left. He could only make out a few dark blobs from the living room. A couch or something was between him and the TV; he could only see the flickering blue light sizzle around the lumps of furniture.

Kevin stepped slowly inside, gently guiding the screen door shut behind him. He straightened, squinted at the TV. He still couldn't tell if anyone was up front or not. Part of the furniture grunted at something witty that the host had said, and Kevin realized that there was a very large woman sprawled on the couch. It was clear she was focused on the TV, and did not realize some ten-year-old kid had just stepped into her trailer.

Kevin felt his mouth go dry. He crouched, and moved in a kind of duckwalk back to the bedrooms. The first doorway on the left was the bathroom, and smelled worse than any Porta-Potty he'd ever used. He figured that the doorway at the end of the hall led to the mother's bedroom, and so that meant that the room off to the right was probably Jerm and his brother's.

He was right. Beer advertisements featuring bikini-clad women and *Playboy* centerfolds had been stapled to the fake-wood laminate walls. The single window had been covered with an old black sheet, anchored to the top of the window with thumbtacks. It kept the room in nearly total darkness. As his eyes adjusted, Kevin saw that the two beds were simply a couple of mattresses thrown into opposite corners. The brothers apparently shared a single dresser, built out of particleboard, but most of the laundry was scattered throughout the room. Kevin wasn't sure if he was more scared of running into Jerm, his brother, or the mother, but he still crawled into the room and started feeling around for the handgun.

Ten minutes later, he was convinced that Jerm had not hidden the gun in his room, and he really wanted to wash his hands. Kevin was disappointed, but not surprised. He didn't think Jerm would hide the revolver someplace where his brother might find it. Still, he had to try. He eased back into the hall.

The talk show had been replaced by some Hollywood gossip show. The dark shape in the flickering shadows of the TV moved. A thick, sleepy voice said, "Who's that?"

Kevin froze, blood coagulating into ice.

"Who is that?" the voice asked again.

"Just uh, looking for Jerm," he croaked, staring at the stained carpet.

"He ain't here. He's at school." A spark from a lighter. "You'll find him there."

Kevin smelled sweet and sour smoke, like burning rotten fruit. He said, "Okay."

The shape held her breath. Exhaled. "Be a sugar on the way out and make sure you close that screen door. Bangs when the wind blows if you don't click it just right. Drives me fucking nuts."

"Okay, sure, no problem," Kevin said, already through the doorway. He shut the door with a solid click, pushed against it to confirm the door handle had engaged the doorframe. He started down the steps. He had no idea where he was headed next. It didn't matter. He was too relieved to care.

He'd figure it out on his bike, once he was long gone.

A pair of hands so white they may have been wearing bleached latex gloves lunged out of the darkness under the trailer and yanked him off his feet. He tried to scrabble backward, but one of the hands closed over his shoe. Jerm's gray face swam into view. "What . . . Why are you here?" His voice sounded garbled, like his tongue was swollen.

"I . . . I . . .." Kevin couldn't form words, let alone explain himself.

Jerm didn't act like he heard anything anyway. His head lolled around on a loose neck, like it was too heavy to hold upright and still. Something was different about his face, but he kept it pulled back from the light, so Kevin couldn't get a good look. He kept talking, mostly to himself. "Thought I shot you at school already. Wanted everybody to see it."

Kevin tried to pull his foot back, but the movement caught Jerm's attention. "Fuck are you doing here?" Jerm nearly shouted, yanking him deeper under the trailer. He leaned over Kevin, and in the dim light,

Kevin could see that Jerm's skin had broken out even
worse than usual. Much worse. Sticky-looking blackheads had exploded across his face, lining every crease
and fold in the puffy skin. Jerm curled his lips back,
revealing yellow teeth and a black tongue. His nostrils
were plugged completely with solid-looking gray snot.
And his eyes. Something was wrong with his eyes.

They bulged unnaturally, as though reacting to some
uncomfortable inner pressure. Tiny gray buds were growing out of his eye sockets, near the inner corners, pushing
the eyeballs out of the way. Kevin got the distinct impression that Jerm was looking in two different directions at
once, and it was confusing the hell out of him.

"Thought I shot you already," Jerm repeated. He
reached down and when he pulled his hand back up into
the faint light, Kevin could see Jerm was now holding
his mom's Smith & Wesson. Jerm clicked the hammer
back and it sounded so loud in the cramped, dusty shadows under the trailer that Kevin was worried his bladder
might give out.

Kevin flopped flat on his back and kicked out frantically with his free foot, driving his heel into Jerm's chin
and nose. The sole of his sneaker smashed against the
blackheads, popping the ripe mounds, releasing a
stinking black paste. Jerm grunted and let go of his
other foot.

Kevin twisted and scrabbled toward the sunlight. He
had nearly reached the edge of the shadows when he felt,
rather than heard, some explosion behind him, and at the
same time, a sledgehammer came down on the back of his
head and darkness overtook him and he knew no more.

CHAPTER 15

The Fitzgimmons were expecting Sandy. The front gate was wide open. She'd been toying with the idea of running along on a code 10-39, which meant full lights and siren, letting everybody know they needed to get the hell out of the way. Then, when she got closer, she could switch to a 10-40, running silent without lights and the siren. Sandy changed her mind because with the Fitzgimmons, sneaking in unannounced might be a good way to get shot. It was better to give them as much advance warning as possible.

Still, they wouldn't have been able to get the gate open in time if they were just now hearing the siren. They knew she was coming and were ready. She slowed to a more respectable speed and turned off the siren.

When she got closer she saw that the tow truck from the garage where Axel worked was hooked up to a white pickup. The back end was off the ground, and Sandy could see large ruts in the driveway where the pickup had tried to drive away. The pickup had a USDA logo on the door; the back was enclosed with multipurpose storage compartments, almost like something the vet drove around to ranches when he was checking on large animals. The driver was still inside the cab, waving frantically at her.

Edgar sat on the hood of the pickup; Axel was behind the wheel of the tow truck. Purcell was standing off in the shade of the oak trees. Sandy shut off the engine and climbed out, trying not to make it obvious she was looking around for Charlie. Purcell's truck was parked over by the barn, so Charlie had to be around somewhere.

Purcell stepped out of the shade and took his time meandering across the driveway.

Sandy stepped over to the pickup, said to the man inside, "Sir, would you mind stepping out of the vehicle?"

"You tell these psychos to unhook me and I'll think about it." He looked to be in his fifties, with a neatly trimmed gray beard. His eyes had narrowed and he jabbed his finger in random directions to punctuate his words. "Fact is, I'll feel a whole lot better when you arrest all of them. You get them facedown on the ground in handcuffs and then I'll get out."

Sandy turned to Purcell, who had gotten close enough to speak with. "Purcell. I'd been hoping I wouldn't have to be back here in a professional capacity so soon."

"Chief." Purcell gave her a nod in greeting.

"What's the problem?"

"What we have here, I suppose you could say, is a failure of communication. Charlie caught this man trespassing, so we decided to hang onto him until the proper authorities showed up."

"I see. Did you call us?"

"Nah. Didn't see any point. Fella in there told us he was calling the cops a buncha times, so I figured that'd kill two birds, one stone and all that. And I knew you folks were busy with the funeral."

Sandy resisted the urge to tell him it wasn't a funeral.

The guy from the USDA shouted through the windshield, "What are you waiting for? Arrest them!"

Sandy tried to open the passenger door. It was locked. "Sir, it would be much easier if you would just step out of the vehicle and we can all discuss this."

"You know what they threatened to do to me? Do you have any idea of the kind of filth that comes out of their mouth?"

"We don't put up with trespassers on my property," Purcell said. "You're awful damn fortunate we didn't just shoot you first, then call the chief."

Sandy asked Purcell, "You say Charlie found him? Whereabouts?"

"Up in the north field."

"We have to take samples if you want to be certified," the USDA guy yelled. "What is wrong with you?"

Sandy and Purcell ignored him. She asked, "Any chance Charlie's around? Like to talk to him."

"He's busy. He can talk later, if need be."

"I'd like to talk to him now."

Purcell hesitated. Sandy stepped closer, lowered her voice so the USDA guy in the pickup couldn't hear. "You and your boys are in some awfully deep hot water here. You want my help, you get Charlie out here now."

Purcell put two fingers to his lips and gave a whistle that scared crows into the air at two hundred yards. Sandy figured her ears would be ringing until evening. It wasn't so much that she needed to interview Charlie immediately, but she wanted him in her sights so he wasn't sneaking up behind her again.

A few moments later, the barn doors creaked open and Charlie stepped out. He dragged a large chain across the door handles and snapped a padlock through the links. Sandy felt Purcell stiffen up beside her, and knew that Charlie had made a mistake. He shouldn't have made a big deal about locking the barn.

Now she was curious. She figured it probably was something that might compromise their chances of being certified organic, and filed the question away for later. Right now she had to deal with getting the USDA man off the farm without too much of a battle.

As Charlie sauntered over, shielding his eyes against the sun, Sandy's radio erupted. "Attention, all units. Attention, all units. Multiple reports of shots fired, Pleasant Prairie Trailer Haven. Repeat, multiple reports of gunfire. Please respond."

Sandy froze. She knew she was at least fifteen, maybe twenty minutes away; all the officers covering the Morton service were much, much closer. As she reached for her radio, she heard Sheriff Hoyt's voice, "Ten-four. On our way."

A flurry of other voices echoed Sheriff Hoyt. Sandy knew she should finish here first, then head into town to assist in any way possible. Still, she wanted to get there as soon as she could. She fixed Charlie with a cold stare and didn't waste any time. "Did you assault this man in any way?"

"Fuck no. He say that?"

"Did you threaten him with physical violence?"

Charlie scratched his head, shrugged. "Not that I remember exactly. All I did is stay between him and his truck until Axe got there with the tow truck. I might have mentioned a few things that could go wrong, him trespassing and all."

She turned back to Purcell. "I'm doing my best to help you out, but you need to listen. This shouldn't be a surprise. You know damn well you cannot take this man and his vehicle hostage. Best you can do for yourself is turn him loose immediately. Longer you keep him up in the air like that, the worse he's gonna sue."

That got Purcell's attention. "He can't sue me. He's the trespasser here. This is my property. Thought that would be clear as daylight."

Sandy shook her head. "He's doing his job. You might as well have invited him over yourself."

Purcell stuck his hands in his jeans and thought about it a moment. "What a pisser. Hard to get ahead when the game is rigged against you right from the start. Boys, you pay attention. There's a lesson to be learned here."

Voices burst over Sandy's radio. "Shots fired! Officer down. Officer down."

Sandy could not have cared any less about the argument between the idiots out at Purcell's farm, but it was her responsibility. It sounded like all kinds of hell was breaking loose in town, and she tried not to let the urgency show on her face. "Look, gentlemen. We need to wrap this up."

Purcell nodded. "Axel. Let him down. Now. See if we can't work something out with the man."

Axel didn't like it, but he flipped a lever and released the pickup all at once. The rear wheels crashed down, and the whole back end of the pickup bounced twice. Sandy knocked impatiently on the window. "Sir, you need to step out here now."

"The hell I do," the USDA guy said. "You people are crazy."

Sandy said, "Next time, I'd research my clients a little closer. Might not be a bad idea to find out if they're liable to shoot trespassers on sight."

Purcell leaned on the hood and waved through the windshield. "Sorry about this little mix-up. Hope this doesn't screw up our certification chances."

"Fuck you!" the USDA man yelled and cranked the engine over.

Sandy's radio crackled. "Suspect is a young male. Thirteen to fifteen years of age. Armed and dangerous."

A cold, spiky feeling grew in the center of Sandy's chest. She pulled out her cell phone and quickly found the contact number for Kevin's school.

The USDA man hit the gas and tore out of the driveway, spraying gravel in his wake. He barely missed Sandy's cruiser and was gone in a cloud of dust that hung in the air like a brown fog.

Sandy heard the prerecorded message and hit the button to speak with the office.

"District seventy-nine, how can I help you?"

"Hi, this is Sandy Chisel. I would like to speak with my son Kevin, please. He is in Mr. Humpher's math class."

"One moment."

Sandy turned to find Purcell and his sons watching her. At that moment, she had no idea what to say to the Fitzgimmon men.

The office secretary got back on the phone and said, "I'm sorry. Kevin is not at school today. His teacher reported him absent."

* * *

Jerm could have sworn he'd already shot the little shit. Several times. That wasn't the only thing he was confused about. He had no memory of coming home last night. The last thing he remembered was that police cruiser whispering out of the darkness and scaring the shit out of him. There was something after that, something about hiding out in a big pipe, but then . . . nothing.

He couldn't tell if he'd been to school already. Wasn't sure if he'd taken the gun. Vague images of floating down the hallway, shooting a bunch of people, especially all those cocksucking teachers, drifted through his head. Something about putting the barrel of his new handgun between Kevin's teeth and pulling the trigger, watching the prick's brains splatter all over the lockers.

Was it real? Was it a dream? It was all getting kind of slippery.

Dream or not, the little fucker was dead now. At least, as best as he could tell. Jerm's eyes weren't working so well. Everything was sort of stretched from side to side. Nothing lined up like it used to. He'd felt and heard the gun going off, no question about *that*. But it wasn't like the memory of when he shot Kevin back in the school. There was no clear moment this time where he saw the back of Kevin's head explode.

He crawled forward. There. There was the punk-ass bitch. Sprawled out across the front sidewalk. Wasn't moving. Looked dead enough. Jerm shrank back. The light bothered his eyes. Daylight made everything—the headache, the weird shit going on with his vision, his memory—made it all worse.

He heard thumping in the trailer above. Heard his mom yell, "What the fuck was that?" She stomped over and kicked open the screen door. He heard her give a girlish little shriek when she saw Kevin's body. She came thundering down the front steps, yelling, "What happened? What the fuck happened?" She caught her breath and managed to bend over and peer into the darkness under the trailer. Jerm was surprised she'd gotten off the couch in the first place. She yelled at him, "What the fuck are you doing?"

Jerm didn't think. It was all a dream anyway. He felt curiously outside himself, as he was merely a casual observer, peering in through some dim windows at someone else's fantasies. Saw himself raise the handgun and squeeze off a round. His mom's face jerked, crinkled somehow, as if she'd just taken a big bite of a sour lemon, and her nose disappeared in a burst of red.

Blue gun smoke swirled hypnotically in the space between the light and shadow. He liked that. Took a breath, pursed his lips, and blew a stream of heat out into the smoke, creating a roiling vortex.

He'd be lying if he said that shooting his mom didn't feel awful damn good. He liked the weight of the gun. Liked how he could simply point the barrel, pull the trigger, and shit in his life went away. It made him feel so good that he crawled out of the darkness and out into the daylight. He didn't like how the light and heat had a sharp edge that peeled him open, but he wanted to feel that sensation again, to feel the gun jerk in his hands, watch the blue smoke circle his head, as he basked in the knowledge that he'd just erased more goddamn useless pain and bullshit from his life.

Jerm walked to the front of the Pleasant Prairie Trailer Haven. Saw that asshole Raleigh standing on his deck, yelling something. Jerm drifted closer, raised the

Smith & Wesson. Watched the man's expression change from hatred to fear. Squeezed the trigger before the asshole could run back inside.

Raleigh spun, a sudden red flower blooming on his chest, and went crashing through his lawn chair before toppling off the deck into the pond. The wide-open blue sky came down and wrapped Jerm in a soft blanket and he sighed, perfectly content.

He wanted more.

He kept walking, straight down the street.

The blast of someone's horn shook him out of his reverie. He blinked and tried to look around. The world still wasn't falling into place like he hoped, but he could manage to make sense of the images his eyes fed his brain, however nonsensical they might look.

That was a dream for you.

There was a car behind him. The driver hit the horn again. Jerm eased around the front of the car, guiding himself along the hood and up the windshield with his left hand. The cranky fat broad inside was squawking something at him, but he shut her down with the handgun. This time, he distinctly saw blood, bone, and brains, explode across the front seat.

It made him feel even better.

He kept walking. And when the first cop car came screeching to a stop, siren wailing, lights spinning, Jerm just smiled and raised his gun. The first time he squeezed the trigger, the driver's door window exploded and the cop inside fell back against the seat. Jerm walked right up through the broken glass and pointed the barrel at the cop's head and squeezed the trigger a second time.

Another burst of bone and blood. All over the steering wheel.

More sirens. Coming from all directions. Fucking pigs. His hands popped open the cylinder, moving all on their own, and plucked out the empty shells. He dug into his pockets and pulled out a handful of loose cartridges, all from the boxes his daddy had left. Most of the shells were either too loose or didn't fit at all. He found five that fit well enough to slide into the chambers, snug and secure, as if they were destined to be fired from the gun. Jerm waited until he could see at least three county troopers roaring up the street right at him before he stepped forward and blasted away.

The cop cars scattered, breaking away from the street and plowing into front lawns. Jerm kept right on tracking the cruisers, squeezing off empties, lost in a series of dry clicks. The effort of standing out in the full sunlight eventually took its toll, and he let his head and the gun drop. He bent over, breathing deeply, as if he'd just sprinted down a football field. He noticed the shadows inside the dead trooper's vehicle and crawled over the corpse, shutting the door behind him.

He slid headfirst into the shadow of the floor of the passenger seat, curling up into a ball, knees up around his ears, arms wrapped tight around his shins, locked around each elbow. Once in tight under the dashboard, head wedged between the seat and the door, feet jammed against the upright .12 gauge, he did not move again.

Jerm exhaled one last time, and his already dim consciousness faded and blinked out.

His flesh did not relinquish the hold on itself.

* * *

Sheriff Hoyt signaled to his men to run forward and surround Bryan's cruiser. Poor bastard. Twenty-one years on the force. Three, four years until a solid pension. Then shot in the head by some underage punk. It was a god-damn waste.

He waited until they got closer before he took off in a crouch from his own vehicle and slid behind the passenger rear panel on his knees. He took a second to gather himself and said, "Go. Unload on that fucker."

Three other county troopers rose and squeezed off a dozen shots apiece, blasting out the windows and un-leashing a firestorm of lead tornados inside the car.

Two bullets caught Jerm in the chest. One went through his head.

A soft summer breeze gently dissipated the blue smoke.

Somebody shouted, "Clear!" and everybody crowded around and got their first good look at Jerm. They saw the blood and bullet holes and Sheriff Hoyt called the time of death. He pulled the nearest trooper over and told the man to get Mike Castle on the phone. Castle was the only doctor in Parker's Mill, and served as the town coroner and pathologist if Chirchirillo was busy.

"Tell him I want him here immediately." Dr. Castle was a little too friendly with Chief Chisel for Sheriff's Hoyt's liking, but he didn't have a choice. "We got our-selves a boatload of national press in town for the god-damn funeral or whatever it is, and they're gonna be on this like flies on shit. You make sure Mike understands we need this fucker in the freezer. They figure out a kid did the shooting, and they're gonna start asking questions." Sheriff Hoyt pitched his voice higher, pretending to be a reporter. "'Why's he so young? What went wrong? Oh, it's such a tragedy.' That bullshit never helps anybody. Let's get his ass out of the equation. Let 'em speculate."

The trooper nodded and went off to call Castle.

Sheriff Hoyt pulled two more troopers over. The street was starting to get crowded with more cruisers, an ambulance, and even that dipshit Deputy Hendricks. At least the goddamn bitch chief wasn't here yet. "You," he pointed at a young trooper. "Get in touch with Chirchirillo. He's in court today, but you get him on the horn. We need somebody on our side to take care of the victims, and the Church is a good man. He'll listen to reason, make sure things get painted the way we want 'em."

Sheriff Hoyt told the second trooper to round up anybody that was left, including that dumbass Hendricks, and seal off the area. "This is a goddamn crime scene. The last thing we need is the press running wild through here, waving their cameras and microphones at anything that moves."

Sheriff Hoyt stuck his head through one of the shattered windows into the sweltering heat of the county police car and shook his head. He spotted the shooter's handgun, a nickel-plated Model 686 Smith & Wesson, down along Trooper Bryan's feet. Something about it seemed awfully familiar, like he should know the gun for some reason. The connection held promise, but he couldn't grasp it, and the image was gone. He filed it away to think about later and focused on the immediate problem. His men were busy with their own assignments, on the phone, or waving off reporters and a few curious townspeople.

And that left Sheriff Hoyt to follow the trail of bodies.

He had a gut feeling where the kid had come from, and started heading south. A block away, he found what was left of Mrs. Perkins. She had been a cranky old bitch, and probably would have been dead in a year or so of a heart attack because of her weight, but it was still a damn shame to go out with your blood dripping from the dashboard. From her car, Sheriff Hoyt could see the body of the trailer park landlord floating facedown in the retention pond, and it didn't take Sherlock Holmes to figure out where the kid lived.

He headed down the narrow center street, passing empty trailer after empty trailer. When he saw the body of the large woman sprawled out next to the warped wooden stairs, he wasn't surprised. He should have known that this particular trailer had someone living there, because it looked so much worse than the rest of the trailers. He stopped, tilted his head like an old dog, and recognized the woman from her bleached blond hair.

Miss Ellie May Higgins. Again, it wasn't a surprise.

Back in the nineties Ellie May was the hottest thing in the county and had the time of her life raising hell. Now she was in her mid thirties, mother of two, maybe three, creeping up on two hundred pounds, and living on frozen cheeseburgers, pot, and TV. She was just one of these people that, for whatever reason, you knew damn well they wouldn't be collecting Social Security and watching the grandkids run around. The bullet had punched through the dead center of her skull, wiping out her nose and popping her brain stem, leaving nothing but a ragged hole in the middle of her face, an astonished lower jaw, and instant death.

Sheriff Hoyt got closer and saw a kid wriggling out from underneath her body.

Now that, *that* was a surprise.

His right hand flew to the special rubber grips of his Ruger Blackhawk. Ever since those two assholes shot up the high school in Colorado and those two sniper spooks crept around Washington, D.C., he drilled his men that whenever they encountered a crime, they always had to be aware of the possibility of two or more suspects.

The kid struggled; Ellie May had let herself go, that much you couldn't argue with. She had always been cur-vaceous, no bullshit there, but in the years since her glory days had faded, she had become a hell of a heavy woman. It took the kid a while to slide out from under-neath a corpse that wasn't in the mood to cooperate.

From a distance, he was maybe nine, ten. Sheriff Hoyt got a look at the kid's eyes. Up close, the kid seemed older than he looked. Maybe twelve or thirteen.

The kid rolled away and stood up, wavering a little when he straightened. Blood ran from a trail of burned scalp that traveled up the back of his neck, skimming off the skull, leaving a straight, shallow gash. Sheriff Hoyt was impressed; the kid had come within an eyelash of a bullet in the brainpan.

The kid fixed Sheriff Hoyt with a stare, for only a blink of a moment, but it was enough. Enough to take in the hat, the badge, Hoyt's face. The kid looked away and didn't say anything. Disrespectful punk.

Just like his mom.

Sheriff Hoyt snapped his fingers. It all came together,

like water spilling down a suddenly unplugged drain. He now knew where he'd seen the gun. At that bitch's trial, before she stole the election.

"Well, I'll be damned," he said to the kid. "What do you think your mother's gonna say about all this?"

CHAPTER 16

Bob Morton glanced at the mirror and got a good look at his face. Now that the memorial service was finished, he could catch his breath, take a moment to try and make sense of everything. It had all gotten so confusing lately.

Under the fluorescent light, he looked tired. Drawn. It was to be expected, he supposed. Mourning his son, hadn't been sleeping right. Color was off. He just hoped his bad complexion hadn't been too obvious this morning. He dabbed at the black spots at the corners of his mouth. He scrubbed harder; they persisted.

Bob double-checked the bathroom door to make sure it was locked, then leaned into the mirror and gave the biggest blemish on the right ride of his mouth, right where his lips came together, a wicked squeeze. It bulged, but wouldn't pop. He tried again. No explosion, no wet splat. He tried on the other side. No matter the angle, he could not express the black circles.

And they were getting bigger, no question. Squeezing them just made things worse; his fingernails tore the skin and increased the swelling in the immediate area. He was starting to look like a squirrel in the fall, cheeks full of acorns. He splashed some more water on his face to calm things down. As the clusters got bigger, he noticed that the darkness inside the spheres faded more and more into a dull gray, like some kind of volcanic ash was slowly erupting out of his pores.

He used the hand towel to dry his face. When he touched his nose, it felt like it was clogged with hard nuggets of snot. Using his index finger, he pushed up on the tip, as if he were trying to make himself look like a pig, tilted his head back, and leaned in closer to the mirror.

Black stalks with conical buds at the tips clustered together in the nostrils like disturbingly thick hair. Bob gave them an experimental poke. They were flexible, and yielded to his touch. He placed both hands flat on the vanity and exhaled, long and slow. He understood that he was balancing on the razor edge of total, abject fear, and the slightest shift would send him screaming from the bathroom. His breath came out in a slight, wavering whistle, like a worried teapot.

He had to stay in control; his family and his reputation demanded nothing less.

He wrapped a wad of toilet paper around his fingers and pressed it to his nose. He took a deep breath and blew air out of his nose as hard as he could. Some air got through, but not much. His ears popped, and even that didn't feel right. He checked the toilet paper and bit down on a bubble of hysterical laughter.

Some of the things had broken loose and were smeared into the tissue paper, along with sticky smudges of black snot. He didn't want to admit it, but they did look like some kind of miniature mushrooms. The soiled paper went into the toilet. He found the tiny scissors he used to trim his nose and ear hairs, and went to work methodically snipping away at the things still in his nostrils.

Another blast into fresh toilet paper. When he pulled it back this time, it was covered with dozens of the mushroom things and more black snot. That went into the toilet as well, and he flushed it quickly. He took another look at his nostrils. He'd cleared most everything out of his nose, at least up front as far as he could reach. He needed a flashlight to check and see if there were more of the things growing deeper in his nasal passages, but he wasn't ready for that. Not yet.

He got a Q-tip from his wife's jar and screwed it into his right ear, rolling it between his thumb and forefinger. The cotton swab made murky, liquid sounds as he went deeper. He pulled it out and wasn't surprised to find more black muck coating the tip. He reversed the Q-tip and stuck the fresh end back into his ear.

Bob went through more than fifteen Q-tips before he was satisfied he was cleared out. They all went into the toilet as well. He crossed his arms, jamming his fingers under each armpit, and bit down on the insides of his lips. He would not scream. He would not.

Then he felt something else, some kind of weird bulge in his armpits. He avoided meeting his eyes in the mirror as he lifted his shirt and found that more of the mushrooms were poking through the gray hair under his arms. He ripped off his shirt, lifted his arm high, and stared at the dark growths popping up. Turning, he twisted his head to look at his bare back. Just skin and patches of gray hair.

Still, he wasn't going to assume anything. Not anymore. He yanked his suit pants down, stepped out of his shoes and socks. Nothing between his toes. Nothing on his legs. Nothing behind his knees. He pulled his briefs out and glanced nervously down at his groin. Nothing there, thank God.

Almost an afterthought, he stuck his right hand around to feel his ass, just in case, because he hadn't been able to move his bowels in at least two days. That need was simply *gone*.

He felt more of the tiny buds pushing up through the tight folds of the skin of his anus. There was a single moment of pure, toe-curling revulsion, and before he could stop himself, he curled his fingers into claws and raked at his flesh.

He brought his hand back up. Black gunk was smeared under his nails. His hand shook. Then he gripped the mirror with his right hand and ripped at the mushrooms sprouting through the skin of his armpits with his left. He leaned closer to the mirror and saw that he was breaking the stalks off at the roots, leaving dark, ominous little craters behind.

There was no blood.

No pain.

Somehow, that was the worst.

Sandy didn't trust herself to speak just yet and they drove home in silence. Kevin wouldn't look at her, and watched the houses slide past his window. He'd barely said anything since Sandy had arrived on the scene and found her son in the back of an ambulance, getting the back of his head patched up.

At least that prick Sheriff Hoyt hadn't locked him in the backseat of his cruiser.

She'd heard enough on the radio driving into town to piece together most of what had happened. But she still couldn't figure out how her son had been involved. There would be time enough for that later, time enough to sort through everything, but not right in the middle of a major crime scene. As soon as she arrived, she hustled Kevin into her own cruiser and a simple glare at the nearest trooper told the man that she was taking her child and no one was stopping her.

She'd switched off her radio, and when her cell phone rang, she turned it off and threw it at the floor. Kevin flinched, and she felt bad. She couldn't take it anymore and whipped into the alley behind the Stop 'n Save. She shut off the engine and turned to her son, reaching out to stroke his hair.

He didn't react to her touch, still wouldn't look at her.

The line of bandages that stretched up his neck across his scalp chilled her. Tears welled up and she closed her eyes, trying to think of something, anything, to say. A simple, "What happened?" wouldn't be enough, wouldn't even begin to crack the surface. She blinked furiously, willing the tears to disappear.

They sat in silence for a few minutes, feeling the summer sun beat down into the cruiser. Finally, Sandy said, "We better go home and make sure Puffing Bill hasn't destroyed the place."

Kevin gave a slight shrug.

At least it was a response. She put the car in gear and neither of them spoke the rest of the way home.

Sheriff Hoyt was waiting for them. He'd parked in the driveway, forcing Sandy to park on the street. He stood, leaning against his rear bumper, arms crossed, eyes hidden behind mirrored aviator sunglasses.

Sandy told Kevin to go inside and let the dog out into the backyard. Sheriff Hoyt's eyes never left her face. They stared at each other for a moment, and Sandy didn't want to dance around the subject. She knew Kevin was a witness to a mass murder, but that didn't explain the scrutiny, the way Sheriff Hoyt had treated him like a suspect. "What do you want?" she asked. "My son has been through enough hell today."

"I don't doubt it. Gonna leave a hell of scar, back of his head, there."

Sandy put her hands on her hips and waited.

Sheriff Hoyt went to the driver's seat and reached in through the open window. He grabbed a plastic evidence bag. Inside was the Model 686. "Know anything about this?"

Sandy recognized the handgun instantly. Ice flooded her veins. Her mouth went dry. "You know damn well I do. It's mine."

"Thought so. Any idea how it got into that little fucker's hands? I'd like to hear all about that."

"I don't know."

Sheriff Hoyt watched her for a moment, face impassive behind those mirrored sunglasses. He used his tongue to dislodge some piece of stringy meat stuck between his upper molars. Eventually, he said, "Maybe you don't, maybe you do. Not sure it matters much, 'cause I'll bet your boy knows. We gonna have to talk to him, down at the station, you understand that, don't you?"

"He's not going anywhere right now."

Sheriff Hoyt considered this. "You do realize that

four people are dead, 'cause of this." He hefted the plastic evidence bag. "Slow news day, this'll be front page on the national news. It's bigger than both of us, bigger than this town, this county. So it shouldn't be a surprise that you are hereby suspended without pay. The county police will take over your duties for the time being." He turned the plastic bag over and over in his hands. "You and your son are in a heap-load of trouble. I hope you know this. Hell, I wanted to, I could take him in immediately, put him in a room, and sweat the truth out of him."

"You could try."

Sheriff Hoyt chuckled. He knew damn well Sandy wasn't talking about his legal right to remove a suspect from his home and take him to the station for an interrogation.

She was talking about him making it out of the driveway alive.

He turned his gaze skyward and contemplated the branches of the elm trees that swayed gently above their heads. "Tell you what. You sleep on it. Get yourself lawyered up. And bring Kevin down to the courthouse tomorrow. We do need to speak with the young man, as I'm sure you are aware." He nodded. "Okay. Tomorrow. Bring him down and we'll get all this sorted out."

He waited for Sandy to agree, or say something defiant, but she stood motionless, drilling him with her stare. He kept waiting, but when it became apparent Sandy had made herself perfectly clear and felt no reason to explain herself any further, he tipped his hat, curled his fingers around the bag, and got back into his cruiser.

She stepped out of the way as he backed down the

driveway. When he drew level with her, he rolled down the passenger window and said, "Tomorrow morning. Nine sharp. Don't be late."

She didn't respond. He rolled the window back up and left.

Sandy moved her own cruiser into the driveway and went inside. Kevin was out in the back, playing with the dog. She gave him a few more minutes and spent them pacing back and forth in the kitchen.

Her gun. Good Christ. Four people dead. Her gun.

She unplugged the house phone and made sure her cell was turned off, then went to the sliding glass back door and saw Kevin on his knees, petting the scarred pit bull. Puffing Bill seemed to know something was wrong, because he was leaning into the boy's touch. Sandy watched for a while, and while she didn't want to disturb them, she couldn't put it off any longer.

She slid the door open and went out to the backyard. Part of her couldn't help but notice the mounds of earth along the fence, covered with leaves. She'd been meaning to get out there and plant flowers in the spring, but had never found the chance. She tried to push that out of her mind, because the last thing she needed was something else to feel guilty about.

Kevin and Puffing Bill were aware of her presence, but neither moved. Puffing Bill seemed to know that the boy needed him, and stood stock still. His eyes found Sandy. She patted his head.

In the end, she didn't have to say anything. She simply sat quietly, both of them petting the dog, and Kevin finally said, "Mom, I took it." His voice quavered, but he didn't cry. He didn't cry as the whole story came pouring out, how he had taken the Smith &

Wesson, and how Jerm had been tormenting him for months, how it had all gotten so twisted and awful, what Jerm had done with his lunch bag, all of it. When he got to how he had finally tried to crawl out of the trailer, and then woke up with Jerm's mom laying on top of him, his voice finally cracked irrevocably, and there was no going back. Sobs erupted out of him and he gasped for breath.

Sandy could not process all of it right away. Part of her brain was still trying to put all the pieces together, but the mother instinct inside her, the part of her soul that recognized that her child was suffering, overrode everything else for that moment, and she took him into her arms and squeezed him tight. Tremors racked his thin body.

She held him for a long time.

"You feeling okay?" Cochran asked. He swiveled from Bob's desk, steepled his fingers in concern on his chest.

Bob shut the door to the bathroom behind him and fixed his attack dog with a grim stare. "I lost my son. How do you think I feel?" He settled himself on the edge of the couch, eyes on the TV news.

"I can only imagine," Cochran said.

Footage of the burning island appeared on the TV and Bob yelled, "Quiet," and turned the sound up. But there was nothing new. Just that distant, grainy footage of the island on fire and a bunch of smug assholes arguing about what could have been done to prevent such a tragedy.

Bob gripped his knees, then sank back into the couch.

Seeing the footage yet again pushed the horror and rage and confusion out of his chest. He realized he was exhausted. "I'm sorry. Exploding like that. I mean . . ." He looked up. "Do you have any sons, or children?"

"No. I have never married. I have no children."

Bob turned back to the TV. "You'll see. Someday. You'll have kids and someday you'll change your mind."

Cochran nodded politely. "Other friends have said the same thing."

Bob said, "There ya go."

They heard the bedroom door open and shut, and Belinda appeared on the stairs. Bob turned the TV off. He didn't want her to have to listen to any more news about the island. She'd changed her clothes, and now wore her usual sweater and jeans, and sensible gym shoes. She headed straight into the kitchen. They listened to her open and close the fridge, then heard the water splash into the sink.

Cochran didn't say anything, just listened for a while, and turned his attention back to the papers on the desk.

Bob wanted to exhale. Thank Christ. His wife was back down where it made him comfortable. He'd listened to those sounds every night of his married life, and they put him at ease, because life was back where it should be. The money was at the bank, the corn was growing under God's blue sky, and his wife was back in the kitchen.

He even felt a little hungry.

Soon Belinda stood in the kitchen doorway. She cleared her throat. "Dinner's ready."

The men stood and followed her into the dining room. She had laid out dinner, trays and trays across the table. Meatloaf. Mashed potatoes. Peas. Salad. Garlic French bread. Ice water. White wine.

"I'm sorry, it isn't much," Belinda said. "Probably nothing like what you are used to." This was aimed at Cochran.

Cochran said, "It's great. Thank you."

Bob waited for more, because he thought his wife deserved a hell of a lot of praise from a guest for showing such hospitality just days after losing her son. When it became clear that Cochran wasn't going to say anything else, Bob had to say, "Much obliged, dear. As always, a fantastic spread."

She stood back, letting the men take their seats. When they were settled, she brought her own plate to the table and sat down, but made no attempt to reach for any food. She spoke, quietly, directly to Cochran. "Why? Why couldn't you leave him alone? Why did you have to go and burn him?"

Bob closed his eyes and tried to think of something, anything, to change the subject.

His wife did not stop. "You burned him up. What happens to his soul, then? What happens then?" She started to cry. "My boy. My boy. You burnt him. Erased him. Couldn't even leave a piece for his own mother." Her voice rose. "Didn't even have the decency to send him home in a box."

Bob stood up. "Honey, please."

She waved him off, focused on Cochran. "What is wrong with you people?"

Cochran said, "I am truly sorry for your loss."

Bob took his wife in his arms. "Honey, you're tired. You aren't yourself. Time to get some rest." He escorted her upstairs. She went agreeably, although she asked,

"Why?" every so often as if she had forgotten the question.

Upstairs in the master bathroom, Bob shook out two more Xanax and gave them to his wife. She took them without hesitation and let him tuck her into bed. He turned off the light, lingered a moment, listening as she started to softly cry. He wanted to say something, but had no idea what, and closed the door on her low sobbing.

He went back down and sat at the table.

Cochran laid his fork on his plate.

Bob said, "Sorry. It's . . . Thought it might do her some good to be in the kitchen. Soothe her nerves, you know? She's just tired."

"Of course she is," Cochran said. "It's okay. Truly. I understand. I am here as an Allagro employee. You and your wife are a part of the Allagro family, and my job extends to helping you as best as I can during this difficult time. Now that we have gotten through the memorial, my job here is nearly finished. I can wrap up the loose ends tomorrow, and leave you good folks in peace."

Bob nodded. "Good. I mean, I appreciate the help, I surely do, but I think my wife and I need some time to ourselves now."

"Of course. I understand. And even after I leave, you need anything, anything at all, you call me. Anytime. Twenty-four hours a day. Like I said, you are an important part of the Allagro family, and we are here for you." Cochran swirled the wine around his glass and smiled.

Bob knew Cochran saw him as just some hick farmer and didn't think he was used to a slick-talking lawyer, but enough bullshit had been shoveled his way from bankers, tractor salesman, and field owners, that he knew when someone was setting him up. He could smell the faint condescension between Cochran's words. So he waited. He knew that the man was circling around to something, the real reason for the speech.

It didn't take long. Cochran put his elbows on the table and leaned forward, concern in his eyes. "And if you don't mind my saying so, you must be awfully tired yourself. How you holding up?"

Bob didn't smile back. "I'm holding up just fine. Second time you've asked me how I'm feeling."

Cochran didn't blink. "I'm not trying to pry. Just concerned. No offense, but you really don't look well."

"And I already told you. I lost my son. You got a problem with that?" The rage and frustration were back, and beginning to build.

Cochran sat back in his chair and studied Bob. "Of course not. I'm just trying to help."

"Help. How?"

"Any way I can."

"You seem awfully preoccupied with my health."

"Again, just trying to help. I certainly didn't mean to cause you any offense."

Bob forced a grin. "Sorry. Getting a little testy. You're right. Must be tired." He stuck out his hand to shake. "Guess I should call it a night."

Cochran smiled right back but made no move to take Bob's hand. "Good night, then. Hope it is peaceful for you."

Bob let his smile die. "What's your problem? I'm not good enough to shake your hand?"

"Of course not."

"Then shake my hand."

"I'd rather not."

"Afraid of catching something?"

"No."

"Then why not?"

Cochran sat back and studied the farmer. "Where are you going with this, Bob?"

"I'm not sure I understand the question."

"I think you do."

"I'm not sure I like the tone of your voice."

"I think that you need to think very carefully about how you want to proceed."

"I think I'm about done with your help."

"You sure you want to do this? Think about your wife. Your farm. My employers are . . . quite powerful, and wield a lot of influence. I would suggest that you take this into account and don't piss your life's work away."

Bob drew his hands into fists. "How dare you . . . how dare you sit here as a guest at my dinner table and threaten my wife and my farm? You've already taken my son."

Cochran was quiet for a moment. "What exactly have you got planted out there in that two acres by the expressway, Bob?"

So that was it. They wanted his son's last crop. "Get out of my house."

"Again, you sure this is what you want, Bob? Think very carefully."

"Get off my property. Now."

Cochran drummed his fingers against the table and watched Bob for a moment. "So be it," he said, dabbed at his mouth with his napkin, threw it on the table, and stood. He left the dining room without another word.

Bob did not move as he listened to Cochran gather

his things and leave the house. He waited until he heard the rented car gather speed as it went down the drive-way, then went to the foot of the stairs, listening up at the bedroom. His wife had stopped crying. The house was silent, save for the ticking grandfather clock in the front room.

He found the right keys on the hooks next to the back door and went out in the fading light to the huge shed where he kept the combine harvesters. It was too early to harvest the crop, but he'd be damned if he let those bastards take his son's corn.

CHAPTER 17

"How sure are you, Mr. Cochran?" The voice on the other end of the phone might have been discussing the weather.

Cochran said, "Ninety percent. He's sick. It's not the flu. Don't know how to diagnose it. He's trying to hide it, but something's going on." He'd pulled the car over in the Korner Kafe's parking lot and called the private number he'd been asked to memorize. They didn't want it written down anywhere.

The men at the other end were quiet for a while. Cochran wasn't sure if they were discussing the situation or merely thinking. He'd worked for them long enough to know that he should remain silent until they reached a decision. Eventually, one of them spoke. "What is your recommendation?"

"If he is indeed growing the strain, then there is no choice."

A new voice spoke. "Rectifying the situation on the

island was one thing. Rectifying a situation like that on American soil is quite another."

Cochran said, "It may be our only chance to contain the situation."

"And if you are wrong?" The voice let the question hang for several seconds. "The consequences could be catastrophic."

"For the organization, yes," Cochran agreed. "However, if nothing is done, the consequences could be catastrophic for the entire northern hemisphere." He let them chew on that for a while.

The first voice spoke. "It would appear then, that we cannot make an informed decision at this time."

Cochran saw where this was headed. "Look, I'm telling you. It's here. I have no doubt."

"You claimed you had ten percent of doubt."

Cochran shook his head. "I'm ninety-five percent positive, okay? Hell, after seeing the man tonight, I'd say I'm ninety-nine percent absolutely sure."

"I, for one, would feel better if you called us back when you were one hundred percent certain."

Cochran bared his teeth at the phone. Then he collected himself, and said in the most even voice he could manage, "Fine. I only hope that we aren't too late." He hit the END button and it was all he could do not to start swearing and throw the goddamn phone out the window. He reminded himself that they probably had his car bugged, as well as tagged with a GPS tracker.

One of these days. One of these days he was going to mail in his resignation letter from some country far, far away, and then he would quietly disappear to a beach in Mexico somewhere. When he had enough stashed away, hidden even from their eyes.

Soon. But not yet.

He pulled the complimentary road atlas out of the rental car's glove box and traced Road G until it dead-ended against I-72. He pulled out into the quiet streets, still not used to how people simply vanished from the streets once the sun went down. It was like a goddamn ghost town or something.

He followed Road G up until the pavement stopped and parked next to the NO OUTLET sign. He pulled out his penlight and unfolded the papers he'd stolen from Bob's house. The two acres should be straight ahead. Cochran clicked off the light, made sure his handgun was secure in its holster, and got out of the car.

He listened for a moment to the wind, then went back to the trunk. His employers had equipped him with the latest biohazard gear, just in case. Cochran slipped into a white Tyvek biohazard suit, thick rubber gloves, and thick-soled rubber boots. He fitted a riot-control gas mask over his face, tugging the straps tight, then pulled the hood over his head and started into the darkness.

The gas mask had an open faceplate, giving him a decent field of vision, but it was too damn dark out there in the middle of nowhere. The penlight worked just fine when going through files in a dark room but didn't illuminate much of anything in a cornfield at night when there was no moon. He stabbed the narrow needle of white light into the rows, making the shadows lurch and sway.

Cochran could see the occasional headlights of a truck flying down the nearby expressway, and it bothered him that he couldn't hear as well as he wanted, not with the hood snug over his ears and his dry, amplified breathing through the respirator. Still, it was better than the alternative.

Breathing the spores.

Cochran recognized that he was just nervous. Better to get this finished, then get the hell out. He headed deeper into the field, stopping every ten or fifteen feet to sweep the light in a slow circle, just to make sure nothing was creeping up on him. He stopped again, trying to peer over the corn. He'd lost all sense of distance. Was the car a hundred feet behind him? Two hundred? Goddamnit. After years of working for Allagro and standing around cornfields, he couldn't believe he still wasn't used to being alone in the endless rows. At least he hadn't lost his sense of direction. As long as he kept the expressway to his right, he would be fine.

He caught movement out at the end of the penlight's beam. It was low to the ground and scuttled out of sight before he could pin it down with the light. It was too big to be one of the insects the scientists had been so worried about. A cat, maybe? Possum? He hoped it wasn't a skunk; even though he was fully protected, and wouldn't smell a damn thing, he still had to get out of the suit eventually, and he'd have to deal with it then.

Cochran took a few steps forward, leaned into the row where he thought he'd seen it. Nothing but wisps of cobwebs. He pushed through two more rows, sweeping the light back and forth.

There. A glimpse of gray fur. Possum, most likely. He almost laughed, then got angry. At the thing. At the cornfield. At himself. Maybe his employers were right and he was getting too old for the job. Scared of a god-damn possum. If he didn't have to unzip the biohazard suit to get at his gun, he would have shot the thing.

He followed it, pushing through another row, and stopped cold.

Whatever it was, it wasn't a possum.

Cochran willed himself to hold the light steady. It was almost the size of a small cat, but there was no body exactly, just six or seven legs jutting awkwardly in all directions, like some mutant crab with a tiny body and fur. The thing froze in the light. At first, he told himself it had to be some poor animal that had been hit by a truck, pulverizing the body, splitting and cracking the legs, and it had crawled into the corn to die.

But as he got a better look, he knew damn well this wasn't an animal that had been hit by a car. There was no head. No ears. No eyes. All the legs gave it away. They were from different animals. Some of the fur was gray, like a possum. Some of the legs were shorter, with black fur. They were glued to a kind of exposed back-bone, short, maybe three inches long, riddled with ropy gray tendrils. In fact, he was now close enough to the creature that he could see more of the tendrils, some nearly as big around as his pinkie, some so tiny they were almost hairlike, wrapped around the center like some horrible biological net.

The thing didn't like the light. It scuttled sideways, heading for the deeper shadows. Its movements were tentative and uncoordinated, as if the legs weren't used to working together. The fact that it was moving at all stirred a wave of revulsion deep within his stomach.

Cochran followed, easily keeping pace since it moved so slowly, keeping his penlight trained dead on it. Again, the suit was a double-edged sword. On one hand, it protected him. But at the same time, he couldn't make a phone call. Not only would he have to unzip the suit, he would have to take off his glove, because it would only unlock once he placed his thumbprint on the screen.

He wanted to let the bastards upstairs know that he was one hundred fucking percent certain now, and to make them understand that the fungus was not only here, it was moving up the goddamn food chain.

He felt for the phone under the suit, just to reassure himself it was still there, and looked down for just a second when he touched the shape. He looked back up. The tiny pool of light was empty, just dry leaves and dirt. He waved the beam around and jumped back when he saw the thing. It was crawling closer. And moving faster. "Son of a bitch!" He took another step backward.

Something touched his left foot.

He whipped the penlight down and cried, "Oh fuck!" as another creature tried to crawl up his leg. He dropped the light trying to shake it off and took another step back. The penlight bounced and as it flipped over, he saw two others scuttling out of the row to his right. Three more of them appeared behind the first one. Cochran stumbled forward, reaching down, but in the suit, he kicked the light before he could grab it. It spun, slashing the light through the corn. What he saw made his blood run cold.

They were everywhere. Dozens, maybe hundreds.

Something broke inside his mind, something ancient, and a primitive reflex took over completely. He bolted, a hysterical shriek echoing around the inside of his face-plate, and he crashed through row after row of corn, trailing leaves, corn silk, and cobwebs, as he ran deeper into the night.

WEDNESDAY, JULY 4th

CHAPTER 18

When Sandy turned on her phone that morning, she saw she had almost twenty-four messages. She wasn't surprised. She checked on Kevin's door. It was shut. She went downstairs and made coffee before bothering to listen to the messages. The first two were from Sheriff Hoyt, before he had met her in the driveway. He was smart enough not to say anything incriminating, but his voice was full of vaguely threatening promises. The next was Liz, checking to make sure Kevin was okay. Sandy closed her eyes; it hadn't taken long at all for the news to spread about her son. The next five were from reporters. She erased them all.

The ninth call was from Dr. Castle. "Sandy, this is Mike. I, uh, tried your home phone, didn't work. I've started the external examination on the, uh, suspect." Dr. Castle was also aware that his voice was being recorded and he didn't want to say Jerm's name. "I, uh, I think it would be a good idea if we spoke. Sooner rather than later. Please give me a call at the office. I'll be here a while, and I've left instructions with the front desk to transfer your call to the basement." Parker's Mill's morgue was located in the basement of Dr. Castle's practice. "Please give me a call as soon as you get this message."

The next two voice mails were from reporters. Then Dr. Castle again. "Sandy, this is Mike. Listen, you need to call me. This, this is not something I feel comfortable taking to Sheriff Hoyt. Please call me back."

The next message was from Dr. Castle as well. "Sandy, this is urgent. Call me."

Every message, Dr. Castle's voice got more and more strained. "What I'm finding, it's nothing that I am prepared for. I don't have the right equipment. This is, I simply don't know. All I do know is that this facility is woefully inadequate. I . . . I've never encountered anything like this." He started coughing. "I'm at a loss. We may need to involve the CDC."

Sandy swallowed. Had her son been exposed to something?

The next message. "I don't think it's contagious." He gave a sad laugh. "Hell, I don't know. It's . . . I called a friend, an expert in mycology, at the Argonne labs. Teaches at the University of Chicago. He wants pictures. I have no idea of the legal ramifications of all this. Please, please call me."

Next message. "This is . . . beyond the scope of my experience. I had to stop the necropsy. It's . . ." His voice softened, and it was clear that he wasn't worried about being recorded. He just needed help from a friend. "I hope to see you here tomorrow morning. I'll be here no later than eight." That was the last message, left around ten o'clock last night.

Sandy checked the clock. Six a.m. After Kevin

cracked and it had all come pouring out—how he had figured out the combination of the Browning gun safe and how he had stolen her key for the trigger guard and all of the preparation he had taken and how it had only worked because Sandy didn't like to look at the gun and left it buried back in the back of the safe—she had held him until he fell asleep.

She had climbed into her own bed and tried to figure out if she should meet Sheriff Hoyt at the county court-house in the morning with Kevin or not. If she took him down there, odds were, he'd end up in juvenile deten-tion, a place full of damaged kids who would eat him alive. If she kept him home, the DA would look at it as if she was giving her son preferential treatment, and would push for a maximum sentence.

Either way, she was screwed.

She poured another cup of coffee and went upstairs to look into Kevin's room. Her son was still sound asleep, mouth open, legs sprawled, arms akimbo. Puff-ing Bill was curled up in a tight coil between Kevin's legs. The dog raised his scarred head and regarded her with calm eyes. Sandy whispered, "Lay down. Go back to sleep." She shut the door softly.

She went downstairs, took a sip of coffee, and even-tually realized that the reason she thought it had taken so long to make a decision was because, deep down, she knew that it wasn't a choice at all. She'd known what she would do from the moment Sheriff Hoyt gave her the order. She opened her closet and looked at her uni-form. Might as well go all the way.

She pulled the uniform out of the closet and got dressed. After dialing Elliot's parents' number, she let the coffee put some cheer in her voice. "I am so sorry to

call you so early, but I'm afraid something has come up.
You know this job," Sandy chuckled, letting that hang,
hoping she wouldn't have to resort to the commitment
to community service speech.

While Elliot's mom dithered about and finally managed a good morning, Sandy cut right in and asked,
"Could you, if it's no trouble, would you mind looking
after Kevin today?"

Slight hesitation from Patty. "I, uh, we, uh, well, um,
no, no that shouldn't be a problem. We . . . we were
going to go to the parade." Her tone made it clear that
she fully expected everyone in town to be there. Then
she remembered the shooting yesterday. "Oh my gosh,
do you think there will still be a parade? I mean, they
wouldn't cancel it, would they?"

Sandy thought about everything she knew about the
mayor and Sheriff Hoyt. "I seriously doubt they would
cancel it. This town will have a parade."

"Well, is it okay if we take Kevin?"

"Of course. Have a great time. I'll take the boys fishing next weekend, give you and Randy a day to yourselves as a thank-you, as one parent to another. I
appreciate it." Sandy decided not to mention Puffing
Bill just yet. "I'll drop Kevin off in a half hour."

Cochran knew it was all his fault. He would admit
that much at least. He should never have panicked.
Never should have bolted from the first sign of the
fungus, never should have run screaming into the night.
He should have headed back to his car, instead of running in the completely opposite direction.

Maybe then he would have escaped.

Now he was stuck.

Fear and adrenaline had fueled his flight as he plowed through what felt like miles and miles of cornfields. He realized now, with the morning sun peeking through the wide, thin windows up near the ceiling, that his panic was the reason that he was now trapped. If he only could have kept his head, he would be out on the expressway, practically in the next state by now, leaving this nightmare behind him.

Instead, he was caught in the dead center of the infection, like a dying fly in a cobweb.

He'd run and run, slapping cornstalks out of his way, until he burst out of the corn onto somebody's lawn. He'd fallen and slammed into the long grass. He worried that the fall had torn a gash in the knee of his biohazard suit, but couldn't tell. Since he'd dropped the damn penlight, he could only see by the faint light of a sliver of the moon and the gleam of stars.

He staggered to his feet and lurched over the closest structure. From the chicken wire he guessed it was some sort of henhouse. He curled his fingers through the holes in the wire, trying to catch his breath under the riot gas mask. He sounded like Darth Vader having an asthma attack.

The henhouse looked empty. Until a single wing laying in the dust and chicken shit decided to go berserk, spinning and flapping at the dirt like a fish gasping for air.

He looked down and found the entire bottom half of the structure covered in white cobwebs. But those pale filaments, the long threads clumped together like cotton candy, they weren't cobwebs. He'd caught enough of what the Allagro scientists had been trying to say, and knew to step back immediately.

He moved too late.

Things that looked like centipedes were already climbing up his boots. He scraped them off, leaving a gray sludge, streaks of wet ashes smeared against the rubber. He turned and started across the wide lawn.

Even over the gas mask's rasping breathing, he heard the buzzing from the barn. A couple fluttered in front of his face mask, and he caught a glimpse of a fluttering ball of brown wings. One landed on his arm. Again, like the insects, it looked like the fungus had taken the wings from grasshoppers, cicadas, even wasps. He didn't look long; he took his gloved hand and smashed it, smearing the insides down the Tyvek material.

A roaring buzz from above made him look up.

The cloud of insects above made the stars blink in and out in a twinkling static, and for a moment, he didn't know where to run. He glanced back to the corn. More of the crawling things came out of the field, like black crabs scuttling up a cold shore. Then the flying creatures were on him, swirling around in a quivering and buzzing storm. He tucked in his chin as far as he could, pressing the respirators to his chest. If they got to the soft skin at his throat, he was finished.

The farmhouse was his only chance. He couldn't see it very well through the cloud of insect wings, and it had no lights on inside. He ran up to the back steps and tried the door. It was locked. He stumbled back, knowing that if he broke a window, they would just fly right in behind him.

The constant jagged humming of the insects swarming over him made it hard to think. He turned and tried to head down the steps but slipped off and fell hard on slanted wood. He realized he'd fallen on the cellar doors. His fingers found purchase and he pulled.

The right door swung up and he jumped inside, slamming it behind him. He sat in total darkness for a few minutes, just trying to slow his breathing. When he heard or felt one of the insects, he smashed it, but otherwise was content to sit for a long time, trying to listen. He didn't think that any were getting through the doors. He kept crushing any that he heard fluttering around his head, but they were growing more and more infrequent.

There was less and less scratching at the door as well. Maybe they had forgotten about him and moved on. Maybe. He didn't want to open the door and find out. So very, very carefully, he scooted down the stairs until he hit the floor. He stood, waving his hand around for a light switch or chain. He found a chain and pulled. A click. But no light. Either the bulb was burnt out or it was missing. By this time, his eyes had peered into the gloom long enough to spot the whisper of light that allowed him to make out the shapes of the windows up near the ceiling.

He got closer, stumbling over and through awkward black shapes scattered throughout the small basement until he stood in the faint spill of moonlight, and tried to peer at the biohazard suit. He couldn't find any more of the insects. If he could just get to his phone, he could use that light to see, but that would involve opening the suit.

He decided that since he was in no immediate danger, he would simply wait until morning. It couldn't be that far off. Then, when he could see, he would take a chance on opening his suit where he could get to his phone. And his gun.

Hours later, when the dark shadows in the basement gradually became gray shapes until golden light finally crept across the rough timbers of the ceiling, Cochran took stock of his situation. He could not find any more bugs on him. Couldn't find any more bugs in the basement. Maybe the sunlight chased them off. He listened for a while at the cellar doors, but he couldn't hear anything else.

He went back to the far wall, put his back against the cement, and unzipped his suit. He quickly pulled out his gun and phone, then zipped back up, straight away. Setting the phone aside for the moment, he checked the clip on his Nighthawk T4. The gun nuts in town might have scoffed that it was only a nine-millimeter, but advances in modern ammunition had made that particular argument irrelevant, as far as Cochran was concerned.

What he was most worried about was that it only held nine shells.

That left the phone. He hadn't wanted to call the men upstairs, not until he had gotten out of town, but now he had no choice. He peeled off his glove, dialed, and as it rang, he put his glove back on.

"Hello?"

Was there a wisp of surprise in the voice? Cochran didn't waste time. "I'm one hundred percent sure."

"You are certain?"

"Without a doubt."

"Very well. We will initiate eradication efforts. An extraction team is on the way. We'll have you out of there shortly."

"Good. I—wait a minute," Cochran said, staring at the phone. "How do you know I need an extraction?"

"Isn't it obvious? We know you have been in the same location for almost five hours, roughly a mile due north from the contamination center. Seems clear that you require assistance."

"Of course," Cochran whispered to himself. He held up his phone and looked at it. They'd been tracking him the entire time. He had been a fool. And now, this extraction team, they were already on their way. He had a feeling that this team wasn't coming all the way out to this farmhouse to escort him out of the area.

The next question confirmed it.

"Paul," the voice asked. "How are you feeling?"

"Fucking fantastic," Cochran said, and whipped the phone into the corner of the basement, where it cracked and bounced back, landing on a square of two-by-fours. It wasn't enough. He got up and drove his boot heel into the shell of the phone, grinding it into the old wood. He grabbed the pieces and flung them away.

He stood and was trying to peer through the grimy windows when he heard a new sound. Something that scratched and scrabbled at wood. He crept toward the cellar doors.

The sound came again. It wasn't on the other side of the doors.

It was from something down in the basement with him.

He went back and retrieved his gun. It didn't make him feel any better.

Something moved in the corner of the basement. He looked to where he had thrown the phone the first time. The square chunk of two-by-fours shifted slightly.

Something was moving it from underneath. It moved again, revealing a dark hole.

A pair of fingers appeared, curling over the edge. A thumb followed. And . . . that was all. The three digits formed a tripod and moved clumsily toward him.

Cochran couldn't breathe. The fingers looked like they'd been glued together with black sludge and held tight at the joints with gray tendrils. A fuzzy patch of white cobwebs hung down from the center of where the fingers were joined.

Another couple of fingers crept over the edge of the hole. This time, it was four fingers and a couple of stubby toes, no thumb. They tipped and swayed as they tried to crawl along.

Cochran found his feet and edged closer. He still held on to his gun. The fingers seemed to sense him and followed his movement. He nudged the thumb and two fingers back toward the hole with his toe. The other four-finger organism, aware of the proximity of his boot, rushed at him. He brushed that one back into the darkness as well.

He stood at the edge and peered down in to the hole. Too damn dark to see anything.

He looked around, found an old dresser with a swivel mirror on top. Dragging it closer, he angled the mirror at the windows, now blazing with the morning sun. He tilted it over the hole, and blasted sunlight down into the void.

At first, he wasn't sure what he was looking at. It was like trying to piece together a painting of a human by Picasso; most of the parts were all there, but they didn't make sense. Until the eyes opened and stared up at him. Then he saw how the head was sunk into an irregular circle of flesh, wreathed in arms, legs, exposed ribs, something that may have been a hipbone, all of it submerged in raw sewage. He tilted the mirror even farther, and saw that the walls of the hole were covered with the finger and toe creatures, along with more of the long, centipede things that scurried along with twenty or thirty different insect legs on each side.

They were all crawling up the rough cement, up to him.

For a long moment, Cochran didn't move. His mind simply couldn't accept the horrors that dripped with human excrement crawling up out of the rural septic tank. But as soon as a pair of tiny cricket legs crested the edge of the access hatch and the rest of the wriggling creature followed, heading straight for his boot, he jumped backward and aimed the Nighthawk.

He squeezed off three rounds before he realized it wouldn't help.

More of the fungus organisms followed, climbing their way out of the septic tank.

Cochran started for the cellar doors, but stopped. What if there were more of the bigger things outside, the ones that were using possum and skunk legs? They seemed tougher than the insect creatures. They moved faster too. His eyes went to the old lumber that covered the basement and served as the floorboards for the house above. He could now see faint light between some of the seams, and how several of the two-by-twelves had long cracks running along their length.

He hefted the handgun. He wasn't entirely sure how many rounds he'd torched off, but there had to be at least five or six left. Not nearly enough to protect himself against the monsters crawling out of the septic tank. He thought of another use.

Thick, sloshing sounds were coming out of the access hatch.

He didn't want to know if that awful flower thing with the horrible open eyes was trying to get out. His eyes went to the ceiling again, following the cracks. He found a spot where several of the cracks intersected each other and dragged the dresser over and set it right under the section that seemed to be the most vulnerable to damage.

Then he took the Nighthawk, squinted, and aimed up at the floorboards. He squeezed off round after round, moving his hand in a tight circle. Turned out there were six cartridges left. When the gun was empty, he had an oval punched through the floor above, like some kind of child's perforated artwork.

He climbed up on the dresser and used the empty handgun to hammer at the wood in the center of the circle. It took a while, but eventually it started to crack. Within fifteen minutes and bashing the shit out of the two-by-twelve, he smashed a hole into the first floor of the farmhouse.

He tossed the gun through the hole, grabbed two sides, and hefted himself up. He crawled out of the ragged hole and found himself in the kitchen. He lurched over to the fridge and seized the top corners. Rocking it back and forth, he toppled it over with a crash. The entire floor groaned and made some teeth-clenching cracking noises, but the structure held, and the hole he had climbed through was now covered with a heavy refrigerator.

He made a quick sweep of the first floor. No firearms.

No shells. The driveway was empty, but he knew that his bosses had given his location to the "extraction" team. They had to be close. If he tried to escape on foot, he wouldn't get far enough.

He needed backup.

There was a phone on the wall in the kitchen.

He dialed 911.

CHAPTER 19

Sandy parked her cruiser in Dr. Castle's lot and walked around to the back of the building. A black awning covered the narrow driveway, protecting a pair of double doors. This was where the two funeral homes in Parker's Mill picked up the bodies.

She knocked and stepped back. As she waited, she noticed a sign taped to the inside of the window. "We're sorry, but we're closed for the holiday. If this is an emergency, please call 911."

She tried the door.

It was open, and swung wide on well-oiled hinges.

Sandy stuck her head inside and called out, "Hello?" No immediate answer. She stepped inside and closed the door behind her. "Hello? Anybody around? This is Chief Chisel. Anybody hear me?"

She went out to the waiting room. It was empty, along with the office behind the counter. She checked the two examination rooms. Nobody. It looked like everybody had gone to the parade.

She went past the freight elevator to the stairs that led to the basement and called down, "Hello? Dr. Castle?"

Ugly fluorescent light spilled out of a square little window in the door at the bottom of the stairs. She descended the narrow stairwell and tried the door handle. Part of her expected it to be locked and another part was hoping it would be, so she could leave.

The handle twisted easily and clicked obediently open. She stepped into the morgue. The place smelled of formaldehyde and bleach. It was a clinical smell, not rotten at all. Sometimes, Dr. Castle had to handle a traffic accident where the body had been laying in the sun for too long, or the occasional suicide that had ripened before being discovered, so he always made sure the morgue was well ventilated and spotless.

The refrigerated drawers waited off to the left. A stainless steel table with several drains set into it and a large utility sink were set off to the right. Sandy wanted to call out for Dr. Castle again, but it was clear that the room was empty.

Except for the body bag on the table in the center of the room.

She'd been in here before, plenty of times, mostly to acknowledge Dr. Castle's findings and sign on the dotted line. Yes, this person had died instantly when their minivan had struck the Christmas tree truck in a head-on collision. Yes, this person had drowned after getting drunk and falling out of his rowboat into the Mississippi River. Yes, this infant had been beaten to death by her father.

Sandy didn't like being down here.

She pulled out her phone and dialed Dr. Castle's

home number. Nobody picked up. She hung up without leaving a message and took two steps toward the table.

The black plastic of the body bag crinkled, shifted. Sandy stopped. Her right hand had dropped to the handle of her Glock, but she had no idea of how her sidearm would help. Still, she didn't let go.

Something moved again inside the plastic.

Despite her training, she got closer. Reached out, pinched a fold of the bag between her thumb and forefinger. She gave it a quick yank, then stood back and brought the Glock out, aimed it at the table.

A lump in the bag rose up, then fell back. Something that sounded like fingernails scraped the inside of the bag.

Sandy stepped back, still holding the Glock up and ready. She supposed it was possible that Jerm had been brought here still alive, and he was simply asking for help, inside a cadaver bag. Possible, but not likely. It was also possible that it wasn't Jerm at all in that bag. Could be that it was someone else entirely.

Sandy didn't think so.

She had no choice. She reached out with her free hand and started to unzip the bag. Something scurried over inside the bag and grabbed at her hand. It felt almost like someone's hand on the other side of the fabric trying to clutch at her. She shifted to the side and unzipped the bag about eighteen inches in one, long, smooth motion.

Fingers unfurled from inside the bag and pulled at the plastic.

Sandy's immediate thought was that she was watching two hands come crawling out, all on their own, like that pet hand from *The Addams Family*. Then she realized they weren't hands exactly. They had fingers and even toes, but no palms; the digits rose up into a mass of gray webbing, like a short, stubby tipi. They scuttled awkwardly out of the bag like spiders that had waded through grain alcohol.

Other parts of the bag were moving now. Bigger parts. Sandy had seen enough to know that whatever Dr. Castle had seen last night, he had been right.

She reholstered the Glock, found a large pair of tongs, and picked up one of the finger spiders. It struggled weakly, and as she turned it over, she could see a mass of what looked like white cotton candy underneath, growing out of the upper pads of the fingers and toes. She dropped it in the bag and quickly grabbed the other one. She used the tongs to grab the zipper and zip the bag shut.

The parts inside continued to move.

Her radio crackled. It was Liz. "Chief, you there? Come back. Chief?"

Sandy wanted to start shooting at the bag, to burn it, something. She hit the button on the radio. "Chisel here. Over."

"Chief, we're getting a ton of calls about people not coming home last night. I'm forwarding them on to the county boys for now, but I just got one hell of a weird nine-one-one call, thought you should hear about this one first." Liz either hadn't heard about Sandy's suspension, or more likely was simply choosing to ignore the command. "Male, says he's under attack from some kind of monsters. I think he's just some tweaker, wandered off the interstate and got lost. He's freaking out, says he needs help."

"Monsters, huh?" Sandy said, watching the body bag.

"His words, not mine. And you'll never guess where he was calling from. The Einhorns'."

"You're kidding."

"Nope. When it rains it pours, huh?"

The Einhorns. Mrs. Kobritz. And now Dr. Castle. All those missing people.

"You want, I can let Sheriff Hoyt know, and he can send one of his boys out."

Sandy knew that she would have to bring Sheriff Hoyt into this mess, sooner than later, but if she could figure out at least a few pieces of the puzzle, it might go easier for her and Kevin later. Never mind that she was unable to act in any official capacity as the town's chief. "No, that's okay. I've got it. Let Sheriff Hoyt handle the parade for now. I'll head out there, see what's what."

"You gonna join us at the parade? I'm outta here in less than . . . twenty minutes. You want me to save you a spot?"

"No, that's okay, thanks. I'll be there soon. I'll find my boy and we'll watch it together."

"See you then. Over and out."

Bob was proud of himself.

It had been years since he'd personally driven the harvester up and down the rows, but the old skills had never left. Even as bad as he felt. Of course the technology had changed, made it easier for one man to do everything. Used to be, he had someone else to drive alongside the combine with a trailer to collect the grain. Now, the combine itself had a trailer, and so Bob could easily harvest acres and acres on his own.

He remembered endless summer days of sitting on his father's lap in the combine, bouncing through one field after another, back and forth, back and forth, as his father taught him what was important in life. God. Farming. Family. Back in those days, there wasn't much to do in the cab of the combine. Now, he still couldn't believe how it had more technology than his office at home. Air-conditioning, for one thing. They'd never had central air put in the house, and so Bob always felt a little guilty using it in the combine. A radio. He'd seen some models that even had little televisions, but he drew the line at that. No sir. You couldn't work and watch TV at the same time.

He didn't bother closing the gate behind him. The field was done. Time to let it sit until next spring. It had been too early to harvest the corn, and it wouldn't be as sweet as it should be, but that wasn't the point. No, he'd harvested his son's corn to show everyone that his son had been a farmer when he died. No one could take that away. No one. Not even Allagro.

And now Bob had the evidence. Two acres of corn that half-filled the trailer behind the combine. That amount was nothing, of course, not when he was used to dealing with hundreds of acres, day after day. It was enough, though, to make sure everybody knew that the Mortons had farming in their blood.

If Bob had turned around, he might have seen the lazy black cloud that jolted and swirled with every bump in the road as it hung like a fog over the trailer of corn.

He passed Cochran's rental car. It was empty. Bob

hoped the son of a bitch had gotten lost out here looking for Bob Jr.'s two acres. He was in no hurry as he eased the massive combine and trailer up to the intersection of Road G and Highway 17. It only had a top speed of fifteen miles an hour anyway. He turned left, toward town.

It didn't matter anymore. Cochran was too late to do anything. Let him call his bosses. Let him make all the threats he wanted. Let him go give those condescending looks to somebody else. Bob had taken care of his farm.

If nothing else, that's what was truly important to Bob. No matter how he looked, or how he felt, he could still take care of his business, his home, his life. And by God, he was going to prove it to everybody. He couldn't think of a better way to show everyone just what a genuine American farmer was made of.

It was time to take the corn to the parade.

CHAPTER 20

Sandy didn't see a car in the Einhorn driveway. It didn't look much different from the last time she had been out here, except for the police tape on the front porch. They'd hauled Kurt's truck back to the county lab to test for any bloodstains. As far as Sandy knew, they hadn't found anything. She didn't think they would.

She pulled around the horseshoe driveway and parked in front of the steps. She got out and stood in the full morning sunlight, taking in the house for a moment. A breeze ruffled the plastic ribbons of yellow crime-scene tape stretched across the front steps. All of the shells that had littered the driveway had been collected. She went up the front walk and saw that the bloodstains were almost gone. One good rain and you'd never know a man had been shot to death on his front lawn.

She ripped the tape away, not worrying too much about disturbing a crime scene. Being suspended, she had no business being out here in the first place. She peered in the window. Nothing moved inside. Knocked on the front door. No answer.

It didn't surprise her. Whoever had been here had taken their car and left.

Still, that comment about the "monsters" wouldn't leave her alone. She couldn't help but feel it had something to do with the missing people and that body bag back at Dr. Castle's. She knocked again. "Hello? This is Chief Sandy Chisel. Anybody here call nine-one-one?"

Still no answer.

She tried the front door. It was open. As inept as the county guys could be, she didn't think they would ever go off and leave the house of a crime scene unlocked. She pushed the door open a few inches. Called out, "Hello?" as she gently unsnapped her holster.

She pushed the door but remained on the porch. The door swung open all the way, revealing a living room exactly the same as she remembered. Her gaze lingered on the kitchen doorway. Something was blocking the bottom of the doorway. Something big, like a metal box. She realized it was the fridge, lying on its side.

Maybe someone had broken in, maybe kicked their way in through the back or broke a window. They could have left through the front door, which explained why it wasn't locked. Still trying to figure out the scenarios, she stepped inside, intent on the overturned fridge in the kitchen.

Something popped her in the back of the head and she felt what could have been a gun barrel jammed into the side of her neck, just under her right ear. A voice said, "On the fucking floor. Now!"

Sandy never took her right hand from her pistol, but she nodded and said, "Okay, okay. No trouble." She bent her knees, preparing to lie down.

A man's hand closed over her right hand, going for

the pistol. She could tell it was his left hand because his right was holding his gun. He had been waiting to the right of the door, and was now behind her. That meant he was off-balance. So she dropped, tucking her head into her shoulder and angling out of the line of fire, and whirled, kicking out with her left leg. She brought her right forearm up and deflected the barrel even farther while rolling her hips at the same time. At this point, the top of her left boot whipped around and cracked the man's knee, knocking him further off balance. With her left hand, her thumb and forefinger found the pressure points in his left wrist, pinning it to her hip.

She crashed to the floor, landing on her back, pulling the man with her. Her right forearm continued up, sliding neatly into the groove between the man's chest and chin, jamming her ulna bone into his throat, forcing him to land sideways next to her. He grunted harshly when he landed and Sandy rolled on top of him, driving her right knee into his groin for good measure.

She saw his eyes go wide and for the first time realized he was wearing some kind of gas mask. Not only that, he was in some biohazard suit as well. The word "monsters" flashed across her mind as she ripped the face mask off and stood up, stomping her boot down on his gun hand.

Without the mask, she recognized him as Bob Morton's Allagro lawyer.

She pried his gun away, tossed it on Kurt's La-Z-Boy. It didn't look like he cared much; both hands went immediately to his groin and cupped his balls. He groaned.

Sandy gave him time to try and breathe. "We were never introduced formally, but you would be Mr. Cochran, I believe. Word gets around in a small town. Looks like you bit off more than you could chew. Should've known better. Been spending too much time in a suit is my guess." She stood over him, hands on her hips. "You want to tell me what's going on or should we head into town?"

"Fuck off."

Sandy shrugged. "Town it is then. You can tell me later." She put her boot on his neck, picked up his arm, torqued it, forcing him to roll over. Then she cuffed his hands.

"Wait," he gasped. "Just wait. You take me to town, I'm a dead man."

"That so?" Sandy wasn't impressed.

"You don't understand. We are out of time."

"Maybe for you. I get the feeling you're wasting my time."

"Men are on their way. And we do not want to be here when they come. Why do you think I called you? Jesus Christ, you think I want law enforcement involved if I can help it?"

Sandy waited.

"Look, I'll tell you everything. Why I'm here, all of it. Help me sit up." She helped him lean against the coffee table. He didn't want to look at her. "What do you know about GMOs?"

"Enough to stay out of any discussions about them in this town."

"You know who I work for. I'm not just here to help out Bob Morton." He started with the island, explaining what they thought had happened, including the two scientists' theories, and even what he thought was happening to Bob Morton, all of it leading to this morning, when he had escaped the basement.

"Where did you say these things came from down there?"

"Some kind of big hole. Smelled like shit."

The septic tank, Sandy thought. Maybe that's where Ingrid had gone.

She snuck a quick look out of the front windows, even though she had her doubts about his story. Never hurt to be cautious. The cruiser sat out there, alone. "Seems to me," she said slowly, "the big question here is where are all of these things that chased you through the corn? Where's all the bugs? What happened to all of them?"

Cochran shook his head. "I don't know. Maybe they don't like the sunlight." He thought one of the scientists had said something about why fungus preferred dark, cool environments, and that was one of the reasons so many of them grew underground. "Look, either you believe me or you don't. We have to get out of here. You want proof, stick your head in the basement. Leave me the keys though, so I can run like hell when you get swarmed."

Sandy didn't want to admit it, but he had a point. Sounded simple enough. She couldn't lift the fridge, so all she had to do was go out back and open the cellar doors. Of course, the smart thing to do would be to call Sheriff Hoyt and get his men out here so they could take Cochran into custody, and somebody with proper equipment could check out the basement.

If things had turned out differently yesterday that's what she would have done.

Instead, she left Cochran in the living room and took one last look out the front windows. Still empty. She went to the kitchen doorway and examined the fridge that blocked it. She wondered if she could slide it over a little, just enough to see the hole. Maybe then she could shine her flashlight down there. She knelt down, squared her shoulder into the fridge, and braced her boots on the wood floor.

"Please don't," Cochran said. "Please. Let's just go."

Something in his voice gave her pause. She eased off the fridge and lowered her head to the floor, pressed her ear against the linoleum. She couldn't hear anything but Cochran's ragged breathing. Then, something else.

It wasn't coming from under the floor.

It was an engine, coming up the driveway.

Animals made Elliot's parents nervous. Sandy hadn't given them much choice about taking Mrs. Kobritz's dog, though. She didn't know how much of the news of the shooting had spread through the town, but she figured by now, everybody probably knew everything. She wanted Puffing Bill to stay with Kevin because the dog might be enough to keep people away from him. The last thing she wanted was some snotty bitch asking if he felt bad about all those people getting shot.

Puffing Bill was more than happy to remain at Kevin's side.

After Sandy left, and they were packing up a picnic basket to take to the parade, Randy tried to convince Kevin to leave the dog in the backyard. "Only while we're at the parade, okay? We'll come straight home after. He'll be happier out there, away from all the noise and people." Elliot's parents were convinced that a pit bull was one of the most dangerous animals in the world, and was only biding his time before sinking his jaws into their son.

Kevin said, "He needs to stay with me. I'll watch him. He'll be good. I promise."

In the end, when it became clear that Kevin would rather stay behind with the dog than go to the parade without the animal, Randy and Patty relented. It was getting late, and if you didn't stake a spot early along the route for Parker's Mill's annual Fourth of July celebration, you wouldn't be able to see the parade, simple as that. So they made sure the leash was tight, forbid Elliot from petting the dog, gathered their supplies, and set off.

They lived only three blocks from Main Street, and walked to Veterans' Park, where the parade culminated. A stage had been erected for the city council and mayor, where they would present various awards and achievement medals after the parade. The park itself was full of local vendors selling everything from fruits and vegetables to corn dogs and pizza and tortilla chips to fresh-squeezed lemonade with more sugar than juice.

Of course, no Fourth of July holiday was complete without buckets of corn on the cob, impaled on sticks, and dunked in vats of warm butter.

The park itself wasn't crowded as usual and when they reached Main Street, Randy frowned. The curbs were half empty. Every year since he could remember, there wasn't a single free inch along the parade route. Residents, especially farmers who lived out of town, set out all their cheap plastic lawn chairs to save their places hours, sometimes even days, in advance. This year he couldn't believe the size of the gaps between the sets of chairs.

Maybe a lot of people were taking advantage of the holiday to go on vacation or visit relatives. Whatever the reason, he wasn't going to complain. It just meant that his family had plenty of spots to choose where they wanted to watch the parade. They even passed up a few until finding a spot not too far down from the stage and got settled.

The parade was almost ready to begin.

Cochran heard the engine too, and struggled to get to his feet.

Sandy went to the front windows. "Stay down and be quiet." She went outside on the front porch and down the steps. Wondered if a little more peace of mind would perhaps be advisable. She didn't want to trust Cochran, but maybe it wasn't such a bad idea to be prepared for anything. She unclipped the shotgun from the dash and stood it upright on the driver's seat. She left the door open, crossed her arms, and leaned against the back door.

A black car came out of the corn, rolling slowly up the driveway as if the driver wasn't sure he was in the right place. As the car got closer, she counted three men inside. Sandy got a fluttery feeling in the pit of her stomach when the car stopped. It was starting to feel just like the time when she had to shoot those two men in the traffic stop.

Except this time there were three men.

The driver turned off the engine and held up his hand in a polite wave. None of the men went to climb out. They stayed put, talking things over. Finally, the driver got out. He was a barrel-chested guy with short cropped hair. Maybe early thirties. Hard to tell his age because of the wraparound sunglasses. It looked like he'd stopped at L.L. Bean during the drive and changed clothes. Brand-new flannel shirt and jeans. Sandy didn't think it made much sense in the heat of summer.

The other two watched her from behind tinted windows.

"Morning," Sandy said.

"Morning."

She didn't say anything else. She wanted to put the burden of explanation on him, instead of giving him a quick and easy excuse, like asking if he was lost.

The man waited for the inevitable question, and when he realized that it wasn't going to happen, that she was waiting him out, he said, "Nice day for the Fourth, huh?"

Sandy gave a noncommittal nod.

The man decided that being lost was the easiest choice. "You know how to get back to I-72 from here?"

This was the moment Sandy realized that Cochran had been telling the truth. These men were not tourists. They were not fisherman. They were here to silence a man who had become a liability. And they would kill anyone who got in the way.

She cocked her head, pretending to think about the question. Both the man in the passenger seat and the man in the back undoubtedly had their weapons out and ready, waiting for Sandy to lift her arm and point. When that happened, they would fire, and the driver would head into the house and finish Cochran.

If she turned and reached for the shotgun in the cruiser behind her, they would shoot her in the back. She thought about dropping and rolling under their car, but they could try and shoot through the floorboards just as easily as she could try and shoot up through the bottom of the car. It wouldn't take long for the driver to realize he could bend over and shoot her as easy as tying his shoes.

She hated to leave the shotgun in the car, but kept her right hand on her Glock and eased up to the front of their car instead, playing dumb and giving a girlish shake of her short blond hair. The longer she kept them off balance, the better. "Well, gee, I'm new here, and I don't really know, you know?"

She backed up to the house, never taking her hand off the Glock. "I can check with the family who lives here. I'm sure they can help." She wanted the men to think there were more people inside, just to make them hesitate that much longer.

"I got a map here," the driver said in an effort to bring her closer to his car.

Sandy went up the stairs backward. "No thanks. Wouldn't help much." She found the door handle behind her with her left hand and twisted it.

The other two men in the car opened their doors. They stood, and Sandy noticed that they all wore long-sleeve flannel shirts, despite the heat.

"Listen," the driver said. "I think we're getting off on the wrong foot here. We just need to find our way back to the interstate. That's all."

Sandy took one step backward, into the house.

The passenger twisted suddenly, revealing that the man in the backseat had a handgun and it was leveled at Sandy. He fired, twice.

Sandy felt the wood chips from the front door spray into her face before she heard the shots. She fell backward, hit the floor, and rolled out of sight.

Cochran had been watching and waiting and now

kicked the door shut. "Keys!" he hissed, holding his cuffed hands out to his side.

Sandy didn't think twice. She fished the key out of her pocket and one of the men fired again. Four holes appeared in the front door, waist high. Cochran rolled over to her and when his back slammed into her, he held the cuffs up as best as he could.

Sandy unlocked the cuffs and said, "Open the door. Quick." She figured they would be expecting them to dig in deep inside the house and wouldn't expect a sneak attack.

Cochran's face made it clear he didn't think it was a good idea, but he crawled back over to the door and waited for her signal. She nodded, and he whipped the front door wide open. Sandy saw that one of the men was coming straight up the stairs and hadn't expected an open door.

She squeezed the trigger three times. At fifteen feet, shooting from a sitting position, resting her Glock on her knee, it wasn't difficult to put all three rounds straight into the center of his chest. The man went to his knees, but didn't drop his handgun. She then understood why they were all wearing long-sleeve flannel shirts.

They all wore Kevlar vests.

So she readjusted, shot him in the head, and yelled, "Shut it!"

Cochran slammed the door.

The windows exploded in a maelstrom of glass and lead.

Sandy tossed the Glock to Cochran. He caught it and gave her a look filled with confusion. "Go." She angled her head at the kitchen. "Out the back door. Hurry. Get around the side before they think about it. Stay low and shoot whoever is on the porch."

Cochran didn't have to be told twice. He scrambled up and dove over the fridge through the kitchen doorway. More gunfire blasted through the front windows. Good Christ. It sounded like one of them had a fucking fully automatic assault rifle out there.

Sandy wriggled on her stomach through the broken glass over to the Einhorns' twenty-six-inch TV on a stand in the corner. She scooted it over the front door and wedged it at an angle under the door handle. The rabbit ear antenna stuck out wildly.

More gunfire, but she couldn't tell where it was going because the glass was nearly gone from the windows. She wanted to stick her head up and see if Cochran had managed to get out the back door but worried she would catch a bullet in the back of the head. Instead, she propelled herself back across the floor using her elbows and toes and slid into place behind the couch.

She'd given up her only gun, but she still had the Taser X26P on her left hip and wondered how well their fancy bulletproof vests would protect them against 13,000 volts. That is, if they didn't shoot her first.

She didn't have to wait long.

A barrage of gunfire erupted and the front door shuddered under the onslaught. Sandy flattened herself into the floor. It sounded like whoever had the assault rifle was emptying the clip into the front door, and sure enough, after a several seconds of mind-numbing gunfire, there were a few moments of relief as he switched magazines.

Sandy got ready.

The man with the machine gun kicked open the front door, knocking the TV aside, and raked the Einhorn living room with automatic gunfire, whipping the gun back and forth, spraying bullets like he wanted to water the flowers but only had a few drops left in the hose.

Sandy closed her eyes and prayed, promising the Universe that she would do whatever she could to raise her son as a decent human being if she lived through this. Splinters of wood and powder from drywall settled over her like remnants from a hurricane. She blinked the dust out of her eyes and watched from under the couch as the man's feet stepped over the threshold.

He froze, watching and waiting for movement. He was big, and she didn't think her nifty little spinning and kicking trick with Cochran would work on this guy. Cochran was a lawyer who spent most of his time in a suit and tie; this man was a professional mercenary.

The back door clicked shut.

The man ran for the kitchen and as he reached the couch, Sandy fired the Taser. Twin electric dragons snaked up and chomped hold of his flesh; one snapped at the inside of his thigh, the other hit his left testicle. He made a surprised grunt and toppled over. The assault rifle flew out of his hands and clattered across the refrigerator in the doorway and landed in the kitchen. His forehead cracked into the side of the fridge, throwing his skull at an odd angle as the rest of his body hit the floor.

Sandy hoped he'd broken his neck. She scrambled up, stepped on him, and hopped over the fridge. If he wasn't dead, she had less than five seconds before he was moving again. She went for the assault rifle and turned around to find the man struggling to his feet.

At some point, sometime after she had shot the first man in the head, she had stopped thinking like a law enforcement officer and now the foremost image in her mind was her son's face. She had left him behind to respond to an emergency telephone call that had turned out to be a lie. And now she would let nothing stop her from getting back to Kevin. She would take him in her arms again or she would die trying.

The man ripped out the barbs and didn't make a sound.

Sandy didn't want to waste any more time with somebody that could pull the end of a fishhook out of his balls without whimpering. She brought the assault rifle around. She wasn't used to the light trigger, though, and squeezed it too soon. The rifle jumped in her hands and bullets stitched across the doorway, right above the man's head, as the recoil raised the barrel higher and higher. She released the trigger and readjusted, but it was too late.

A dull click; the rifle was empty.

He wrapped the Taser wire around both fists like a boxer wrapping tape around his knuckles, then put one knee on the fridge, keeping his eyes locked on her the whole time.

Sandy heard gunfire out in the front yard but couldn't worry about Cochran now.

She dropped the assault rifle, wondering if she had enough time to reload the Taser. She needed something, anything, to use as a weapon, because the man was going to take her apart with his bare hands.

She grabbed the knife block off the counter and

cracked him in the skull with all three pounds. Butcher knives spilled all over the floor. The blow dazed him for only a half second. Blood pooled and started spilling into his eye. He blinked, shook his head to clear it, and crawled completely onto the fridge.

Sandy was already scrabbling for the knives. Her fingers curled around a thick handle and she leapt at the man, coming down on him like a lithe little grim reaper. The steak knife sliced the side of his face open from temple to jawbone; the flesh peeled away from the bone like a rotten orange.

A giant fist, bound in Taser wire, came out of nowhere. It caught her on the chin like a one-hundred-mile-an-hour fastball and lifted her off her feet. She landed flat on her back amid the rest of the knives and she heard a deep, wrenching crack from the house itself.

The floor dropped several inches.

Sandy lost her knife and scrambled for the back door as she heard the man roar and leap from the fridge. He landed a few feet behind her kicking legs and she wished she could have seen his expression as the floorboards gave way and he crashed through to the basement in an avalanche of rotten timber, linoleum squares, and knives.

She had just grabbed hold of the back door handle when the floor collapsed, and was able to hang on. She swung it open and caught herself on the threshold. She pulled herself over and glanced back down into the basement.

The man had landed on the mirror and dresser, cracking it with the impact, and rolled off to the floor as debris rained down around him. He stirred, and reached out to grab at his left leg.

Through the cloud of dust, Sandy thought she saw something else moving down there. She caught flashes of what looked like long black centipedes crawling through the wreckage, all drawn to the struggling man. The human fingers followed, crawling over and under the linoleum and splinters, exactly like the spider creatures in the body bag back at Dr. Castle's office. Then things even bigger crawled out. These had longer tentacles than the insects, moving along with two uneven rows on both sides of the legs of small rodents like rats or squirrels. They cautiously crept out of the septic tank and slithered through what was left of the floor. Sometimes she could see exposed backbones along the tendrils.

They swarmed the man as he rolled and tried to get away, and she saw that his left leg was bent horribly just below the knee. A shard of startlingly white bone jutted out from just under his kneecap. Sandy knew that he wasn't going anywhere anytime soon and rolled away from the kitchen.

The shooting out front had stopped. She stayed low and crept around the south side of the house, keeping the barn to her right. One of the doors was open, but she couldn't see far into the darkness inside. She slipped into the bushes that had grown wild up the side of the house and crept under their canopy to the front corner of the house, trying to catch a glimpse of the third man or Cochran.

In the driveway, the third man was out in the open. He was dragging his dead comrade, the guy Sandy had shot in the head, back along the walk to the vehicles. Sandy wondered if he was taking the body to their car, removing the evidence. But he opened the cruiser's back door and rolled the body into the backseat. He slammed the cruiser's door and went to the rental car's trunk.

He pulled out three large tanks, all strapped together with a backpack harness in the front. The man bent over and spent a few minutes attaching some sort of hose-and-gun-looking thing to the tanks. A pool of dread grew in Sandy's stomach, and sure enough, when the man stood, he carried a goddamn flamethrower.

Sandy wondered what the hell else they had in the trunk.

The man stood back from the cruiser, then opened up with a jet of flame that blasted through the open front windows and incinerated everything inside. So much for the shotgun.

Satisfied, the man turned back to the house and marched back up the walk. He stepped out of sight, and for a few seconds she couldn't see because the steps were in the way, but it wasn't long before he dragged Cochran over to the porch. Sandy shrank back, lowering herself to the dirt and watching with one eye through the rose thorns.

Cochran was still alive. He moaned as the man left him at the bottom of the front steps. The front of Cochran's white shirt was stained red.

The man called out, "Jack? You in there, Jack?" He didn't give Jack much time to answer, stepping back and spraying the second floor with flames. Sandy could feel the heat from the flamethrower even twenty feet away. The roof caught with a dry, muffled *whump*.

The man circled around the house, heading south, moving to Sandy's right, between the house and the barn. He gave the gable a fresh coat of fire as he moved. When he could see both the front and back doors, he yelled, "I know you heard me, Miss Police Officer. You're listening to me. You come on out here before things get bad in there. You and me will talk. We will reach an agreement much better than what you will experience inside, I promise you that. Come out right now and you will live."

Sandy grew flat into the dirt and turned her head away.

He gave the house another spray.

She felt something against the back of her thigh. A tickle at first. Then warmth, pressing down, harder and harder, until it erupted into full burning. Part of her knew it was just a tiny spot, just an ember, just a piece of the roof, but it still felt like her entire leg was on fire. She bit down on her sleeve and tried not to scream.

The man was on the move again. "You make me wait much longer, I might lose my temper." He circled around the back, maybe worried that she was trying to get out a window on the other side of the house.

As soon as he passed the back corner, she jerked around with a fistful of dirt and slapped at the burn. The ember was about the size of a dime. She bit down on another scream as she pushed harder, filling the wound with cool soil and extinguishing the glowing wood.

She stuck her head back around the front to see if the coast was clear and saw that Cochran was on his feet, stumbling to the rental car. Sandy was impressed. He'd been playing possum. Not entirely, though, as she watched him lurch along. He'd taken a bullet in the gut somewhere. He bent down and picked up something in the grass. The first man's gun. Cochran made it to the car and opened the front door, dropped into the front seat.

Start the car, dumbass, Sandy almost said aloud. She was trying to decide if she should try for the car and escape or use him as a distraction while she ran for the cover of the corn. If he saw her, the man might use the flamethrower to try and burn the whole field, but the plants were strong and green. The fire wouldn't spread.

Then she heard Cochran saying the cornfields were full of monsters.

She'd also been thinking of trying for the barn, and now wondered if it was full of bugs. The darkness inside didn't look so inviting anymore.

That left Cochran and the car.

He was still just sitting there, and she finally realized Cochran didn't have the keys. She was worried she might have to take her chances in the corn when she heard Cochran yell something. The third man came into view, yelling back, "Thanks for contaminating the car, asshole." Liquid flame spurted out of the end of his weapon.

Just before it reached the car, Cochran fired. An explosion of fire blew out the windows of the rental car at the same moment the bullet took out the third man's forehead. He collapsed, finger still tight on the trigger. The jet of flame arced over his head and burned a streak in the lawn.

Sandy thought she heard Cochran screaming for a moment, then all she could hear was the crackle of flames and the hissing and popping of the old wood of the house as it burned. She tentatively emerged from the bushes and took it all in. The house was fully engulfed in flames.

Both cars were on fire, sending black, poisonous-looking smoke into the cloudless blue sky. The flamethrower finally ran out of fuel, and the grass smoked in the sunlight.

She pulled out her cell phone and saw that it had been cracked from one of her falls. The screen wouldn't respond to her touch. At least she still had her radio. She hit the button, "Liz? Liz? You there?"

"This is an official channel. Identify yourself. And this better not be who I think it is," Sheriff Hoyt's voice came back.

CHAPTER 21

Bob was happy.

He felt like he was back in high school, in the home-coming parade. He'd been voted Homecoming King, and Carol, the Homecoming Queen, had red hair and a curvy figure and a reputation for drinking beer with the boys and getting frisky in her daddy's Chevy. All was right with the world.

Something jostled him and he looked down at the surprisingly modern controls of one his combines. He had to remind himself that this wasn't 1976. All the red, white, and blue that covered the town wasn't for the bicentennial. This was the Fourth of July parade, and he was bringing in his son's crop to show everyone in town that his son was just as much of a farmer as his father and grandfather before him.

This was perhaps the proudest moment of his life.

He just wished he felt better. There was a coldness in his chest, and something was wrong with his eyes. They wouldn't focus. And his arms and legs wouldn't respond for about two or three seconds after he tried to get them to move.

Good thing the combine pretty much drove itself.

He couldn't remember signing up for the parade, but the antique car club stopped and gave him plenty of room to follow Troop 2957. He gave all the scouts a cheerful wave. At least, he hoped it was a wave. It was getting a little hard to tell what his arms were doing. The combine was still moving; he could feel it rumbling along at least.

That was all right, though. He could make out the green of the park coming up on the right, and that's where he wanted to stop and rest for a while. Maybe he would let one of his men drive the combine home.

He was feeling a little tired, after all.

Sheriff Hoyt had just about had enough from this self-entitled bitch. "You were warned and I guarantee you this: I will see you in jail before sundown."

"Listen to me, asshole. You've got bigger problems. Arrest me later. Right now, we have an emergency. There's something in the corn. Look southeast. You'll see the smoke. There's—"

Sheriff Hoyt cut her off. "I know you think you're something special, but you are gonna find out the hard way that . . ." He trailed off, still keeping the button on his radio down. The sound of grinding metal overpowered the halfhearted theme from *Raiders of the Lost Ark* as the local high school marching band stomped past the viewing stage.

He had been standing back behind the stage, and now pushed and elbowed people aside to reach the curb. The mayor was up at the microphone, making calming gestures and talking, but the mike wasn't turned on. Nobody was paying much attention anyway; they were all standing and pointing down the street.

Sheriff Hoyt took a step off the curb and saw that some idiot was driving a goddamn combine corn harvester up the middle of the street, scattering panicked Boy Scouts before the giant tractor like it was a sleepy dog that had wandered into a rabbit warren. The driver must have been drunk, because the massive combine was drifting across both lanes, scraping the shit out of the parked cars on either side of the street.

He started toward it. Somebody had to stop the dumb son of a bitch. In nearly thirty years of law enforcement, Sheriff Hoyt had never seen anything quite like this. He'd arrested drunks driving nearly every make and model of vehicle on the highway, hauled in punks drinking on those troublesome ATVs, even had to put the cuffs on a wasted cowboy on a horse. The only thing that even came close to this mess was when he caught a couple of Mexicans drunk on a John Deere, but that was in a field, not even on one of the back-county roads.

This, this took the goddamn cake.

Sheriff Hoyt hit the button on his radio. "Chisel, you sit tight. I'll deal with you soon enough. We got a situation in town that requires real law enforcement." He didn't bother to listen to her response and turned his radio off for the time being. Just until he got this new mess sorted out.

He got close enough to see inside the combine's cab. It almost looked like that was Bob Morton himself in there. *Shit*. Well, this situation just got a hell of a lot more complicated. Sheriff Hoyt resnapped his holster.

He'd been thinking he might have to make an impression on the driver, but now that he saw it was Bob Morton, well, his job was going to require a bit more finesse than simply sticking a pistol in somebody's face and telling him to grab the pavement.

He looked up and down the street, but the only law enforcement he could see right away was that pussy town deputy, Hendricks. He raised his arm, got the numbskull's attention, and pointed at the combine. The dumbshit waved back. Sheriff Hoyt shook his head. It was a wonder the man hadn't shot himself cleaning his own weapon.

At least they didn't have to jump onto a moving vehicle. Bob took care of that.

The combine veered away from the left side of the street, scaring away a whole flock of parade watchers, and smashed the twelve-row header right into Phil Larkins's 1957 Chevy pickup. Four of the header's conical snouts impaled the poor old antique like a pitchfork sinking into a bale of hay. Sheriff Hoyt winced. Larkins's insurance guys were going to raise holy hell. The trailer couldn't take the sudden turn and twisted helplessly behind the combine, spilling two acres' worth of corn into the street.

Bob sat in the cab and it didn't look like he was moving much.

Deputy Hendricks finally got the hint that he was supposed to help out. He joined Sheriff Hoyt at the foot of the huge, bright green John Deere combine. Damn thing had tank-like treads for the front drivers, instead of regular wheels. A six-foot ladder rose to the cab. Hendricks hung back and made it clear that he didn't want to be the first one up there.

Neither paid much attention to the gray cloud that swirled from the spilled corn and rolled out across Main Street.

Sheriff Hoyt started up the steep stairs. He got up to the catwalk and was surprised to find the windows of the cab fogging up or something. It was hard to see inside and he could just make out Bob's shape, sitting in the bucket seat. He gave it a minute, giving the man a chance to collect himself before he came out and embarrassed himself in front of the whole damn town.

When Bob didn't move, Sheriff Hoyt knocked on the glass, still polite. He gave it a few moments, but his patience was running out. He knocked again. "Mr. Morton? Bob, that you? Fun's over. Time to come out now."

Sheriff Hoyt looked down the ladder at Hendricks, who shrugged. Sheriff Hoyt shook his head. The deputy was about as useless as tits on a boar. He took hold of the door handle, when some instinct, born out of decades of standing guard at the threshold of law and order, keeping the forces of chaos and wild, merciless rage at bay, whispered quietly in the back of his mind. It was the kind of voice he would listen to very carefully if it spoke to him when approaching a strange vehicle or knocking on a quiet door. A sixth sense that he took seriously, but would never acknowledge out loud.

Only this time it had Sandy's voice.

So he ignored it and opened the cab door.

It took Sheriff Hoyt a few seconds to recognize Bob Morton. He'd never seen anybody this bloated and gray still sitting upright. If he hadn't seen the man only the day before, Sheriff Hoyt would have sworn that Bob had been pulled out of the Mississippi River after a week or two of festering on the bottom. His first thought was that this was some kind of sick joke, and somebody had stuffed Bob's dead body in the combine cab.

But then Bob moved his head, and tried to say something.

Sheriff Hoyt leaned closer to listen.

Unintelligible words came out as a kind of wheezing moan. It didn't look like Bob could fully retract his tongue, and so it poked out from between black teeth, swollen and discolored. He opened his mouth wider and Sheriff Hoyt could see dozens upon dozens of little gray nubs erupting out of his tongue, his gums, the insides of his cheeks. The smallest were the diameter of a single grain of rice, the largest the rounded end of a Q-tip.

Up close, Sheriff Hoyt could now see more of the tiny buds sticking out of Bob's nostrils, his ears, even pushing out of his eyelids. Bob couldn't even blink with all those things in the way. From a distance, it looked like someone in a hurry had applied cheap, clumping eyeliner to the farmer's eyes.

Bob had never been a fitness model, but he had kept himself relatively trim for a man in his fifties. Now, though, his distended stomach almost reached the steering wheel. His fingers were swollen, like sausages that had been left on the grill too long. He wheezed again, his arm flopping against the control console.

Sheriff Hoyt realized he should remove the keys, just in case Bob hit the wrong button. He didn't want to get any closer, but reached in and as his fingers brushed against the keys, Bob started to make deep, retching sounds.

And just as Sheriff Hoyt managed to twist the keys and kill the engine, Bob's head exploded in a dry mist, as if someone violently twisted a desiccated orange, popping it open, spitting dried seeds and dusty pulp into the air.

Bob's torso was next, splitting open in four or five wrenching cracks, spraying the inside of the cab with a dark, wet cloud. Gray slime slid down the windows and dripped from the ergonomic controls.

Sheriff Hoyt caught the blast full in the face and was dead before his knees collapsed. He pitched off the combine and landed on his head in the middle of Main Street.

Deputy Hendricks leaned over him and asked, "You okay, Sheriff?"

The gentle winds took the gray cloud from the cab and the trailer and pushed it playfully every which way into the crowds, up and down the street. There was a single scream, but the spores were met primarily with stupefied confusion. A few people understood that something bad was blowing through the town and tried to gather their families and run.

By then, it was all too late.

Sandy spun in a circle, taking it in, the hulking barn, the burning house, the smoldering cars, the dead man on the lawn, and surrounding it all, the green, whispering, waiting corn. She'd seen Cochran's monsters crawling over the man in the basement, and now she had no doubt that the fields were full of them. And maybe even worse things.

She had to get to town to find Kevin. Something in Sheriff Hoyt's voice, just before he clicked off, had raised the hairs on the back of her neck. She had no doubt that whatever havoc this corn fungus was wreaking out in the fields had spread somehow to the center of Parker's Mill.

But she had no vehicle, no phone, and even the radio was useless now, thanks to Sheriff Hoyt. She took one last glance around, making sure she wasn't forgetting something, and started down the driveway at a jog. As she ran, she kept her eyes at the edge of the corn on either side of the gravel driveway. She hoped Cochran was right about the things wanting to stay out of the sunlight. Either way, she stayed in the center of the driveway all the way out to the highway.

The Johnsons had to have heard all the shooting and Sandy wouldn't have been surprised if Meredith had been keeping an eye on all the unfamiliar traffic heading up the driveway to the Einhorn farm. Sandy hoped she had already called 911 again. The call would have been rerouted to the Manchester County Sheriff's Department, but she didn't care as long as they sent somebody out to investigate.

Sandy crossed Highway 17 and ran up to the front door. The possibility that the Johnsons were at the parade occurred to her as she ran. Sandy didn't know if that would be considered too secular or just patriotic. If they were in town, she didn't think it would be difficult to smash a window and climb inside to use their phone. Meredith would undoubtedly file some sort of official complaint, but Sandy didn't particularly give a damn.

Sandy hit the doorbell and listened for movement inside. They had to know she was here. She knocked first, then pounded on the door. No response. The house was silent.

She knew this place didn't have a basement and went to the big picture windows, cupped her hands to her eyes, and peered inside. The windows looked out from the combination living and dining room. The living room had a simple couch and a recliner. The ancient TV was still a piece of furniture in and of itself, wedged into a corner near the front door. A small, circular table filled the dining room. A beige and yellow kitchen waited beyond. All were empty.

She ran around to the back and saw that the big Suburban was still parked in front of the garage and a huge pile of firewood. It looked like they were still home. She went up to the sliding glass back door, stopping a moment when she noticed a stack of fire extinguishers on the patio. Peering at the gauges, she saw that they were all empty.

Sandy tried the sliding glass back door and it slid open. She stepped inside. "Meredith? Albert? You guys home?" It felt like an echo of the Einhorn farmhouse; no one was there. She left the door open and searched through the rest of the first floor. It smelled like something had died under the house. The kids' rooms were full of bunk beds and crayon drawings of Jesus, but no children.

She stopped at the bottom of the staircase. Knocked on the wall. She'd learned the hard way not to sneak up on people in rural areas. Too many carried loaded firearms, and were liable to shoot you if you surprised them. "Hello? Meredith? Albert?"

No answer.

Sandy took her Taser out and went cautiously up the stairs. At the top, she checked the first door on the left.

Bathroom. It was a mess, but empty. Sandy recoiled from the stench, raised her wrist to her nose, and tried to breathe through her mouth.

Unraveled brown and gray bandages had been strewn across the sink. Strips of medical tape festooned the counter like shriveled snakeskins. The gray crust that coated everything reminded her of what she had seen on the floor in the Einhorn kitchen. Clumps of toilet paper had been scattered throughout the bathroom as if somebody had been throwing them like confetti. They coalesced into a tiny mountain near the toilet at the far end. The pile of white paper had stuck together in winding lines, as if the darkened, soiled globs had drawn together like magnets. This left the clean tufted edges of toilet paper to unfurl like pale wisps of flowers on knotty gray vines.

Sandy wished she had her latex gloves but the box was back in the cruiser. She thought back to that night when Meredith had called 911 on Kurt Einhorn. Albert had been bitten or something. Sandy tried to remember. He'd said it was a possum. She'd been worried about rabies, but now she wondered if it had something to do with the fungus.

She didn't touch anything and backed out of the bathroom. At the end of the short hall, there was one door left. It was closed, of course. It had to be Meredith and Albert's bedroom. Suddenly, she didn't want to open it. Didn't care what was on the other side. She wanted to run downstairs and find the phone in the kitchen and call in the county boys. But they'd ask her if she'd checked the whole house and she didn't want to have to tell them that she'd lost her nerve.

So she opened the door. Slow and careful.

The room was almost completely dark. Heavy curtains covered the windows. She couldn't quite tell in the dim light, but it almost looked like they had been duct-taped to the window frame. The door continued to swing open, spilling more light into the room.

There was a circular pile of bodies on the bed. She realized it wasn't bodies, not exactly. A tangle of children's arms and legs were wrapped around a central gray mound. For some reason, the mound seemed fragile, like the crown of a jellyfish. It was nearly three feet across and fluttered with the slight wave of air that came as the door swung open.

Surrounding it, the arms and legs intertwined each other in a horrible, frozen wreath. Sandy looked closer and knew why she hadn't seen a dog or cat in the house; their legs intermingled with the humans'. The whole thing was like looking at some rotten pustule skulking in a badly infected wound. Even after trying to make sense of the thing for several seconds, she still couldn't see any heads. Instead, it was just limbs wrapped around a strangely raw, unfinished center that was covered with a thin gray membrane, like some half-cooked rotten egg, sunny-side up.

Sandy couldn't tell if the number of arms and legs accounted for all the children or not. She tried to get a rough count, but it was impossible. They were far too tangled, twisted around each other in shapes that could never be achieved when they were alive. She doubted anybody would know how many of the family had been absorbed into this huge mound until they performed a careful autopsy. She knew that this was something they would be studying for years.

She stopped. Did that arm move? She watched it a while, but it was still.

This was definitely above her pay scale. It was time to call somebody.

The door flew at her, knocking her back into the doorframe. Meredith popped into view from behind it with wild eyes, swinging a fire extinguisher across her body, like an amateur swinging a tennis racket. The bottom rim caught Sandy in the shoulder and slammed her into the wall. With a speed only possessed by the truly disturbed, Meredith raised the tank over her head and brought it down like a sledgehammer.

If Sandy hadn't gotten her arm up, it would have crushed her skull. As it was, it damn near broke the two bones in her forearm, and drove her to the floor.

Meredith shrieked, "They are going to heaven. They have been saved!"

At the sound of her voice, the twisted mosaic of limbs shivered and twitched. A fragment peeled away from the rough circle, and a number of children's arms and legs unfurled from a central gray tentacle, like a palm frond that had decided to reach out and go exploring. When the gray, pulpy mass that ran along the center of the branch could no longer support the weight of the tiny limbs, it drifted down to the floor and the arms and legs grabbed hold of the shag carpet and pulled the tentacle forward. It rippled awkwardly along, searching for the voice.

"No, no, not Mommy," Meredith said sweetly, and gave the crawling thing a quick blast from the fire extinguisher. "Over there. I brought you some food. To give you strength to reach heaven, my darlings." The tendril shrank away from the puff of frost.

More branches were starting to unfold from the center mass, crawling off the bed, using the children's arms and legs to propel the tendrils in the same way Sandy had seen the centipede creatures in the Einhorn basement use insect legs. The bigger ones down there had worked the same way, growing into individual fingers and toes and making them dance, connecting two long chains of human fingers and toes and rat and squirrel legs that scurried along in ragged waves, alternating sides as to snake along for prey in S-shaped patterns.

Eight or nine tendrils pulled themselves away from the jelly-like mass and came after Meredith. She gave Sandy a kick and slammed the door, preventing Sandy from getting out. She jumped back to the first corner of the bed and gave the crawling tentacles quick flashes from the extinguisher, directing them at the door and Sandy.

Sandy got mad and rolled to her knees, raised the Taser. Fired. The barbs grabbed hold of Meredith's right hip and breast and dropped her like a dead tree in a tornado.

A tip of tendril bumped into the bedroom door, rebounded, and then curled up toward her. The tip was a misshapen child's fist. Too many little fingers unfurled from the center and grabbed at her.

Sandy exhaled, and knew the trick was to keep moving. But two other tendrils joined the first, the floor between the bed and wall bristling with irregular lines of children's limbs.

She went with her first motion and lunged for the closet. She ripped it open with her left hand and yanked out the pepper spray with her right. The tentacles didn't like when she blasted them; the fingers curled back together, and the tendrils shrunk into themselves, each pulling back into itself like a firefighter's collapsible ladder. The space between each of the children's arms and legs grew shorter and shorter until the limbs slapped against other, back against the main bubble on the bed.

They were still for a moment, as if the center was tasting the pepper spray. Different tentacles crawled off the bed and came for her.

Sandy jumped inside the closet and pulled the door shut. She backed into long dresses and sweaters. The thin strip of light at the bottom broke apart as the things came closer. She held onto the door handle just in case those chubby digits could open doors and heard Meredith whimper.

Sandy knew it wouldn't be long before Meredith simply walked over and opened the closet to let her family inside.

But Meredith said, "Oh babies. Oh no. No. Please. Not this. Over there." Her voice took on a pleading, strident tone. "Please. Not me. Babies. Please."

Sandy let go of the door with her right hand and patted her belt. She replaced the pepper spray and found the flashlight. She splashed it around the closet for a second, and was slightly disappointed to see a double-barreled .12 gauge leaning against the back wall. She'd been hoping for an assault rifle or something equally indicative of a family with a healthy fear of God's wrath. Still, she wasn't going to complain as she shut off the light and checked if it was loaded by feel. It was.

Sandy, as the police chief of Parker's Mill, felt a momentary reflexive pang of anger at Meredith and Albert for keeping a loaded gun in an unlocked closet in a houseful of children. She checked for more ammo and found none.

Meredith started to scream.

Sandy knew it might be her only chance to get out of the closet. She made sure the safety was off and opened the door. A few of the tendrils were still agitated and exploring her side of the bed, but most seemed to be concentrating mostly on Meredith's head, leaving her body to flop around. Sandy couldn't quite see what exactly the tendrils were doing to Meredith because her upper half was hidden behind the bed, but she realized she was fine with that. She didn't want to know.

She shouldered the shotgun, found the closest tentacle and squeezed the trigger. The cloud of lead balls blasted the tiny fingers into a gray mist and left greasy strings flopping from the ragged end. There was no blood. Sandy wanted to put the second round into the center mass, but she was worried it might release spores or God knew what, and didn't think she should be breathing in the same room. So she fired at another tentacle creeping closer and went through the door. She slammed it shut behind her.

At the top of the stairs, she glanced back at the bedroom door to make sure the tentacles weren't flowing down the hall at her. It was still closed. Meredith wasn't screaming as loud anymore.

Sandy ran downstairs and in the kitchen found a phone from her youth with buttons in the handset and a fifteen-foot spiral cord to the base. She grabbed it and went through the sliding glass door. Slammed it behind her in case any tendrils came downstairs. She dialed 911.

"Nine-one-one. What is the nature of your emergency?"

"This is Chief Chisel. I need—"

"Oh, hello Chief Chisel. Sheriff Hoyt told us all about what you need. If you insist on wasting our time at the dispatch center, we were instructed to inform you that charges will be filed. Thank you." A click and the line went dead.

Sandy looked at the phone in disbelief. "Motherfucking BITCH!" She tried dialing the FBI. Job protocol made her memorize the number, along with a dozen others. This time, she couldn't even get a dial tone. She tried the CDC. The phone was out.

Sandy found the keys to the Suburban and was about to leave when she looked up at the ceiling. The thought of what was happening upstairs, how the entire family had been consumed, transformed, *swallowed*, made her nauseous. She'd be damned if she let it continue. Even if she had no power as chief anymore, she couldn't let it go.

She lifted the range on the stovetop and blew out the pilot light, then cranked all the burners on. The slight hiss and telltale odor of natural gas filled the kitchen. Under the sink she found an aerosol can of Raid. It was full. She shook it up and put it in the microwave, punched in thirty minutes, and turned it on. The metal started sparking immediately.

Sandy shut the door behind her, got in the Suburban, and took off for town.

CHAPTER 22

When the combine hit the old pickup, Puffing Bill went berserk. He'd been whining and pulling back on his leash as the massive harvester grew closer and closer up the street, and when it finally crashed to a stop, he dug his three feet into the grass and whipped his head back and forth to pull away from the leash.

All it took was for Kevin to move toward him. Instead of backing away, trying to wriggle out of his collar, he turned and began to pull the boy forward, as if he was trying to drag Kevin across the park.

"Maybe he has to go to the bathroom," Patty said. It was clear that she wanted nothing to do with that particular act and preferred that it happened far, far away from her. "Go. Go."

Kevin knew this wasn't Puffing Bill trying to tell him that he needed to go take a shit. The dog wasn't shy, and would do his business wherever he felt like it, as long as he was outside. This was something close to panic, and it scared Kevin. He held on to the leash and allowed Puffing Bill to lead him wherever the dog wanted to go.

They raced through the park and across the street and
down through the residential streets.

Kevin thought he could hear something happening
back at the parade, but they were blocks away before
Puffing Bill slowed down. Despite this, the dog was still
uneasy, whining and constantly keeping his head
moving. His ears flicked at the rustle of every leaf, the
creak of branches rubbing in the breeze.

Tuned to the quiet of the street, Kevin eventually
realized he couldn't hear any birds. No squirrels chasing each other around. In fact, no dogs barked. It was
like the town had been emptied of anything that moved
on its own when no one was looking.

He stopped on a corner and realized that he was
across the street from the high school. The place filled
him with a vague unease, as if the halls were filled
with students like Jerm, all looking for someone weak.
Although, Kevin reflected, Jerm himself would never
be swaggering through these halls. He didn't know how
that made him feel, and he briefly touched the bandage
on the back of his head. Part of him knew that Jerm had
been sick, that something was wrong, and therefore
didn't blame him, but the other part, the part he didn't
want to acknowledge, was glad Jerm was gone.

He started down the narrow access street that ran between the school and the administrative parking lot, cutting between the buildings and a row of a dozen or so
school buses. It felt good to walk through the shadow
cast by the gym and get out of the heat of the day. He
thought they could hang out in the coolness under the
baseball stands again, give Puffing Bill a chance to calm
down, then go back to Elliot and his parents before the
end of the parade.

Puffing Bill growled. Kevin couldn't see anything. Just the empty street, the silent buses, the side of the gym. School was closed for the holiday. There was no one around. "What?" he asked the dog. "What is it?"

Puffing Bill growled again and pulled away from the shadow cast by the gym. He backed up to the buses, barking at the side of the building. Kevin didn't understand. He couldn't see anything. He dropped Puffing Bill's leash and took two steps toward the side of the gym. The dog didn't run, but his barking grew louder, more insistent.

Kevin couldn't hear anything over the barking, but movement caught his eye. He'd been keeping an eye on the double doors to the gym and had missed it at first. Down in the old leaves that coated the three or four storm drains that stretched along the gutter, he caught a flash of something. Something like a snake, maybe? Whatever it was, something was moving underneath the leaves.

When it came crawling out of the storm drain, Kevin thought it was some kind of big furry spider. Then it kept coming, endless rows of scrabbling small legs, scurrying at them with surprising speed. Kevin froze. He thought he could see the legs of cats, some small dogs, raccoons, and others that he couldn't identify, as if some sadistic taxidermist had sewed them into two long rows on either side of a long gray tube.

Another one squirmed out of the next storm drain farther down.

Puffing Bill turned and was now barking at the other side of the street. More of the things were climbing out of those drains. The tendrils stayed low, moving from side to side the same way a sidewinder skims across sand, keeping to the shadows.

Kevin unclipped the leash from Puffing Bill so it wouldn't catch on anything. They both turned and ran.

Sandy stopped at the police station on the outskirts of town and tried the front door. It was locked. She pulled out her keys, then saw the chain wrapped around the push bars on the inside. Same thing for the back door. She knew Liz would have had a fit, and hoped she was smart enough to not get in too much trouble with Sheriff Hoyt.

She thought about trying to break a window, see if she could trigger the alarm, but ultimately decided it wasn't worth it. It wouldn't help her get inside. She climbed back into the Suburban and drove a few blocks to her house.

Kevin was not there.

She sat in the kitchen for a while, trying to think. She got back in the Suburban and drove out to Highway 67 and turned north, stopping at the Korner Kafe.

The CLOSED sign was up in the window. She was surprised; she couldn't ever remember a time when it wasn't open during the day. Her dad used to bring her here for the lunches. He'd get a BLT, and she'd get the mac and cheese. For some reason, she always remembered coming here with him during the winter, when the farmers had too much time on their hands. He must have brought her here during the summer, when there was no snow, but the only images that came to her were sitting at the counter while the winter winds howled outside, sheeting the big windows in intricate spiderwebs of ice.

Sandy tried the front door. It was unlocked, which didn't make much sense. She went around the register and set the phone on the counter. She tried calling the FBI and CDC one more time, but got the same hollow, echoing message that told her the call could not be completed at this time. She called Randy and Patty. Their answering machine picked up and she hung up without saying anything. Just for the hell of it, she tried to call her house. It went through and rang until the answering machine picked up. "Kevin, if you get this, stay there and wait for me. I will find you."

She dug around under the counter and found the phone book, turned the pages until her finger stopped at the Fitzgimmon number. She dialed it and waited as it rang a long time.

Finally, a woman with some kind of accent answered. "Yes?"

"I need to speak with Purcell. Immediately."

The woman put the phone down for a moment. When she came back, she asked, "Who is calling, please?"

"This is Sandy Chisel."

Again, the phone went quiet. Sandy could hear low talking in the background. A man picked it up. "Yeah?"

"Purcell?"

"What do you need, Chief? Kinda busy right now."

"I know you have at least four firearms registered with the county. I need you and your boys to meet me in the Korner Kafe parking lot right away and bring as many shotguns to as you can."

Purcell took a moment, asked, "Why?"

"It'll be easier if I show you." Inside, Sandy was praying that she was wrong, that the sick fear that gripped her when Sheriff Hoyt had mentioned a situation in town had nothing to do with the fungus.

He was quiet again, so she said, "I wouldn't ask if it wasn't an emergency. I need help to get to my son."

This time, she waited through the silence.

Finally, he spoke. "Do you want me to bring those guns I registered or do you want me to bring as many shotguns as I can?"

"I want you to bring as many shotguns as you can."

"See you in a few." He hung up.

The door to the church basement was stronger than Sandy expected. She'd known it would be locked, but figured it was a simple door to the basement of the Church of Jesus Christ of Latter-day Saints, not Fort Knox. She figured a well-placed kick would be enough to crack either the doorframe or the door itself. So far, she'd given it three or four kicks, but it held fast. She looked around for something she could use, but found nothing but a well-manicured lawn and tastefu landscaping surrounding the church.

She ran back to the empty parking lot to check the back of the Suburban. She didn't think there was a lot of room in the back because of all the rows of seats, but maybe Albert had a toolbox or something back there. She didn't see a toolbox, but found something better.

A goddamn chainsaw.

It wasn't huge, just a 38cc orange Husqvarna with a sixteen-inch bar. She checked the gas. It was full. She started it on the run back to the door and it burst into life with a terrific, mean little purr. Even better, Albert had taken off the tip protector, so she could plunge the entire bar straight into the door.

Sandy was tired of wasting time and simply sawed the entire door in half and kicked the bottom half down the basement stairs. She ducked under and hit the lights. As she went down the stairs, she went to kill the engine, but remembered the basement in the Einhorn house. She decided to keep the engine idling for now, at least until she got back into the Suburban.

After Cochran had panicked over his own gas mask being removed, he'd explained that the fungus could infect you with spores that floated in the air. She'd immediately thought about how she'd helped Troop 2957 with their disaster drill and knew where she could find at least a dozen gas masks. She still had no idea why the church needed them, and had never wanted to deliberately make waves by asking.

Luckily, they hadn't moved the gas masks. They were still in a green Army duffel bag hanging in the walk-in utility closet.

She slung the duffel bag over her shoulder and charged back up the stairs into the sunlight. On the lawn, walking to the Suburban, she finally relaxed enough to turn off the chainsaw. It made her feel better, though; the gas masks went into the backseat and the chainsaw went on the front passenger seat so she could keep it close.

As she pulled out of the parking lot, she couldn't understand why no one had come out of the church itself or the connected offices to check on the noise. The parade should have been finished a while ago. Where was everybody?

Purcell was waiting with folded arms while his three sons stood in the back of the pickup. They were parked in the Korner Kafe lot. No shotguns were visible. She pulled in next to Purcell's pickup, got out, and opened the back door. She tossed the duffel bag into the back of the pickup.

Charlie unzipped it and pulled out one of the gas masks. "We going to some kinda weird sex party?" he asked, spinning the mask on his index finger.

"Aw yeah," Axel said. "Count me in, baby."

Edgar gave a little uncontrollable dance, like a toddler that had to take a leak.

"Gotta admit," Purcell said, staring at Sandy. "You got me a little curious here, with guns and gas masks."

"You bring your guns?" Sandy asked.

Purcell smiled. "Guess that all depends on what you mean. If you're talking about those coupla guns I registered just to make the political fuckers happy, then . . . not so much. Those are family heirlooms. They belong above the fireplace, so we can pass the stories down from generation to generation. When these boys have families of their own, they will explain to their children why these guns are important to us." He gave her a grin. "If you're talking about simple firepower, well then . . ."

He pulled a shotgun off the front seat. The stock

and forestock were built of black plastic and from a distance, it looked like a standard military semiautomatic .12 gauge. Purcell had a look that echoed the same joy that boys across the world experience when blowing shit up. "This," he said with a grand air, "is an AA-12, a fully automatic shotgun."

He brandished a circular magazine; it reminded her of one of the clips that Al Capone and his gang had used for their .45 caliber Thompson submachine guns. "Twenty rounds. You'll go through this in less time it takes to blink. Guaranteed to turn anything in front of you into a bad dream."

Despite herself, Sandy was impressed. She'd been hoping for a few sawed-off .12 gauges that held seven or eight goose rounds, not this machine gun that sprayed shotgun shells like a fire hose. She didn't know what to say. "I'm not sure that's legal," she finally managed.

Everybody laughed like she'd made a hell of a joke.

Purcell said, "Of course it isn't. Are you kidding me? Of course it isn't legal. We have three."

"Good," Sandy heard herself say.

He threw the AA-12 into the back of the truck; Charlie caught it. Edgar and Axel proudly held up each of their own. "And just in case," Purcell said, "we brought a couple of SPAS-15s. They don't make 'em anymore, but I couldn't resist." Purcell brought out another shotgun that resembled a machine gun. "This one isn't fully automatic, but it'll fuck shit up, no question." He racked the pump back and smiled at her. "Whether you use it as a pump shotgun or as a semiauto, either way you're a happy camper."

"You can drive," Sandy said. She reached into the Suburban and pulled out the chainsaw. At this, the

Fitzgimmons could hardly contain their glee. Purcell raised his hands as if he was surrendering. "Damn, Chief. I'd hate to get on your bad side."

Sandy hopped into the passenger seat, leaving the sons to ride in the back.

Purcell went around the front of his pickup and climbed in behind the wheel. He put his hand on the keys but didn't start the engine. "I appreciate you bringing the boys home on Saturday night and letting me deal with 'em first. That's the only damn reason I'm here. That said, you get us into some kind of trouble in town, get our dicks in a wringer, you ain't gonna like *my* bad side."

"Okay. I'll explain. On the way."

Chapter 23

Purcell drove slow and listened. He only had one question. "Them fellas that came looking for Morton's lawyer. You think that's all that'll show up? Sounds to me this is not an organization that leaves loose ends."

"I have no idea," Sandy said. She considered it for a moment. "I tried calling the FBI and the CDC from the Johnsons'. Couldn't make any long-distance calls. Same thing from the Korner." She thought about the man with the flamethrower back at the Einhorns'. He'd torched his own vehicle without a second thought, so he either had another one stashed nearby or he was fully expecting to be picked up. She could have kicked herself for not checking to see if he had a cell phone.

"Something to chew on," Purcell said. "Tell you the truth, I thought it all sounded a little far-fetched when you started talking. Now I ain't so sure." He indicated with a tilt of his head the quiet streets. They turned right at the only stoplight onto Main Street. It was utterly empty. When they got to the start of the parade route, they found the street lined with vacant lawn chairs, half-empty food wrappers, napkins fluttering in the breeze.

Sandy put her hand on the dash. "Hold up. Might be a good time to be cautious." She got out and had Charlie hand gas masks to his brothers. She took two and gave one to Purcell. They pulled them on, adjusted the straps until they fit so tight it was almost painful, and took a few experimental breaths. The filters made everything dry and stale, but they could breathe.

Purcell drove around the sawhorses. They passed flatbed trucks with overturned folding chairs on the back, a 4H float, convertible sports cars, and a pickup emblazoned with giant Rotary Club banners and a mountain of candy in the back. The Shriners' go-karts were spread out all over the street as if the men had all gotten bored at the same time and left the karts wherever they felt like it.

They got closer to the park and saw the reason for the traffic jam; the giant combine angled against a line of antique vehicles, the trailer behind it sideways, the load of ears of corns spilled across the entire street.

"I don't know if you want to drive over that or not," Sandy said. Her voice sounded distant and hollow behind the mask.

Purcell threw the gearshift into neutral. "Suits me." He killed the engine, and for the first time, they all could hear how truly quiet the town had become. Sandy and Purcell got out. Purcell went to the front of the pickup and dragged the toe of his boot through the gray dust that coated the pavement.

"Y'all gonna let us in on what the hell's happening?" Charlie asked from the pickup bed.

"Chief here says Allagro went and built themselves a

corn seed with built-in pest control, some kind of super fungus," Purcell said. "Doesn't look like it worked out like they wanted. Now keep your mouth shut and eyes open."

"Okay. But what are we looking for? Nothin's here."

"Awfully sure of yourself, ain't you?"

Charlie rolled his eyes but kept his mouth shut.

"Supposedly this fungus'll infect you one of two ways," Purcell continued. "Breathing the spores, which is why we're wearing the masks, or . . . something else. Make sure you're loaded. Mind you, I want those safeties on, boys." He pulled one of the SPAS-15s out of the cab, checked the clip, and slammed it back into the shotgun. He turned to Sandy. "Well, you got us in town, armed to the teeth, and ready to rock and roll. What's the plan?"

Sandy turned in a slow circle. "I don't know." The reality that everyone in town was missing was starting to sink in, ripping her apart a tiny bit at a time. The utter hopelessness she had been fighting against was creeping through her defenses like cold, skeletal fingers clutching a balloon, tighter and tighter. Eventually, it was going to pop. "I just don't know."

Everyone had simply vanished. She saw how people had abandoned their seats, leaving everything behind. Food, cans of soda, sparklers, little American flags, ice chests full of beer. She walked over to the curb, found an open purse. After lifting the bottom with her boot and spilling the contents into the grass, she saw credit cards, even cash. She turned back to see all four of the Fitzgimmon men watching her.

She went back and grabbed the second SPAS-15 and started up the street without saying a word. She was afraid if she started talking, started trying to explain, to work it out in her head, she would be forced to the conclusion that everyone along the parade had been overcome with the spores. Including Kevin. She couldn't face that, not yet.

She avoided the corn and picked her way along the curb around the combine crash, stopping just long enough to get a good look at the gray, slimy mess in the cab, then continued searching for clues all the way to the temporary stage at the edge of the park. Purcell and Charlie followed at a distance, using the barrels of their shotguns to move overturned chairs and crumpled blankets.

A distant thumping made them look up. Possibly a helicopter. They couldn't see anything but a cloudless blue sky. The sound evaporated and died in the stillness. They went back to the search.

She spotted a small gym shoe and her breathing seized up, but it was too small to fit Kevin. She didn't want to think about the child that had been wearing it. It was too much, and she was worried if she broke down crying in front of the Fitzgimmons they might decide they'd had enough and leave.

She stopped and looked back to the combine, shielding her face mask against the late afternoon sun. She assumed it had been Bob Morton who had driven the combine through the parade and crashed into the cars. From what Cochran had said, the corn Bob Jr. had sent had mostly likely infected his father. And then Bob Sr. had gone and dragged a trailer full of death straight into town and dumped it in everybody's laps. The spores had done their job, and then . . .

She thought back to the Einhorns. Thought about

how Ingrid had disappeared. Wondered if that had been her fingers crawling out of the septic tank. Thought about the curtains drawn tight in the Johnsons' bedroom. Cochran had said something about the fungus, that maybe it didn't like the light. She thought back to last summer, when her and Kevin had replaced the kitchen floor and how they found mold when they peeled up the cheap vinyl tiles.

Maybe she couldn't find Mrs. Kobritz because she had crawled off somewhere to hide from the light. The thought chilled her, despite the summer afternoon heat.

She crossed the street and knew Purcell was watching. His patience would only last so long, and since he didn't give a damn about the town, it was only a matter of time before he rounded up his sons and went back home across the river.

The old brick building had been City Hall for decades until they moved their offices into a more modern building north of town. Various wings and additions had been built over the years until it was now the sprawling home of Parker's Mill's library. It was closed today, of course. Sandy cupped her hands and peered through the glass doors but couldn't see anyone inside.

She thought of the Einhorn basement and went along the front wall, peering down into the window wells. It was too dark to see anything. She knew they didn't let the general public down there; the basement was used mostly as a storage area for the newspaper collection and old equipment like mimeograph machines and the retired card catalog system. The library had transferred everything over to a computerized system that linked up with the rest of the public libraries in the state a few years ago, but the head librarian didn't have the heart to throw all the cards out.

The third window was simply gone, leaving nothing but a few shards of glass glinting in the gravel at the bottom of the window well. She leaned the shotgun against the building and pulled out her flashlight. She got on her knees and bent over, shining the light into the basement. Cool, air-conditioned air brushed against her fingers and face.

She couldn't see anything beyond dusty bookshelves and a stack of broken chairs. She gave a whistle and waved Purcell over. Charlie followed. "I got an idea that if they got a lungful of those spores, they might try to get out of the sun. Find someplace dark and cool."

Sandy lowered herself into the four-foot window well and pushed her feet through the window. She slid her butt off the window frame, rolled her hips over, and rested on her stomach. That way, she could lower herself into the basement, going slow, until her boots touched the floor. The waffle treads made crunching sounds on all the broken glass. Purcell handed the shotgun down to her, stock first.

The library basement was quiet enough she could hear the rumble of the air conditioner out back. She kept the shotgun in her right hand and swept the flashlight beam around with her left. Drops of blood speckled the glass shards scattered across the cement floor.

Purcell stuck his head into the window. Upside down, he asked, "Anything?"

Sandy shook her head and moved deeper into the gloom, past the chairs and through a narrow corridor flanked by empty bookshelves. She thought she heard something and whipped the light back around at the window. Purcell was gone; he'd sat back upright. But she didn't think it had been him anyway.

It seemed like it had come from deeper in the library.

The sound came again, under the air-conditioning, something soft that rose and fell, fading in and out. It reminded her of waves somehow, the way a boat's wake will send small waves out to the riverbank. It sounded almost like someone struggling to breathe, but there would only be a singular rising and falling. This sounded like . . . a crowd, all whispering, spreading ugly gossip.

She crept forward until she came upon a large conference table that had been pushed against the wall. Stacks of boxes covered the top. Shadows cloaked the bottom. Sandy brought the flashlight up.

The first thing she saw was a single, overturned flip-flop. Then a bare foot. A plump ankle. A woman's leg. There was a thin patch of soft hair up near the back of the knee, where the woman had missed a spot shaving.

The light traveled up the leg and revealed a mass of bodies clustered under the conference table. Arms, legs, heads stuck out in random directions. There was no sense of order, no modesty, no indication that there was any cooperation between anyone. It looked as though they had all somehow decided this was a good spot and had wedged their way into the group somehow. Everyone, children, women, men, they were stacked under there like flexible firewood, squeezing into any available space.

Sandy thought that all this weight pressing down on the people on the bottom was the cause of the labored breathing. She got closer and saw that she was wrong.

Things were growing out of their mouths. The gray

tips looked like narrow mushrooms. As she played the flashlight over the living tangle of flesh, she saw that the mushrooms weren't only growing out of their mouths. Gray tendrils had also sprouted from nostrils and ears. Some were even peeking out from the waistbands of jeans, or emerging from the darkness where the shorts and dresses had been pulled tight across flabby thighs.

Worse yet, they were starting to grow into the nearby orifices of anyone lying nearby. An especially thick cluster was inching steadily out of a toddler's sugar-crusted mouth and nose and growing into an old man's ear. Not that Sandy could see them growing or getting bigger. Not really. But if she looked away and came back, the tendrils had stretched. It was like staring at a clock. The minute hand won't move if you're watching, but if you look away for a minute and go back, you'll notice it was progressing after all.

Sandy figured this was how the mound of limbs in the Johnson bedroom had started. She wondered how long it had taken the mound to reach that stage. A day or two at the most. This mass was bigger, with maybe twenty or thirty people jammed together under the long table.

She got closer. She didn't want to touch anyone, but she had to know. Had to know if her son was under there. She kept the flashlight moving, searching for any sign, one of his shoes, a wrinkled twist of his shirt, a glimpse of his hair. *Shit*. She'd been so preoccupied this morning she couldn't even remember what color shirt he'd been wearing. She wondered if she would recognize his hand, his fingers.

Someone gasped behind her and she dropped the flashlight and whirled around and almost fired the shotgun into Charlie's chest.

"The fuck is that?" he wanted to know.

Sandy let her breath out in one long shaky whistle. She picked up the flashlight and backed away. "It's the spores. It's what they do."

Charlie squinted behind the bug-like goggle eyes of his mask. "Fuck me sideways."

"In a day or two, this will somehow produce more spores, I think."

"I think we oughta burn 'em."

Sandy didn't have anything to say to that. The thought of trying to save these people was laughable, only it was the kind of laughing that once you started, you couldn't stop until you were whooping and sucking in great gusts of air and somewhere along the way, the laughter skidded into a series of wavering screams.

She spent another few minutes trying to see if she could spot any sign of Kevin in the mass. Every time she moved the light and then brought it back, the tendrils had grown. She got close to the wall and knew there were at least fifteen bodies under the table that she couldn't see. She flicked the light back at Charlie. "Help me slide the table out. Just a little."

He pulled the table away from the wall, sliding it out slow about seven or eight inches. The metal studs on the center feet screeched as it was dragged across the cement.

She bent over the bodies. A man in his late forties who had been jammed right up under the bottom of the table blinked and opened his eyes. He blinked, but that was all; he didn't move another muscle other than those around his eyes. Sandy suddenly recognized him as Randy, Elliot's father. If he was down here, then . . . She refused to follow that line of thought any further.

Randy's eyes rolled back and fluttered as if he was having a seizure.

A fat seven- or eight-year-old girl, her head stuck sideways in his armpit, also blinked and opened her one visible eye. More eyes, sunk into faces under the man and girl, began to blink.

Sandy looked back up at Randy and found that his eyes were staring right at her.

She stood up.

His eyes followed.

All of the eyes focused on her and the flashlight. Sandy found she was unable to move the light away. Their eyes weren't blank, unfocused. They seemed horribly, horribly *aware*.

Sandy jumped back to stand next to Charlie. Her voice shook. "I think, I think they know. I think they are all awake, they can feel what is happening, but they can't move."

Charlie regarded the table for a moment. Nodded. "That . . . sucks."

They found two more clusters of people as they moved deeper into the basement. They weren't quite as big, and Sandy could see that Kevin was not a part of them. Still, she found people she knew, people she had seen in town, not only folks that she'd had to visit late night to calm down a fight or bust for pot, but people she'd seen in the Stop 'n Save, parents and children she'd met at Kevin's school. It left her feeling raw, like her insides had been scraped and left in a steaming pile on the floor.

She didn't want to leave them, but knew she had no choice. If she tried to say, "I'm going for help," she knew it was a lie. Her only path was locating her son. She would find Kevin or die. If she found him, she would take him far, far away, and leave all this to some-one else. If he had been infected, she would make that decision only when she found him.

When they climbed back out of the broken window, the sun was creeping toward the horizon. The shadows were getting longer; much like the fungal tendrils in the basement, you couldn't see them moving, but they were getting bigger and longer, no question.

After Sandy and Charlie told Purcell what they had seen, he said, "That can't be all of them. Look at all them chairs. A few of 'em went down there, but not everybody."

"Yeah. And that's not the only thing that's bothering me," Sandy said.

"It gets better?" Purcell asked.

"For a couple days now, we've been getting calls. Missing persons. Folks weren't coming home after work out in the fields. People weren't showing up for work. Lot of cranky wives thinking their husbands were out spending the rent on strippers."

"They were probably right."

"That's what we thought. Hell, that's what everybody thought. But what if they ended up like those people? And that was two days ago."

"Maybe so. Either way, nothing we can do about it now. We need to figure out where everybody went so we can find your boy and get the fuck out of town. Getting tired of wearing this mask."

Sandy walked up the street, past the stage, into the intersection of Main Street and Fifth Street. The pavement was littered with trumpets, saxophones, a few trombones, clarinets, and a single bass drum. Beyond that was another flatbed truck. The engine was still idling. A large, papier-mâché statue of a bird of prey with a huge, scowling head had been set up on the back as the falcon mascot for the high school.

Hundreds of people, gone.

They were infected and couldn't have gone far. They sure as hell didn't get into their cars and drive off. She didn't think they were capable of getting farther than they could walk in five minutes, tops. They would look for sanctuary, for someplace to nest, someplace to gather, someplace dark.

She kicked one of the flutes in disgust. It went spinning away under the School Spirit flatbed, where it hit something and produced a cheerful ding. It didn't sound like it had hit a wheel. Sandy bent over and saw that the flute had banged into a short crowbar. Just beyond that was a manhole cover.

The cover was off. The sewer was open.

Sandy straightened and looked down at the street beneath her feet. "I know where they are," she called, and when Purcell and Charlie looked over, she pointed at the pavement. Charlie didn't get it, but Purcell did. He started looking for another manhole cover, found it half a block down, on the other side of the Future Farmers of America truck. It was open as well.

Purcell sent Charlie back to the truck to collect his brothers and some flashlights.

While they waited, Sandy got into the School Spirit truck and pulled it forward, exposing the open manhole. She turned off the engine, climbed out, and joined Purcell in the center of the intersection. They looked down into the darkness.

Purcell said, "We find him down there, you know it'll be too late to save him, right?"

Sandy didn't say anything. If she said no, they both knew she would be wrong. And if she agreed, then she would be admitting that her son was probably dead.

Purcell said, gentle, "If you want, I can take care of him. Make sure he doesn't suffer."

Sandy met his eyes. "You touch my son and I will kill you."

Purcell nodded. "Your call. I'm old enough to know that you never mess with a mama bear."

CHAPTER 24

Sandy didn't bother waiting, and started down; she had her own flashlight and firearm and didn't see the point. She carried the shotgun in her left hand and used her right on the cool iron rungs. The temperature dropped at least fifteen degrees as she descended beneath the surface of the street and even before she reached the bottom and saw anything, she knew in her heart that they had found everyone.

It still didn't prepare her for the reality of actually seeing the twisted knots of bodies, stretching away as far as her flashlight could throw the beam. The brick sewer had been built in the shape of a tube, with curving walls and a trough running along the center of the bottom. She turned in a slow circle, flicking the flashlight beam over the small mountains of bodies, and saw with horror that she was in the middle of a junction, same as the intersection above. People were strewn throughout all four of the huge pipes. The sewer tunnels followed the streets, and Sandy realized that it would take her hours to search through the hundreds of bodies.

They weren't all clustered together in one huge mass. Instead, ten or twelve people had curled tightly together, gathered in curious clumps, then four or five feet farther along, there was another mound of bodies. Sometimes a few of the heaps would be collected along the shallow trench that ran along the bottom, then several mounds would coalesce on one side before they drifted back to the other side. Sometimes it appeared that a few single bodies had laid down between the mounds, as if they were connecting one circle of bodies to the next. The whole tableau could almost be seen as a vine of some sort, growing along from one flower to another, culminating in a tight ring of clusters that encircled the sewer junction.

Sandy stood in the middle of this and felt despair crash over her shoulders like a tsunami. She would never find her son, not among all these bodies, down here in the dark. Her hands shook and she almost went to her knees.

Purcell climbed down, SPAS-15 strapped to his back, a Maglite duct-taped over the barrel. He splashed the light around and muttered, "Holy fuck," under his breath. "Believe I'm gonna be writing a letter to the editor about this."

Charlie was next. He had on a backpack filled with extra ammo and magazines for the AA-12s. Edgar and Axel followed. Each had his flashlight taped to his shotgun and each was struck speechless. Edgar didn't move far from the ladder; he looked like he was about ready to climb back up and get the hell out of town.

Purcell said, "Take a good look around, boys. This shit is why we're going organic."

Charlie said, "We'll never find him. You know that,

right? Not with . . ." He flung a hand to indicate the abomination of all the bodies, locked together in the gloom.

Edgar nodded vigorously, said, "Come on. If he's down here, he's done. Finished. No chance. I don't want to die for somebody that's already dead."

Sandy got close, stabbed a finger into his chest. "Go then. Run."

"Hang on, hang on," Purcell said. "Let's keep our heads here. What we need is a plan. I think we should split up. Cover more ground. Quicker."

"We don't even know what the kid looks like," Charlie pointed out.

"His name is Kevin," Sandy said. "And splitting up is a bad idea. We don't know enough about these things. Just because we haven't seen them move doesn't mean they won't. We should stick together, take our time, and do a methodical search. We get separated down here, there's no telling what could happen."

"I ain't arguing with you," Purcell said. "You got a point. But here's the thing." He looked up the ladder at the fading circle of light. "Sun's going down. You said yourself you didn't think these things like sunlight. What happens when it's night out there?"

Sandy didn't have an answer.

"So let's split up," Purcell said. "Cover as much ground as we can, try and find him, okay?"

"We still don't know what the hell he looks like," Charlie complained again, but Sandy was already unbuttoning her chest pocket. She pulled out a square photo that she'd run through the laminating machine at the office, securing it in plastic. Kevin's face smiled awkwardly out of his school photograph. It was clear that she didn't like folks knowing that she carried it with her on duty.

The Fitzgimmons passed it around. Purcell asked, "What was he wearing?"

Sandy closed her eyes, tried to remember. It felt so long ago. "Shorts. Blue gym shoes. Cheap knockoffs, all I could afford. T-shirt."

"What color?" Purcell asked.

Sandy let her breath out slow and didn't open her eyes. Finally she shook her head. "I don't know. Black? I don't remember."

"Shit," Charlie said.

"Well, let's make the best of what we've got," Purcell said. "Daylight's wastin'. Charlie, you take that branch." He pointed south, down along Fifth Street. "Ed, you and Axe take that one." He indicated the northern tunnel, opposite of Charlie. "I'll head this way." His flashlight swept east, under Main Street. "Chief, you check down that way."

Purcell said, "You see anything, you sing out. Take your time, don't rush, and go as far as you can in fifteen minutes. At the end of fifteen minutes, you start back, you got that?" His boys nodded.

He looked at Sandy. "I'm sorry, but that's all we can give you. Fifteen minutes, we haven't found him, that's a goddamn shame, but my boys are alive, and I intend to keep them that way."

"I understand," Sandy said in a small voice.

"Gonna do my best to keep you in the land of the living too, Chief," Purcell said. "Okay then. Check your watches. See you back here soon. Good luck."

* * *

Sandy found it was possible to walk along on the lower edge of the curved walls and avoid stepping on the bodies. She would stop at each cluster, sometimes leaning over it, sometimes able to circle it completely, looking for any trace of her son. Her little flashlight had a strong beam, but it was small, made for hanging from her belt, and each step took her farther and farther into absolute darkness.

She didn't want to check her watch, didn't want to know how much time had passed. The beam caught a flash of something familiar. Not anything connected to her son, but it still triggered a pang of recognition. She swept the flashlight back over the tangle of arms and legs, moving slower this time.

There. A hand. Long fingernails, elaborately painted with red, white, and blue stars and stripes. The beam of light found the woman's face and revealed eyes wide and staring. Sandy's hand flew to her mask and she turned away, squeezing her eyes tight.

It was Liz.

Sandy tried to take a breath, struggled with the gas mask. She had a powerful urge to rip it off and take a deep gasp, sucking in as much of the air in the sewer as she could. As she struggled to calm down, she heard a yell back down the tunnel.

It was Axel.

Oh God. Had they found Kevin?

Sandy started to run. She realized she was calling Kevin's name, over and over, in a kind of chanting mantra as she ran. She leapt over splayed bodies and splashed through the muck at the bottom of the trough. Soon she was back at the junction, trying to remember which way Axel and Edgar had gone. Straight ahead,

she saw Purcell's flashlight sweeping back and forth as
he came back down his tunnel.

To her left, she saw a distant light. That was Charlie.
Axel and Edgar were to the right, in the southern tunnel.
It didn't take long to reach the two brothers. Edgar stood
over one of the clusters, while Axel was sitting on the
ledge farther along, his feet in the trough. The search
had taken its toll on them. They looked as if they'd just
toured an abattoir on their hands and knees and had
been asked to do it again.

"There," Edgar said simply, his voice flat, pointing at
the mound of bodies.

Sandy pulled up, panting, trying to see through her
mask that was suddenly fogging up. It must have been
because she had been running. She forced herself to
slow her breathing, but it was difficult with her heart
thumping like a machine gun. She closed her eyes, focused on inhaling through her nose, exhaling through
her mouth. When she was ready, she opened her eyes.

For a second, she thought it was Kevin. Same dark
hair. Same skinny build.

Wrong shoes.

She looked closer. It wasn't him. "Oh, thank you,
thank you," she breathed.

Purcell and Charlie splashed up behind her. "Well?"
Purcell said, sounding panicked.

Sandy couldn't speak. She could only shake her
head.

Purcell aimed his flashlight at the boy. "You sure?"

Sandy finally managed, "Yes. It's not him."

Purcell took a deep breath himself. "Well, that's . . .
that's good, I suppose." He pointed his shotgun, shining

his light back down the tunnel. "Let's see, we have, five minutes left. I think we should—"

Axel cried out and jerked his legs out of the trough and scrabbled up the side of the sewer. There was a hand holding tight to his left ankle. An arm was connected to the hand, but up where the shoulder should have been part of a torso, there was only a mess of gray tendrils sprouting from around the white bone ball joint.

Axel shook his foot, but the hand refused to let go. He brought his AA-12 shotgun over his shoulder, rested the end of the barrel on the severed limb's wrist, and squeezed the trigger. Three blasts, so close together they might have been a single explosive sneeze, vaporized the arm in an explosion of blood and viscous, gray slime.

The fingers did not relent and clutched his cowboy boot with a tenacity that enraged Axel. He scraped them off with his other boot and fired again, disintegrating the flesh, blowing the knucklebones into the trough. The sound of the shotgun blasts echoed down the tunnels and for a moment, silence reigned.

"You good?" Purcell asked.

"Fuckers!" Axel shouted.

"Okay," Purcell said. "I think—"

"Shhh." Edgar put a finger to his lips. "Listen."

Purcell and Charlie turned their flashlights back down the tunnel. For a moment, all they could hear was their own rasping breathing inside the gas masks. Then, way, way down the tunnel, a splash. Something heavy. More splashing. It got louder. Then a whole cascade of wet slapping, almost like bare footsteps.

"Whoever it is, there's more than one of 'em," Charlie whispered.

"Maybe it's somebody coming to help. National Guard, somebody like that," Axel said.

"Might be more boys from Allagro," Purcell said.

"Great," Axel said. "Let them clean up their mess."

Sandy shook her head. "We're part of the mess. They'll kill us all."

Something emerged into the very edge of their lights, then backed away into the darkness. Whatever it was, it was down low, as if someone had been crawling along on their hands and knees.

"I wanna try something," Purcell said. "Point your lights at the floor for a sec."

Sandy said, "I'd rather keep an eye on whatever is down there."

"We will. Just for a quick second. Want to see if I can draw it any closer. Let's get a better idea of what we're dealing with here."

One by one, they all aimed their flashlights at the trough. Sandy was last. She stared into the blackness, straining to hear whatever was down the tunnel. She finally couldn't take it anymore and brought her light back up. A yelp burst out of her before she could stop herself.

The Fitzgimmons whipped their lights up.

The tunnel was alive with crawling tendrils. Human limbs had been stretched out along each tendril, sprouting from each side in random arrangements, like crumbling teeth in a rotten mouth. Pale, bare legs slapped through the shallow trench, arms reached out and clutched at the wet bricks. There were too many tendrils to count. They skittered and scrabbled and clawed over each other, undulating over the mounds of inert bodies, sometimes crawling up the sides of the sewer pipe.

Axel was the first to let loose, unloading his clip in less than three seconds. Charlie and Edgar were next, unleashing a blizzard of lead. Purcell and Sandy started shooting as well. An unholy firestorm of destruction exploded down the tunnel.

The arms and legs shattered in bloodless spatters of meat and gray muck.

The shooting died down and everybody reloaded. The trough and bottom of the sloping walls were littered with empty shotgun shells. Blue gun smoke hung around them in a thick haze.

The tendrils did not stop. They sloughed off the ruined limbs, leaving them behind like a plant sheds dead leaves. Fresh, undamaged arms and legs continued to propel the tendrils forward, surging ahead in a clumsy, hungry motion.

"Go," Purcell said. "Go!"

Nobody argued; they turned and ran. Edgar and Axel charged through the sewer, side by side, Sandy on their heels, followed by Charlie and Purcell. They sprinted through the darkness, jumping over mounds of bodies, flashlight beams bouncing off the curved walls.

Axel stepped on the kneecap of one of the bodies stretched between the mounds. The sudden weight twisted the vulnerable joint, pitching Axel sideways into the wall. He rolled into a mound, flailing and kicking. Sandy grabbed the back of his jeans and yanked him upright. Charlie crashed into her and they all stumbled.

Purcell fired a few rounds back down the tunnel behind them for the hell of it.

Edgar ran on ahead, panic fueling his flight. He looked back to make sure that everyone was following, and when he turned back around, his head smacked into low concrete. His feet kept going and he flopped flat on his back in the center of the trough. Sandy and Axel reached him and Sandy jerked his head out of the filthy water.

Blood ran from a gash in his forehead, spilling down between the two circular lenses of the mask. He was out cold, limp as an abandoned marionette. Axel and Charlie lifted him up and they turned to see what lay ahead.

The sewer grew smaller here; the larger pipe collapsed down into a pipe only four feet in diameter. Purcell pulled a road flare from Charlie's backpack and struck the tip. Everybody flinched from the burst of sizzling light. "Might slow 'em down," Purcell said, and tossed it into the center of the closest mound behind them.

Sandy went first. At least the mounds of bodies had tapered off and stopped, leaving the pipe clear. She could walk through the pipe fairly quickly, keeping her head down and back hunched. Charlie and Axel had to bend almost in half at the waist; they were dragging Edgar anyway, so it didn't matter as much. The flare sent their running shadows flickering before them like black flames.

Sandy saw something coming up, some irregularity in the top of the tunnel. She got closer and saw that it was another pipe, leading up to a new manhole. She yelled, "Here!" and climbed up. She reached the cover and tried to lift it. It was too heavy. She went back down, saying, "I can't budge it." Charlie pushed her out of the way and clambered up. They heard him grunt and a sliver of faint light spilled down around him. He came back down and together with Axel, they lifted Edgar up the vertical conduit.

Sandy followed them and crawled out to a night sky and pavement still warm from the heat of the day. She saw that they had emerged three blocks south on Fifth Street, near the high school. The sun was only a red glimmer on the horizon. The streetlights along Main Street were on. Down here, it was all residential houses, and there were no lights. Night was gathering in the deepening shadows, spreading like ink.

Edgar moaned and tried to sit up. He rolled onto his hands and knees and began to retch.

"Shit," Charlie said. "Don't have any choice now." He ripped Edgar's mask off. Vomit spilled out it, dripping off Edgar's nose and chin. He sucked in a ragged breath and vomited again.

Purcell jerked his legs out of the manhole and Axel helped slide the cover back into place. It settled with a loud thunk.

Edgar sat back and spat. "Dizzy," he said.

"You've probably got a concussion," Sandy said.

"Can you walk?" Purcell asked. "We gotta get back to the truck."

Sandy helped Edgar to stand. He looked a little unsteady, but gave them a thumbs-up.

"We'll take it slow, but we need to get moving," Purcell said.

They started back up Fifth Street. Sandy said, "Let's cut down Franklin. I don't want to get any closer to that damn corn than we need to."

Purcell was about to say something when he suddenly stopped short and aimed his shotgun at one of the cars parked along the street. He squatted, sweeping the light back and forth under the car. "Huh. Thought I heard something."

Then they all heard it. The scraping of bare feet and hands over pavement. The sounds came from all around them, creeping through the shadows, slithering through dark yards, crawling through bushes, squirming under vehicles.

Sandy spun, and they found themselves forming a tight circle in the middle of the street, shoulder to shoulder, trying to watch everywhere at once.

They were surrounded.

Charlie had two flares left. He stuck them in his back pocket, then shrugged off his backpack and gave it to Axel. "I'm going for the truck." He racked the bolt back on his AA-12, making sure there was a shell in the breech. "Get him," he pointed at Edgar, standing but still swaying, "someplace where you can hole up for a bit."

Purcell reached out and patted Charlie's shoulder. Father and son shared a look for a moment. Charlie said, "You're gonna hear some shooting. Don't sweat it." He sparked one of the flares and took off running, raising the flare over his head with his left and holding the shotgun by the pistol grip with his right.

A dozen tendrils rippled across the street and followed. More of them, maybe a hundred, seethed out of the darkness and came at them. Purcell and Axel opened up, blasting a hole in the mass of creatures. They pulled Edgar along, struggling to run, heading south on Fifth Street.

Sandy had a flash. "There!" She pointed at a hulking

shape that rose above the houses, silhouetted against the stars. "The water tower! These things, they can't climb. We'll get up there and wait for Charlie."

"I don't know," Purcell draped Edgar's arm over his shoulders and they shuffled along. "We get up there, we're trapped."

"Better than down here," Sandy said, slamming her shotgun into her shoulder and squeezing off two quick shots at a couple of tendrils crawling into the street between two cars.

"Can't argue with that," Purcell said.

Axel emptied his clip into the horde that crept across the street. He dropped it and fumbled for a new one.

Sandy heard distant gunfire.

They ran along the gym and passed a row of school buses. Sandy noticed that tendrils of all sizes were tracking them. Most were large, moving along on human limbs. Some were smaller, lower to the ground, using dog, cat, and possum legs. They flowed over each other as if oblivious to the other tentacles. The effect was like a mass of giant, wriggling centipedes, all scurrying to reach the food first.

"Over there," Sandy said, panting. "At the edge of center field. Near the trees." They ran onto the baseball diamond. The tendrils followed, and their scrabbling across the dry grass raised a cloud of dust and line chalk. Axel hung back and sprayed the closest fungus tentacles with another twenty rounds. The tendrils kept coming.

And more were rushing out of the darkness of the trees to meet them.

Sandy fired at those, trying to open up a path to the base of the water tower. She kept squeezing the trigger until the shotgun was empty, no way to reload now. They reached the waist-high chain-link fence and threw themselves over. She hoped the fence would slow the tendrils behind them, at least for a minute.

But it was low enough that the first few rows of arms on each tendril were able to pull the long line of limbs over and create enough momentum to keep flowing over.

Sandy's steps faltered and she almost gave up when she saw how many tendrils were swarming out from the darkness of the trees. Dozens upon dozens, maybe hundreds. Moving through the grass, they made no sound. In some ways this silence unnerved Sandy the most. There was no warning, nothing until they were crawling up your legs. A dog will growl or bark to let you know they are scared or angry, a pissed-off cat will hiss at you, hell, even a goddamn rattlesnake will shake its tail to warn you off, but these things came after you in total silence. You blinked and they were suddenly upon you.

Axel managed to reload and blew the closest tendrils into a fine gray mist. Then the water tower loomed overhead. They pushed Edgar up the ladder first. Purcell was next, sticking close to Edgar in case he fell. Axel continued to fire, sweeping the shotgun back and forth in wild, frantic movements.

Sandy turned and put one foot on the flat piece of steel that jutted from the northwest leg of the water tower. She went to push herself off the ground, and heard a cry, a sound that struck the very core of her soul. She froze. The cry came again.

"Mom!"

It was Kevin.

CHAPTER 25

Sandy jumped off the water tower and whipped her flashlight around.

The tendrils crept closer, closer.

"In the tree!" Kevin yelled.

She raised the Maglite, flashing it into the branches. And twenty yards away, across a heaving mass of tendrils, she saw her son, standing in the crook of an old oak, fifteen feet off the ground. Puffing Bill carefully straddled the branch next to him.

She started toward him, lowering her shotgun and jerking the trigger. Nothing happened. Axel grabbed her. "You're empty! Get up there!" He shoved her at the ladder.

She knew he was right. She called out to Kevin, "Stay put! I'll get you. Just stay there!"

She put her foot on the ladder and started climbing. A fresh wave of emotion burst inside her mind, leaving her dazed. Sweet relief and raw fear ricocheted through her body and she had to stop for a second to collect her thoughts. Axel slapped her ass. She started moving, realizing that falling off the water tower wouldn't help Kevin.

Down below, the tendrils wrapped around the spindly legs of the tower, and even though some of the arms grabbed listlessly at the ladder rungs, they could not climb.

She yelled, "Stay there!" in case he hadn't heard her the first time. "We'll get you. Just as soon as I can." Her promise sounded hollow and desperate. She kept going, hand over hand, until she reached the catwalk.

Axel was right behind her. They crawled out onto the narrow ledge that ran around the top of the water tower. Purcell had pulled Edgar over to make room, and now Edgar sat with his feet dangling over the edge, clutching the railing.

Sandy sidled along the other direction until she was facing Kevin. "Are you okay?" she called.

"Yeah, Mom. We're good."

She almost wept as joy swept through her. "Just stay put until we figure something, all right? Just stay put."

"Okay, Mom." He might as well have said, "Well, *DUH*." Of course they were going to stay put. Where else would they go?

She inched back to Purcell. He looked up at her and gave her a tired smile. "That your boy?"

She nodded.

"Good, good."

Axel dropped the backpack on the catwalk and slumped back against the cool metal of the water tank, trying to catch his breath. Purcell opened the pack and inventoried the contents. There wasn't much. Three full clips for the AA-12s. Four more clips for the SPAS-12s. No water. No food.

They were high enough that they could see the entire town, and looked northwest, trying to see if Charlie had reached the truck. It was impossible, though, and all they could really make out were the streetlights spaced along Main Street.

Despite herself, Sandy slumped down and sat next to Axel. Exhaustion spread throughout her body, filling her muscles with lead. She watched the sun sink below the horizon and sometime later, she slept.

Sandy scared everybody, including herself, by screaming out, "Don't fall asleep!"

"What?" Purcell grabbed her. He'd thought she was falling off the tower.

Axel had a shotgun up and ready to go, "What, what?" echoing his dad.

Before Sandy could answer, reassure them, they all heard a thumping come out of the northern sky.

Three lights opened up on them all at the same time, freezing Sandy, Purcell, his boys, pinning them to the side of the tank. The lights came skimming along the horizon, and swept past them in the roaring wash of three helicopters thundering past the water tank over one hundred miles an hour.

As they passed, the lights vanished at the same time and the helicopters went dark again.

Purcell said to Axel, "You hear them helicopters come back around, you hand me one of them double As. Fuckin' black helicopters. And you thought I was nuts, telling folks about 'em."

Two miles to the south, they could see a flash and hear a *whoomp*, as the hundreds of acres of corn around

the Einhorn, Kobritz, and Johnson houses and barns
started to burn. Sandy watched as the fires lit the sky
with an orange glow.

Edgar said, "What the hell's that?" He pointed back
to the north, back toward Main Street. They saw flashes
of a pair of headlights winding their way along the
parade. Heard a horn, pressed over and over.

"Charlie?" Sandy asked.

"Yeah, it is. I oughta recognize the sound of my own
truck." Purcell used the railing to help him stand up.

The sound of the rotors grew louder. The helicopters
were sweeping back around. The headlights of the truck
turned south on Fifth Street, heading toward the high
school. If anything, it seemed to be gathering speed.

"What's he doing?" Purcell asked, mostly to himself.

The helicopters roared overhead. Gunfire crackled
from underneath each chopper, splitting the night wide
open with tracers. They swooped down and blew Purcell's truck apart. It was like watching popcorn explode
in the microwave. Momentum carried the burning truck
along, where it eventually scraped along parked cars and
smashed into a tree.

Purcell brought Edgar's AA-12 up and fired at the
helicopters, screaming in rage.

One of the helicopters veered away from the other
two and banked toward them.

Sandy cringed. "I think you got his attention. Let's
get—"

Purcell yelled, "Gimme another fucking clip. Gonna
light this son of a bitch—"

The helicopter opened fire. Tracers singed through
the air a dozen yards away from the tank to the west,
sweeping closer.

Lightning streaked up from the ground, back near the library, and jolted the chopper. It farted pale smoke and faltered, pitching and starting to spin. The tracers sailed over the top of the water tank. The helicopter kept spinning, faster and faster. Near the end, the pilot almost got it under control, pulling it out of the tailspin, but the tail rotors clipped the edge of the roof of the baseball stand and that was all it took.

The helicopter went sideways and exploded across the pitcher's mound.

Purcell howled.

The massive spinning blades struck the grass and shattered, sending great shards of metal into the night. One six-foot piece whipped out and caught the north-western leg of the tower, connecting with a deep, thrumming sound and shearing the strut in half.

The water tower swayed like a small boat going sideways in an approaching storm.

The other two helicopters split apart and shot away, disappearing in the night sky.

"Fight, cocksuckers!" Purcell shouted, shooting at them.

The tower started to dip and rock, easy at first, as if getting used to the idea.

Sandy took hold of the railing with both hands and squeezed as hard as she could. The water shifted and slammed into one side of the tank behind her, then the other. As it rocked back, she felt that same drop in her stomach that she felt on a roller coaster, when it slowed down at the first apex, right before plummeting at the ground.

When the tower reached the point of no return, and started to topple over in slow motion, she scrambled up the tilting catwalk, trying to balance on the tank itself as it tilted at the earth and went down. Axel braced himself and wrapped one arm around his brother. Purcell put his back to the tank and closed his eyes.

The tower hit one of center field's light posts on the way down and spun.

Sandy went flying, flung fifteen feet into the air. She hit third base with an impact that made something snap inside her right shoulder and rolled, flopping and bouncing, down the concrete steps into the visitors' dugout.

Four hundred thousand gallons of water burst from the ruptured tank, sending a three-foot wave across the infield, washing away the tendrils. It hit the low front wall of the dugout and exploded, most of it going straight up or to the sides. Still, the impact was enough to drive her into the concrete bench.

She tried to rise from the churning water. Her back had been wrenched, and it hurt to breathe. Moving her right arm sparked agony. She couldn't see any tendrils right away. She raised herself up to sit on the concrete bench. After cautiously feeling around her right shoulder, she found a lump over her right clavicle.

She'd broken her collarbone.

She carefully put her right hand in her front pocket and tried to stand. She found she could only move if she kept her arm tight to her side. Her gun was still in its holster. She reached across her stomach with her left hand and fumbled with it a while before unsnapping the strap. The Glock felt alien and heavy in her left hand.

Tendrils twisted and flailed around the dugout, all those rotten limbs quivering in the muddy water.

The Fitzgimmons rose from the receding water near second base in various states of consciousness.

Axel helped his brother and father up and they went staggering back to the crumpled tower. Sandy didn't understand why they would try for the tower again, until they passed the heap of metal and headed for the trees.

She looked up, wondering if she could climb onto the roof of the dugout with one arm. Water trickled into the dugout down the steps. She got one foot on the front wall, stood on it and got her chest and left arm over the edge, hung there for a moment, then managed to throw her left leg onto the roof. She pulled herself over from there, right shoulder jolting her with every movement.

Soon the water had washed away, leaving nothing but wet grass and muddy sand. It only took a few seconds for the first tendril to explore the dugout roof. The tip came up from the home base end, a dozen fingers open and grasping like a bristling flower. Gnarled arms clawed at the cement and hauled more of the tentacle onto the roof.

Sandy squeezed off four rounds at point-blank range, pumping bullets into the cluster of fingers. The tendril shuddered and curled to the side. Broken and torn fingers dropped off the tip like ejected shells.

Drawn by the gunfire, more tendrils appeared, crawling up over the edge. Sandy emptied her Glock at them and only attracted more. She didn't bother trying to put the handgun back in its holster and dropped it, feeling around her belt.

She found the Taser, fired at a tentacle at her feet. The limbs twitched for a second, then shrugged it off and crawled closer. She realized she couldn't reload a new cartridge with one hand and dropped the Taser. That left the Mace.

She pulled it out and spun, finger frozen just above

the trigger. The dugout was now completely surrounded. Beyond the grasping, clawing tendrils wriggling onto the roof, she could see hundreds more, all swarming closer. Her hand shook. She didn't want to turn around and look at the tree where Kevin waited. She hoped he couldn't see what was about to happen.

She abruptly reversed the can of Mace and sprayed her legs, moved up to her stomach and back. It started to sputter and hiss air so she tried to get the remnants into her hair. She was grateful that she wore the gas mask.

The tendrils shrank back at first, but then hunger overcame the stench of the Mace and they crawled even closer. They came up from everywhere.

Sandy tried not to scream.

A pair of headlights burst upon her as a tow truck roared through the parking lot, towing an old tanker trailer. Holes the size of golf balls had been blown in its sides, and some kind of liquid was spilling out, spraying the outside of the truck and at least six feet into the air on each side. It smelled like bleach and dried kale. The truck whipped around and jerked to a stop near the dugout, splashing the chemical everywhere.

The tendrils shrank away.

"Run!" Charlie shouted from the driver's seat of Axel's garage tow truck. Sandy jumped off the dugout and went to her knees in the liquid. It seeped into her cuts and burned. She threw herself into the front seat and Charlie hit the gas, slipping and sliding through the mud. Once in the outfield, he did his best to run over the tendrils, crunching the arms and legs under the wheels.

The whole time, liquid continued to spray from the tanker trailer. If any part of the tendrils touched the liquid, they would immediately shed that part and pull away.

Charlie drove over the outfield fence and pulled around the trees in a tight loop. He kept going, circling around and around, creating a kind of soggy DMZ, free of the tendrils.

Eventually, Axel climbed down out of the tree with his shotgun and blasted the closest tendril into three pieces. Purcell followed and got close enough to the smaller chunks and put one or two well-placed rounds into the center, leaving the limbs to mindlessly twitch in the grass.

Sandy yelled out of her window at Kevin. "Don't you dare come down until I come get you."

Charlie pulled close to the base of the tree and everybody piled into the back of the tow truck. Kevin helped Puffing Bill down onto the roof first, saying, "Once I helped him up the first couple of branches, he climbed like he was part squirrel."

Sandy pulled off her own mask and put it on her son. She knew it was probably too late to make a difference, but didn't think it would hurt. Then she pulled him tight. Tears spilled silently down her cheeks. Puffing Bill sat quietly and leaned into her.

They heard the distant sound of helicopters. After a moment, though, the noise faded and was gone. She said, "We should go."

Purcell knocked on the roof. "You waiting for them to come back? Move it." Everyone in the back arranged themselves around the large boom and got comfortable.

Charlie pulled away, and they dragged the old, leaking tanker back through the town, following his original path through town. It was easy to see; he'd left a swath of broken limbs and ash-like decaying tendrils.

"That's your pesticide," Sandy said to Purcell. "From your barn."

Purcell nodded. "But I wasn't using it in the fields. No, no. I emptied all my fertilizer and pesticide into that tank so I could show 'em the empty containers for the certification. Thing is, you know how expensive it is to dispose of all that shit? Figured I'd find someplace safe for all of it."

Sandy gave him a look.

Purcell drew back, pretending to be insulted. "What do you take me for? You think I'm gonna pour that crap in the nearest ditch? No, I woulda found a good spot for it. Like in Beverly Hills. Someplace in Hollywood at least. Get folks' attention."

She fiddled with her radio, spinning through the different channels. Occasionally, she caught glimmers of the conversation between the helicopter pilots and three or four agencies vying for control of the situation. It sounded like the helicopter pilots were reluctant to go back through the town.

Once she heard, ". . . not prepared for that kind of armed response . . ."

"Roger that." The creeping fuzz of static obscured the rest. Then, ". . . subjects will be neutralized as soon as quarantine measures are finalized."

They listened, but couldn't hear anything else.

"They're coming back," Sandy said.

Purcell was quiet for a while. "Might be. Might not. Thinking they woulda been through here by now, if they were coming back. Something else is going on."

They stopped by the Korner Kafe, out where the

streets were clear and empty. No tendrils were visible. They left the tow truck and the tanker trailer in the middle of the highway and everybody piled into the Suburban. Charlie got in behind the wheel and they rolled out of town in the gray light of predawn.

THURSDAY,
JULY 5th

CHAPTER 26

Charlie could see lights flashing ahead and yelled through the back window. "It's a roadblock."

"Slow down. But don't stop. Keep going. We stop, we may not get going again," Purcell said.

"It's a roadblock, I'm telling you. We have to stop."

"Keep going." Purcell made it clear that he wasn't arguing.

Interstate 72 waited ahead, with four on- and off-ramps curving between the expressway and Highway 67. The highway on both sides of the expressway had been blocked off with blinking sawhorses and concrete barriers. New lanes of traffic had been marked with traffic cones. A number of military vehicles waited under the overpass.

Despite Purcell's order, Charlie pulled up and stopped.

They couldn't see anything moving. The vehicles were empty. Everyone had disappeared.

A radio squawked from one of the Humvees. "Station thirteen, come in. Come in station thirteen."

Sandy turned her gaze to the cornfields that surrounded them. The green stalks almost glowed in the morning light. The effect made her think of the field as a vast emerald ocean, and predators lurked in the depths.

Purcell felt her unease. "We should keep moving."

Charlie pulled through the checkpoint. He eased the Suburban to the right, following the on-ramp as it curled around to head east on I-72. The expressway was empty. Billows of black smoke roiled across the road.

Nobody said anything.

Sandy looked to the north, back to Parker's Mill. Smaller wisps of black smoke still smoldered in the town itself.

Then, something else. A gray cloud, erupting like ash from a volcano, rose into the pale blue sky. It twisted and swirled, almost as if it was alive. Sandy took Kevin's hand and leaned forward. She tapped Charlie's shoulder and pointed at the ominous gray cloud. "Drive faster."